Praise for **TRAPPED!**

★ "Seventh-grade sleuths visit their local libraries and unmask a Russian spy ring. The pleasures of watching the young sherlocks once again deduce rings around the grown-ups (using a technique they call TOAST, for 'Theory of All Small Things') are just as rich in this trilogy closer as they were in Volume 1. A top-shelf test of courage, friendship, and ingenuity."
—*Kirkus Reviews*, starred review

Praise for **VANISHED!**

2018 EDGAR AWARD WINNER

★ "As in *Framed!* (2016), fast brain- and footwork saves the day at the last moment, but watching Florian wow everyone . . . with Holmes-style connecting of dots along the way is just as satisfying. A splendid whodunit: cerebral, exhilarating, low in violence, methodical in construction, and occasionally hilarious."
—*Kirkus Reviews*, starred review

Praise for **FRAMED!**

2017 EDGAR AWARD NOMINEE
2016 PARENTS' CHOICE AWARD WINNER

"Mystery buffs and fans of Anthony Horowitz's Alex Rider series are in for a treat. . . . With elements of Alex Rider, James Bond, and Sherlock Holmes stories, this is likely to be popular with mystery and action/adventure fans." —*School Library Journal*

BY JAMES PONTI

The Framed! series
Framed!
Vanished!
Trapped!

The Dead City trilogy
Dead City
Blue Moon
Dark Days

TRAPPED!

A FRAMED! NOVEL

JAMES PONTI

ALADDIN
New York London Toronto Sydney New Delhi

ALADDIN

An imprint of Simon & Schuster Children's Publishing Division

1230 Avenue of the Americas, New York, New York 10020

First Aladdin paperback edition September 2019

Text copyright © 2018 by James Ponti

Cover illustration copyright © 2018 by Paul Hoppe

Also available in an Aladdin hardcover edition.

All rights reserved, including the right of reproduction in whole or in part in any form.

ALADDIN and related logo are registered trademarks of Simon & Schuster, Inc.

For information about special discounts for bulk purchases, please contact Simon & Schuster Special Sales at 1-866-506-1949 or business@simonandschuster.com.

The Simon & Schuster Speakers Bureau can bring authors to your live event. For more information or to book an event contact the Simon & Schuster Speakers Bureau at 1-866-248-3049 or visit our website at www.simonspeakers.com.

Cover designed by Laura Lyn DiSiena

Interior designed by Laura Lyn DiSiena and Steve Scott

The text of this book was set in Janson Text LT Std.

Manufactured in the United States of America 0819 OFF

2 4 6 8 10 9 7 5 3 1

The Library of Congress has cataloged the hardcover edition as follows:

Names: Ponti, James, author.

Title: Trapped! / by James Ponti.

Description: First Aladdin hardcover edition. | New York : Aladdin, 2018. |

Series: Framed! ; 3 | Summary: Middle schoolers Florian and Margaret are determined to catch a spy who is implicating their FBI supervisor, Marcus Rivers, in a variety of crimes—even if they have to break into, and out of, the Library of Congress to do it.

Identifiers: LCCN 2018005076 | ISBN 9781534408913 (hc) | ISBN 9781534408937 (eBook)

Subjects: | CYAC: Mystery and detective stories. | United States. Federal Bureau of Investigation—Fiction. | Friendship—Fiction. | Spies—Fiction. |

Library of Congress—Fiction. | Washington (D.C.)—Fiction. |

BISAC: JUVENILE FICTION / Mysteries & Detective Stories. |

JUVENILE FICTION / Action & Adventure / General. |

JUVENILE FICTION / Humorous Stories.

Classification: LCC PZ7.P7726 Tr 2018 | DDC [Fic]—dc23

LC record available at https://lccn.loc.gov/2018005076

ISBN 9781534408920 (pbk)

For librarians everywhere:
Without you, our world
would be so much smaller.
You are my rock stars.

1.

Geek Mythology

YOU CAN'T JUDGE A BOOK BY ITS COVER.

My name's Florian Bates, and if you looked at me, you'd see a twelve-year-old boy and think, *Seventh grader.* And while that wouldn't be wrong, it wouldn't begin to tell you the whole story. For example, it wouldn't tell you that, in addition to doing homework and mowing the lawn, my list of chores typically includes solving cases as a consulting detective with the FBI's Special Projects Team.

And if you looked at the copy of Albert Einstein's *Relativity* that was checked out from the Tenley-Friendship branch of the DC Public Library nine days ago, you'd think, *Science book.* (Okay, first you might look at the picture of

Einstein on the cover and wonder how he got his hair to look that way, but then you'd think, *Science book*.) However, you'd never guess that the book triggered an international incident involving a Russian spy ring, the theft of national treasures, a European crime syndicate, and a joint task force of the FBI, CIA, and National Security Agency.

And finally, if you looked at our plan to break into the Library of Congress, evade its state-of-the-art security system, and somehow find the single piece of information necessary to solve our case, you'd think my best friend—Margaret—and I were absolutely bonkers.

Okay, so sometimes you *can* judge a book by its cover.

The plan was totally nuts.

To be honest, it wasn't so much a plan as it was a list of nearly impossible objectives with no idea how to accomplish them. We knew it was bad. We just couldn't come up with anything better. We had to unmask a spy who'd spent decades as a deep-cover agent stealing US government secrets. But more important, we had to help Marcus.

Marcus Rivers was in charge of the Special Projects Team. But he wasn't just our boss; he was family. He was also an amazing agent who never once hesitated to risk his life and his career to protect us. It was our turn to return the favor.

At some point during the case, we slipped up and the spy used our mistake to make it look like Marcus was guilty of theft, corruption, and espionage. Marcus who'd spent his entire career fighting criminals was now accused of being one.

Desperate times called for desperate measures.

"You're the mastermind," I said to Margaret as we approached the library. "What are we going to do?"

"Get inside, find the evidence, and prove Marcus is innocent," she said.

I gave her a sideways glance. "You have any specific details about how we should do those things?"

She shrugged. "I figured we'd just make it up as we went along."

Like I said, *absolutely bonkers.*

OBJECTIVE 1:
Crash the "It's All About the Books" Gala at the Library of Congress

First, we had to get inside the library by crashing a gala reception in the Great Hall of the Thomas Jefferson Building. When we arrived, there were about fifty people in tuxedos and gowns waiting to pass through security.

"How are we going to do this?" I asked.

"Clothes and confidence," Margaret answered as if that were a complete sentence.

"What are you talking about?"

"I looked up 'crashing a formal party' online, and it said the two most important things were clothes and confidence. You've got to dress like you belong and act like you belong."

Between my tuxedo and Margaret's dress, we had the clothes part covered. It was the confidence component that had me worried.

"Speaking of clothes," she said. "Why do you have a tux?"

"Because it's a formal event," I answered, stating the obvious.

"No. Not why are you wearing it. Why do you have it in the first place? What twelve-year-old owns a tuxedo?"

I couldn't believe it. "Let me get this straight. You're giving me a hard time for having something we need?"

"I'm not giving you a hard time," she said. "I just think it's a little . . . unusual. Call me curious."

"Both my parents work in museums," I explained. "I've been dragged to more fund-raisers and exhibition openings than I can remember. They're usually formal events like this one, so they bought me a tux."

"Okay, that makes sense," she said. "It's also good news. Since you've been to a lot of these things, you should fit right in."

"Well, there's one big difference between those events and this one."

"What's that?"

"We had invitations."

She gave me a conspiratorial smile and said, "You're not going to let a little piece of paper stop us from solving the mystery and saving Marcus, are you?"

She always knew what to say to get me to go along with her schemes. "No, I'm not," I answered. "Let's do this."

There were two lines with security guards manning metal detectors. At the head of each line was a woman with a computer tablet checking invitations. One of the women looked to be in her mid-twenties and wore a black cocktail dress and very high heels. The other wore a longer dress with shoes that were nice but more comfortable. She also had a wedding band on her ring finger.

"The odds are better that the one on the right is a mom," I said. "That might mean she's nicer to kids."

"True," answered Margaret. "But the one on the left is more likely to think all kids are stupid."

"Good point," I said as we got into the line on the left.

During an FBI training session called Outsmarting Your

Opponent, we were taught that the biggest advantage you can have is for the other side to underestimate your abilities.

"When she asks for our invitations, we'll tell her our moms have them but are already inside."

"If our mothers are inside, then why are we out here?" I asked.

"That's where the stupid comes in." Margaret suddenly adopted the voice of an airheaded middle schooler who spoke in endless run-on sentences. "I was texting my friend Maddie about the party but I had trouble getting good reception so I started walking around trying to get more bars but it just got worse and worse so I went through a door and accidentally got locked outside. OMG, my mom's going to kill me if she finds out."

"Do people really think kids talk that way?" I asked.

"I'm counting on it," Margaret said.

"And why am I outside if you were the one on the phone?" I asked.

"You're my best friend. You go wherever I go."

"So we're both stupid."

"That's the plan unless you've got a better one," she said.

I exhaled slowly. "Tragically, I don't."

We were about halfway through the line when she realized we had a potential problem. "Uh-oh."

"What?" I asked nervously.

"She'll probably want a name to check against the guest list. We'll need some TOAST help on that."

TOAST stands for the Theory of All Small Things. It is the method we use to read people and situations in order to solve cases. The idea is that if you look for little details, you can add them up to discover otherwise hidden pieces of information. At the moment we needed the names of two potential "mothers" who were already inside the gala.

"I got it covered," I said.

I pulled out my phone and started searching.

"What are you doing?" she asked.

"Looking on social media for any pictures tagged with that." I pointed to a banner that read, #ITSALLABOUTTHEBOOKS.

"Oh, that's kind of brilliant," she said as she did likewise.

Even though the party was barely an hour old, there were already dozens of photos to scroll through of people inside having fun.

"Find one posted by someone with an unusual name," I said. "It'll seem less likely that we made it up. Also, find out where they work in case that's included on the guest list."

By the time we reached the front of the line, we were ready to go. Margaret's airhead act worked like a charm, and when asked, I became the son of a kids' book publisher named Mara Anastas. I even spelled it out for her so that she could find it on her tablet.

"See what I mean," Margaret said as we walked through the entrance. "Clothes and confidence."

OBJECTIVE 2:
Avoid Detection While Sneaking into the Library's Secure Area

It was amazing how different the Great Hall looked compared to when we'd come during normal hours. Multicolored lights gave it a party feel, and giant reproductions of famous book covers were hung as decorations. People mingled in clusters while a jazz quartet played on a stage.

A waiter walked past us carrying a tray of finger food, which caught Margaret's attention. "Ooh, those look delicious."

"We're working a case," I reminded her, "not going to a party."

She gave me that Margaret smirk. "Actually, we're blending in at a party so that we can work the case. Besides, if I pass out from starvation, that will attract even more attention."

She chased after the waiter, and I scanned the room. Now that we were inside, we needed to find the computer server. The library had an automated system that kept detailed records of its secure areas. If we could access them, we thought we could prove Marcus's innocence.

Margaret returned carrying a little plate with two toothpick skewers of beef. "The waiter said it's called *bulgogi*, and it's amazing," she said as she tasted one. "I think it's Korean."

"Is that one for me?" I asked, pointing to the untouched skewer.

"I thought you said we weren't at a party."

"Well, now I'm worried about passing out due to starvation."

She reluctantly held up the second skewer, and I snatched it before she could change her mind. It was delicious.

"You're right," I said between chews. "We've got to track him down and get more."

"No, no, no," she said. "This is not good."

"What do you mean? It tastes great."

"Not the food," she replied. "Him."

She nodded over my shoulder, and I turned to see one of our suspects about fifteen feet from us. It was Alistair Toombs, the director of the library's Rare Book and Special Collections Division. Luckily, he was facing the other way. We had a run-in with him earlier during the case and couldn't risk being seen.

We worked our way to the opposite side of the room and tried to disappear into the crowd of people milling around chitchatting.

"We've got to find the server room fast," I said as I studied the building's layout, trying to logically deduce where it should be. "It has to be cool and dry, which means it won't have any exterior walls. Humidity can seep through those. They'd also stay away from the lower basement to avoid potential flooding. As far as wiring . . ."

"I hate to interrupt your little Sherlock moment," Margaret said. "But it might be quicker if we just follow him."

Next to the stage a computer tech was making adjustments to the audio and lighting boards. He looked like he was just out of college. As soon as he was done, he took his tool kit and left.

"Change of plans," I said. "Let's follow him."

The guy led us back across the room before he got into an elevator labeled STAFF ONLY. After the doors closed, we rushed over to watch the display to see where he got off.

"Two floors down," said Margaret. "Now we're getting somewhere."

"Yeah, except we're not getting anywhere on that elevator. At least, not without a key card."

The call button was attached to a card reader.

"Not a problem," she said. "We'll just hang around here until somebody gets off the elevator. Then we'll slip in before the doors shut."

It was a good plan. At least until Alistair Toombs spotted us. Because we'd followed the computer tech, we were no longer hidden in the crowd. I could tell by Toombs's expression that he recognized us. He looked angry and was headed our way.

Luckily, at that moment the elevator dinged, and the door opened. We had to wait for a man as he struggled to push an oversized catering cart. We helped him by giving it a tug, and by the time he was finally gone, Toombs had almost reached us. We jumped into the elevator and pushed the buttons as quickly as we could.

"Wait one moment!" Toombs called out as the doors finally closed and we began to descend.

"We're not going to have much time before he takes the next elevator down and starts chasing us," said Margaret.

When the doors opened, we hurried out into the hallway. We didn't want to run because it might attract attention, but we did our best speed walking.

"What are we looking for?" Margaret asked in a hurried whisper.

"Any place we can hide," I said.

Down here the building showed its age. Over the course of 120 years, it had been built and rebuilt so many times the hallways and storage rooms were mazelike in their complexity. The good part was that that would make it harder for Alistair to find us. The bad part was that it meant it would be difficult for us to find our way around.

When we heard the ding announcing the elevator's return, we picked up the pace even more. We just kept making turn after turn until we ran into a dead end. Behind us we could hear Alistair's footsteps in the distance. We had three doors to choose from. Amazingly, one was marked COMPUTERS.

Margaret and I shared a smile. Fate had shined on us.

"Better lucky than smart," she whispered.

We slipped into the darkened room as quietly as we could and closed the door tightly behind us. We didn't dare turn on the lights for fear he'd be able to see the glow under the door.

We could hear him getting closer.

More frightening, we could tell that he was trying each door along the way. Most of them were locked, and we heard the rattle of the handles.

"What do we do?" I asked. "Hide?"

Next to the door was a small electronic display that had a keypad and a glowing red button marked LOCK.

I pressed it, and we heard a click.

I cringed at the sound, hoping it wasn't too loud.

We stood silently in the darkness. Through the space underneath the door, we could see a pair of shoes come to a stop. On the other side, Toombs jiggled the handle, but it didn't budge. He tried again, but it still didn't open. Finally he went on his way.

We remained motionless for at least two minutes, and all I heard were Margaret's slow, measured breaths.

"You think it's safe to turn on the lights?" she whispered.

"Yes," I said tentatively.

I found the switch and flipped it. As the lights turned on and my eyes adjusted, I realized that our "lucky" find wasn't so lucky after all. We weren't in a computer room. We were in a room full of books about computers. This was, after all, the world's largest library. Books were everywhere.

"Maybe it's better to be smart than lucky," I joked.

"It's okay," she said. "At least he didn't catch us."

"Should we keep trying to find the server?"

Margaret shook her head. "No. He's not going to stop looking. Or worse, he'll alert security. I think we've got to get out of the building before someone catches us. We're not going to be able to help Marcus if we get arrested."

"Good point."

We waited another minute to make sure he was gone, and then I opened the door.

Or rather, I turned the handle to open the door, but nothing happened.

"Stop messing around. It's not funny."

"I'm not trying to be funny," I said. "It's locked."

"Duh," she said, shaking her head. "Because we locked it."

She reached over to the keypad and pressed a green button marked OPEN. But it didn't respond. She tried again but had the same result. I jiggled the handle some more. Nothing happened.

"Margaret," I said nervously. "I think we may be trapped in here."

OBJECTIVE 3:
~~Access Information in the~~
~~Computer Server Room~~
ESCAPE!

Not surprisingly, we had to change our third objective. We were locked in a storage area half the size of a classroom. It was filled with books about the history of computers, manuals that explained how to build computers, and biographies of famous people in computer history. (If only we'd stumbled into the room with the books about lock picking and prison escapes.)

We tried not to panic.

"Maybe we should call our parents," said Margaret. "They can come get us."

It almost certainly meant getting grounded for life, but she was right. That's when we realized being trapped in the basement of a massive marble building filled with metal bookcases totally disrupts your cell service. No matter where we stood in the room or how much we waved our phones in the air, we couldn't get any sort of connection.

"Remember when we were pretending to be so stupid that we got locked out of a building?" I said.

"Yeah."

"It turns out we are that stupid. Only, even stupider because we got locked in."

It was becoming harder and harder to keep calm.

"It's Friday night," Margaret said, panicked. "What if no one comes back here until Monday?"

And harder still.

"Let's not think that way. Let's stay positive."

"You're right," she said with only slight believability. "We can figure this out."

I tried to flip the lock like they do in movies by sliding

my school ID through the slot between the door and the jamb. After about ten tries, the lock remained completely unchanged, but my ID was mangled beyond repair.

Margaret began typing codes into the keypad. She started with 0000 and then tried 0001, 0002, 0003 . . . well, you get the picture.

"You realize there are ten thousand different potential combinations," I said.

She gave me the evil eye and asked, "Is that you staying positive?"

"Sorry," I replied sheepishly as I backed away. "Keep up the good work."

I started scanning shelves looking for anything about electronic locks or keypads, but I couldn't make sense of how the books were organized.

"Margaret, can you look at this?"

"I'm kind of busy over here," she said, focusing on the keypad and trying to make sure she didn't skip a number.

I took a book off the shelf and brought it over to her.

"I don't understand this," I said, holding up the spine for her to see.

She stopped and read the title. "*Geek Mythology: The Real-Life Legends and Gods of Computer History.*" She looked up. "What about it?"

"I'm not confused by the title. I don't understand the call number."

"QA76.16.W69."

"Exactly," I replied. "I've never seen anything like that in a library before. Shouldn't it be something like 791.43?"

Margaret smiled when she realized why I was confused.

"You'd think so," she said. "But that's because most libraries use the Dewey decimal system. The Library of Congress has its own classification system. We learned about it last year in English."

"Seriously? That's so confusing. Why would they do that?"

"I think the Librarian of Congress is upstairs at that gala," she said. "As soon as I crack this code, we can go ask her."

I stared at the book, and my mind started piecing together the puzzle. I must have had a far-off look because Margaret reached over and touched my shoulder.

"Are you okay?" she asked.

"Let me see your phone," I said urgently.

"I'm pretty sure there still isn't any cell service down here."

"I don't want to make a call. I need to check your photo gallery."

She handed it to me, and I quickly swiped through all the pictures she'd taken during the case, their colors streaming by in a blur. There were two in particular I was looking for, and when I found them, I switched back and forth between them to make sure I was right. Even though I was, I didn't know what it all meant.

I closed my eyes, and the pieces of the case flooded through my mind. FBI, CIA, NSA, Russian spies, Library of Congress, Albert Einstein, Alistair Toombs, and then . . . books. There were so many books throughout the case. Rare books. Science books. Children's books. Massive volumes of Shakespeare's works. A book that belonged to Thomas Jefferson. And now *Geek Mythology*. Maybe the hashtag was right. Maybe it was "all about the books." I remembered my mother once telling me, "No matter what you're searching for, you can always find the answer in the library. The secrets of the world are hidden in books," she'd said. "All you've got to do is look for them."

And then everything went dark, and I saw the answer right in front of me. I opened my eyes and looked at Margaret.

"We've got to get out of here!" I exclaimed.

"Yeah, I realized that a while ago. That's why I'm typing ten thousand different codes."

"No, I mean, we've got to get out of here because I may have just solved the case."

"Really? How?"

"It's hard to explain," I said. "But the first thing you have to understand is that *Geek Mythology* changes everything."

2.

Toastbusters

One Week Earlier

I PROMISE I'LL EXPLAIN HOW *GEEK MYTHOLOGY* changed everything. But for it to really make sense, I first have to explain what everything is. That means going back one week earlier. It was a Friday afternoon, and the FBI wasn't treating Marcus like a criminal; it was awarding him one of its highest honors. And Margaret and I weren't trapped in a room beneath the Library of Congress; we were going head-to-head in an epic battle of Toastbusters.

The object of the game was to see who could uncover the most hidden details about people using nothing more than the Theory of All Small Things. Normally we played in the school cafeteria or at one of the Smithsonians, but those locations weren't particularly challenging because the two easiest groups of people to read were kids and tourists. This match was different. We were at the J. Edgar Hoover Building in a room full of FBI agents who dressed alike, had matching haircuts, and were specifically trained to avoid detection.

This was our Super Bowl.

"The guy with the red tie getting punch," Margaret said, trying her best to talk like a ventriloquist without moving her lips. "I think he's recently gotten divorced."

We both turned to Kayla, who was standing between us and serving as the official scorer. She was an agent and the "unofficial" fourth member of the team. Since she worked at the Bureau, she was able to tell us when we were right or wrong. A correct observation was worth two points; an incorrect one meant minus one. I could tell from her expression that Margaret had scored again.

"About a month ago," Kayla whispered. "How'd you know?"

"There's a pale stripe on his finger where his wedding ring used to be. And he keeps going back to the hors d'oeuvres table like he hasn't had a decent meal in weeks."

"Very nice. That's two points."

"Which means the game is tied," Margaret added with a little fist pump.

"Not for long," I replied. "So enjoy it while you can."

I carefully scanned the room, which was one of the nicest at FBI Headquarters. It had marble floors, two massive stone fireplaces, and large paintings depicting famous moments in American history. It was used to welcome visiting delegations and hold special events. Today it was hosting the reception for the Bureau's annual awards ceremony. We'd come to see Marcus receive a Director's Award for Excellence, which was a huge honor. He was still in the auditorium posing for pictures, so we'd taken a spot near the dessert table, which gave us plenty of opportunity to observe people. (And, you know, eat lots of dessert.)

"I've got one," I whispered. "The tall guy in the pin-stripe suit munching on carrot sticks."

"Okay," Kayla said. "What can you tell me?"

"He's recently lost between thirty and forty pounds."

She was impressed. "That's two points for Florian."

Margaret gave me a curious look and then studied the man to see how I figured it out. "His jacket," she said, realizing. "It's too big."

"And even though he's only eating carrots, he keeps staring at the dessert table like he's going to tackle it."

"That's a good one," Margaret admitted.

"And it means I'm back up by two."

"Yes, it does. . . ." She took a deep breath as she considered her strategy. "Which is why . . . I'm going for a three-pointer."

Three-pointers were rare. To get one, you had to first identify the person and then give your opponent a chance to steal. It was risky because not only could it cost you points but you'd also lose your turn.

"Who is it?" I asked.

"There's a man with a beard sitting in the far corner. He has a slice of chocolate cake and is drinking a bottle of water." She turned to Kayla. "Do you know him?"

"I do. We were in basic training together at Quantico. Florian, you're on the clock."

I had sixty seconds to make an observation about him, but it wouldn't have mattered if I had sixty minutes. I looked for anything interesting, but he seemed absolutely unremarkable.

"I've got nothing," I admitted reluctantly. "What is it?"

Margaret paused for a moment to increase the drama. Then she leaned forward and whispered, "He works in the field as an undercover agent."

"Okay, wow!" said Kayla. "You're not supposed to know

that. In fact, almost no one in this room knows that."

Margaret beamed with pride. "Don't worry. I won't tell anyone."

I was stunned. "How could you possibly . . . ?"

"It started with his fingernails," she said. "I noticed them when he was getting the cake."

"What's significant about his fingernails? That he has ten of them?" I asked.

"Most agents keep theirs neat and short. But his are long and kind of dirty. Add that to his hair, which needs to be cut, and his beard, which could use a trim."

"And you get someone who's messy," I suggested.

"But he's not messy," she replied. "Look at his suit. Tailored and pressed. It's impeccable. His natural instinct is to be sharp. That tells me his subpar grooming is a job requirement, not a personal choice. And the only requirement that makes sense is that he's undercover. It's so he can blend in better out on the street, where a manicure and crew cut would make him stand out."

I was blown away.

"That's three points," Kayla said, holding up three fingers as punctuation. "Three very impressive points."

"And Campbell takes the lead," Margaret announced like a sportscaster.

Like I said, this was our Super Bowl, and she was playing like a superstar.

I used all my best spy tricks as I scanned the room, hoping to counter with something equally impressive. There was a woman who kept turning her head slightly as she talked to a friend, and I thought she might be deaf in one ear. And I wondered if a man with mismatched socks was color-blind. But nothing seemed particularly TOAST-worthy. And certainly none was as cool as unmasking an undercover agent.

Then, when I swept the room again, I noticed we weren't the only ones spying.

"See the guy in that group over there with his back turned?" I asked, subtly motioning to where four people stood in a cluster about twenty feet away from us. "The one in gray?"

"What can you tell me about him?" asked Kayla.

"It's not part of the game," I said. "It's just that he's watching us. Very carefully. I noticed him earlier in the auditorium. I didn't think much about it at the time, but now I'm sure he's following our every move."

"How's that possible if he's facing the other way?" asked Margaret.

"He's using that mirror."

There was an ornate gold-framed mirror hanging on the

opposite wall over a table with two punch bowls and a large flower arrangement. When you looked in it, you could see his eyes and tell that his attention was focused on us instead of the people he was with.

"I think you're right," said Kayla.

"Any idea who he is?" I asked.

"I've never seen him."

There was a moment of quiet, and then Margaret said, "That's fascinating and all, but you don't get any points for fascinating. So, is that your way of declaring me the winner? 'Cause I have a new victory dance I want to show you guys."

"Not yet," I said defiantly. "Let me look a little bit more."

I tried to get back into the game, but I was too distracted by the man. I wondered why he was so interested in us. I still hadn't spotted anything by the time Marcus came into the room. In the short distance from the door to where we were standing, he must have been stopped by at least a dozen people congratulating him with a handshake or a slap on the back. He seemed a bit embarrassed by all the attention.

"Where are your parents?" Kayla asked him.

"They had to go," he answered. "They're watching my sister's kids tonight."

"You should've seen their faces when you were up there," she said. "They're so proud of you."

"We all are," Margaret said as she gave him a hug. "Congratulations!"

"Thank you."

"Yes, congratulations," I added. "Can I see it?"

He handed me the award, which was glass and shaped like a diamond on a base. The FBI seal was engraved above an inscription, which I read aloud. "'FBI Director's Award for Excellence presented to Special Agent Marcus Rivers in recognition of your outstanding contribution to our nation through exemplary service and dedication. With deepest appreciation.'"

I looked up at him and smiled. "Wow! It's so well deserved."

"Where are you going to put it?" asked Margaret. "On a podium in your office with a little spotlight on it?"

We all laughed.

"I was thinking something a little more low-key," he said. "Like the closet or at my parents' house."

"Well, I'd go with the podium," she replied. "But that's just me."

"It's a good thing you got here when you did," said Kayla as she gave him a congratulatory hug. "Margaret just identified an undercover agent. A few minutes longer and there'd be no telling how many government secrets they might've exposed."

Marcus picked up a piece of cake from the table and ate happily as we walked him through the Toastbusters highlights. He was rightfully impressed by Margaret's fingernail identification, and I decided to concede the match and declare her the outright winner.

Her celebratory dance was surprisingly restrained.

I was still laughing about it when the man who'd been spying on us approached Marcus. He was average height and built like a wrestler. (Not the ones on TV who break chairs over each other's heads, but compact and muscular like the ones you see at the Olympics.) He had a thick black mustache and was bald on top with hair on the sides.

"Congratulations," he said, offering a powerful handshake. "The Director's Award is huge. I hear you've closed some amazing cases lately."

"I think a lot of it was luck," Marcus said modestly. "'Right place at the right time' kind of thing."

"Oh, no," he said with an odd smile. "I'm sure *luck* had nothing to do with it."

He just stood there for a moment creating an awkward silence.

"I'm sorry," said Marcus. "I don't think we've met. I'm Marcus Rivers."

"Dan Napoli," he replied. "I'm with the organized crime

division. I transferred down from the New York office six months ago."

"Nice to meet you, Dan."

Napoli turned to Margaret and me. "And who do we have here?"

Even among agents in the Hoover Building we weren't allowed to discuss our role with the Bureau. So instead of telling him that we were covert assets on the Special Projects Team, Margaret went with our standard cover story.

"I'm Marcus's niece, and this is my best friend."

I noticed she didn't offer our names.

"Well, I'm sure you're proud of your uncle."

"Very much," she replied. "And you're right. *Luck* had nothing to do with the cases he's closed. He's just that good."

Napoli lingered a bit before saying, "Well, it was nice meeting you all. I'm sure our paths will cross again."

I thought that was an odd closing line, and I waited until he was far enough away before I turned to the others and said, "There's something about that guy I don't trust."

"I'm right there with you," Margaret added, her eyes glued to his every move.

When we told Marcus about Napoli spying on us in the mirror, he didn't find it nearly as curious as we did.

"I think one of the drawbacks of playing Toastbusters is that it can make you suspicious of everybody," he suggested. "Just because you're spying on someone doesn't mean they're spying on you."

"If he's not suspicious, then why was he staring at us?" asked Margaret.

"Oh, I don't know. Maybe because you're the only twelve-year-olds in a room full of FBI agents?"

Our lack of a response indicated that he might've been on to something.

"He congratulated me just like half the room," continued Marcus. "And the fact that he included you in the conversation may just mean he's trying to be polite. Besides, you've got to cut those organized-crime guys some slack. They're always locked in a surveillance van spying on low-lifes. It messes up their people skills."

Suddenly everyone's attention turned to the man who'd just entered the room. Admiral David Denton Douglas would have been imposing even if he wasn't the director of the FBI. Tall and fit, he took long purposeful strides as he made a beeline to us. I was impressed with how well he was able to make eye contact and acknowledge people without stopping to chitchat. No doubt it was a necessary skill for officials in powerful positions.

"Sorry to interrupt the festivities," he said. "But I need your help with a situation."

"What type?" asked Marcus.

The admiral looked around the room at all the people, most of whom were now looking our way. "Not here," he said. "We need to use a skiff."

Marcus and Kayla exchanged a serious look.

"Do you want all of us?" Marcus asked, motioning to Margaret and me.

Admiral Douglas thought about this for a moment and nodded. "Yes. Let's bring the whole Special Projects Team."

My pulse began to race, and a smile of anticipation formed on my lips.

As we followed him out the door, Margaret asked Kayla, "What's a skiff?"

She raised her eyebrows a bit and answered, "A spy-proof room."

This was beyond exciting. But the last thing I noticed before we left the room was Dan Napoli watching our every step.

3.

The SCIF

THE ADMIRAL MAINTAINED HIS BRISK PACE DOWN the hall, the heels of his shoes clicking against the marble floor, his posture so perfect his shoulders barely seemed to move as he walked. He bypassed the main bank of elevators and turned into an alcove where a private one was already waiting, its doors open, a uniformed guard inside.

"Good afternoon, Admiral," said the guard.

"Good afternoon, Thomas," he replied. "Subbasement four, please."

"Yes, sir."

The doors shut, and as we descended, I felt a knot of excitement grow in my stomach. In a matter of moments the mood had gone from celebration for Marcus winning an award to anticipation for a case so sensitive we had to go into a spy-proof room just to hear about it. For the first few floors everyone stood quietly, and the only sound was the whirring of the elevator motor. Luckily, we had Margaret there to break the tension.

"You guys are great when it comes to solving crimes but kind of lousy at naming things," she said.

"What do you mean?" asked Marcus.

"Why would you call a spy-proof room a skiff? A skiff is a type of boat. My dad took me fishing in one once, and believe me, there was nothing spy-proof about it. There was nothing mosquito-proof, either. I used an entire can of bug spray and still wound up covered in bites."

The admiral laughed. "I'm with you, Margaret. But the government loves acronyms. Everything's some sort of alphabet soup. 'Skiff' comes from SCIF, which stands for Sensitive Compartmented Information Facility."

A ding announced our arrival. "Subbasement four," said the guard as the doors opened.

"No bug spray necessary," added Marcus as we stepped out into the hallway.

Unlike the reception area or the main hall, there were no marble floors or works of art down here in the bowels of the building. In fact, there was no decoration of any kind, just a long narrow corridor with pea-green walls and tomato-red doors. It was as if the building's color scheme were dictated by the soup menu in the cafeteria.

"You think of a room as a separate and independent location," the admiral explained as we walked. "But it's connected to the outside world in so many ways—windows, walls, wiring."

I know my brain's a little strange, but when he said that, all I could think of was that all three of those words start with *W*.

"The problem with those is that people on the other side can listen in," he continued. "An ear to the wall, a microphone pointed at a window, or a listening device connected to the wiring. So when we discuss things of a top-secret nature, we sometimes use a SCIF. It's a soundproof room enclosed in layers of metal on both sides of the wall, floor, and ceiling." He stopped at a door marked SB4-2051. "A box within a box, wrapped up as tight as a present on Christmas morning."

He opened the door to reveal a waiting room manned by a guard behind a desk who told us that electronics weren't allowed beyond that point. We had to place our phones inside little lockers that looked like post office boxes. As we did, we noticed four were already in use.

"Company?" asked Marcus.

"Good to see they've arrived," said the admiral. "We can get started right away."

My curiosity level was off the charts imagining who might be waiting for us in the room. I wondered if it was a team of undercover agents like the one Margaret identified at the reception. Or maybe there were secret operatives from a foreign government. The possibilities were endless, but never would I have guessed whose faces we saw once he opened the door.

"Mom? Dad? Mr. and Mrs. Campbell?"

"Please enter," encouraged the admiral. "We have to be inside the SCIF to take advantage of its soundproof qualities."

The room had a wooden conference table with eight chairs. My parents were seated on one side with Margaret's on the other while yet another guard kept an eye on them. Once he left the room and the admiral closed the door, we simultaneously asked, "What are you doing here?"

"We don't really know," said Mrs. Campbell.

"The admiral didn't give us too many details," added my father.

"I assure you that nothing's wrong," he said. "We just need to take care of a little business in private. Everyone, please sit down. I don't mean to rush things, but there's another group returning in about forty-five minutes. They've been using the room all day, and I managed to squeeze us in while they're on a meal break."

He moved to the front of the room while we filled in the empty seats.

"Do you know what this is about?" I whispered to Marcus as I sat next to my mother.

He just gave me a smile and a wink.

"I'm sorry for all the subterfuge," said the admiral. "But something unprecedented happened a few weeks ago when I informed Marcus that I was presenting him with a Director's Award for Excellence."

"What's that?" asked Margaret.

"He turned it down."

We all gave Marcus a look of disbelief.

"Why would you do that?" I asked.

"Because I didn't think I deserved it," he replied.

"Special Agent Rivers felt that he was getting recognition and credit for the work of others," explained Admiral Douglas. "Namely, for the work you two have done. And the more I thought about it, the more I saw his point. You both deserve recognition for what you've done. But I think we can all agree that it might have been a bit problematic doing so out in the auditorium in front of all those people. So I convinced Marcus that I would take care of you down here, and in exchange he agreed to accept the award at today's ceremony."

Margaret and I were beyond confused.

"I'm sorry, but I don't understand," she said.

"Maybe this will help."

He unlocked a cabinet and pulled out a pair of flat jewelry boxes, which he placed on the table.

"Margaret, Florian, would you please join me?"

We stood next to him, and he opened one of the boxes to reveal a gold medal engraved with the Great Seal of the United States and attached to a ribbon with red, white, and blue stripes. It was stunning.

"This is the FBI Medal for Meritorious Achievement," he explained. "It's awarded for extraordinary accomplishments in connection with criminal and national security cases. It's one of the highest honors the Bureau can bestow on a civilian, and it is my great privilege that I get to present it to each of you."

Margaret and I were speechless. We just stood there with dazed looks on our faces, which the adults found quite amusing.

Finally Margaret was able to mutter, "You're giving us medals?"

"Yes, I am," he replied. "Now, if you'll bow your heads a little, we can make it official."

He hung the medals around our necks, just like they do at the Olympics, and said, "The Medal for Meritorious Achievement is presented with honor and distinction to covert asset Florian Bates and covert asset Margaret Campbell for their dedicated service to the Federal Bureau of Investigation and the people of the United States of America."

Next he gave a glowing account of the role we'd played in solving several cases, and I was touched by his attention to detail. He talked about me overcoming my fear of helicopters and climbing aboard one during an emergency. He spoke of Margaret's loyalty and quick thinking in a crisis.

"Not only are they brilliant and brave," he concluded, "but I believe that TOAST is without question the most impressive mystery-solving technique I've ever witnessed."

By this point all four parents had tears in their eyes, and although the lighting in the SCIF wasn't great, I'm pretty sure Marcus and Kayla did too.

"I don't know what to say," I responded, dazed by it all.

"How about 'thank you,'" suggested my mother.

"Yes, of course," I replied. "Thank you very much."

"It's a lovely honor," added Margaret, "and greatly appreciated."

"It's my privilege," Douglas responded. "It's a great thing for this country that you two became friends."

"I don't know about that," I said quietly. "But it was certainly great for me."

It was a perfect moment. For about ten seconds. Then the admiral added, "I have bad news, though."

"What?" asked Margaret.

"You can't take the medals out of the SCIF."

Suddenly it all made sense. That's why we needed a spy-proof compartment. We'd received a huge honor, but no one outside that room could know about it. I was a bit disappointed. It must have shown on my face, because Margaret gave me her "cheer up" smile.

"*We* know," she said. "And that's all that matters."

"You're right. To be honest, that's not even the part I'm most disappointed about."

"What do you mean?"

"I thought we were coming down here because we were getting a cool case."

She laughed. "So did I. But this is still pretty nice."

"It's great. But a supersecret spy case would've been great too."

Everyone got up to take a closer look at the medals and congratulate us. It didn't take long for the tinge of disappointment to fade. I don't think I'd ever seen my parents look so proud.

"I don't know about you guys," Marcus said, "but I think this moment calls for barbecue."

"Texas Tony's?" I said excitedly.

"I may have reserved that little private room in the back," he said with a smile. "It's not spy-proof, but the ribs are amazing."

Texas Tony's was a favorite among agents. Not only was it just a few blocks from the Hoover Building but also the food was delicious, which is why Margaret and I repeated her victory dance from earlier.

"Want to join us?" Marcus asked the admiral.

"I'd love to. But I'm afraid there are still a few cases that need my attention tonight." He paused for a moment. "I don't want to interfere with your dinner, but there is one thing that I'd like to discuss while we have the SCIF."

"Of course," Marcus replied.

"We'll just head over to the restaurant and order some appetizers," said Kayla.

"It won't take long," assured the admiral. "Ten, fifteen minutes tops."

Kayla opened the door, and we all started to leave.

"This is where we say good-bye," Margaret said jokingly

to her medal as she took it off, gave it a kiss, and handed it to the admiral.

"It was nice knowing you," I said to mine as I did likewise.

"One day you'll get them back," he said. "There'll be a time when your help here won't have to be secret anymore and they'll be waiting for you in a vault somewhere in this building."

"I can wait," I said as I handed mine to him. "The real reward for me is getting to work on these cases."

"Me too," said Margaret.

He gave us a long look before saying, "Why don't you two stay in here while we discuss the newest one?"

"Really?"

"Really."

First a medal, then the promise of ribs, and now a supersecret case. It was better than a birthday. Kayla left with our parents, and the four of us sat down around the conference table. No one spoke until the door was shut and the room secure.

"I'm about to bend some serious rules, so it's important that we keep this conversation to ourselves," said the admiral. "You understand?"

"Yes, sir," I replied.

"Absolutely," answered Margaret.

"Two days ago a man named Herman Prothro stopped by the Tenley-Friendship branch of the DC Public Library looking for a book about Einstein's theory of relativity. When he got home, he felt something in the spine of the book. He bent back the cover, and a small key fell out. It was the key to a PO box located at the Friendship Station Post Office on Wisconsin Avenue. His curiosity aroused by the mysterious key, Mr. Prothro went to the post office and unlocked the box."

The admiral stood up and walked over to the cabinet, where he pulled out a white cardboard storage box marked EVIDENCE. He placed it on the table right in front of us and started to open it, pausing for a moment to say, "The instant he realized what he'd found, he alerted the FBI."

4.

The Russian Imperial Collection

MARCUS, MARGARET, AND I WERE ON THE EDGE of our seats as the admiral opened the lid to the evidence box and pulled out a thick black binder. He set it on the table with a heavy thud.

"This is what Herman Prothro found in that post office box," he said. "It contains hundreds of pages of top-secret information about ongoing operations being run by the CIA and the National Security Agency."

"Wow!" said Margaret.

"You got that right," said the admiral. "Apparently, we have a pair of spies on our hands who are using the library and post office as a two-step dead drop."

"What's a dead drop?" I asked.

"It's a secret location used to pass information between people so they don't have to meet face-to-face," he explained. "It helps them keep the relationship hidden."

"How does it work?" asked Margaret.

"Spy number one gets the documents, places them in the post office box, and hides the key in the library book."

"Then spy number two gets the key from the book and retrieves the documents," said Marcus, figuring it out. "The two people never come face-to-face, so it's virtually impossible to connect them. And there's nothing suspicious about going to a library or a post office, so they don't attract any attention. It's brilliant."

"But how does spy number two know when or where to check?" I asked.

"That's the million-dollar question," said the admiral. "Usually there's some sort of prearranged code or alert."

"I read about a spy who would signal a pickup by using a piece of chalk to mark a mailbox or tossing a soft drink can on the ground next to a specific park bench," said Marcus. "And there was another who would signal the need to have a meeting by moving a potted plant on the balcony of his apartment."

"So you're saying it could be almost anything?" said Margaret.

"Pretty much," said Marcus.

"What about the person who checked the book out before Prothro?" I suggested.

"We're trying to re-create the history of the book as we speak," said the admiral. "But it hasn't been checked out for nearly a year."

"I wouldn't think a spy would risk something so obvious," added Marcus. "It's more likely that he or she would've come into the library and hidden the key without actually checking the book out. That way there's no record of him being in contact with it."

"You're beginning to see our problem," said the admiral. "There's really a wide variety of possibilities on this one."

I was both excited and overwhelmed. "Are you assigning us this case?"

"No," he replied. "I can't do that. A joint task force of agents from the CIA, NSA, and FBI Counterintelligence Division is handling the investigation. They're the ones who've been using this room. They're spy catchers, the best of the best. But I'm concerned that the other agencies are trying to manipulate the investigation because they're worried some of their people are to blame."

"Then how can we help?" asked Margaret.

"I'd like to show you some of the evidence that isn't

classified," he replied. "So you can run it through the Toaster."

"The Toaster?" I asked.

"You know, let the three of you put your Theory of All Small Things to work."

We laughed. "I like it. 'The Toaster.'"

"Sounds good to me," said Margaret.

We put on white cotton gloves so we could handle the evidence. First he showed us the library book. Based on the copyright it was nearly twenty years old. Although the pages were yellow with age, it felt almost like new and was crisp to open.

"You said it hasn't been checked out in nearly a year," I said.

"That's right," answered Douglas.

"That makes sense," said Marcus. "You'd want to use a book that rarely circulates to make sure no one else gets it by mistake."

I opened the back cover looking for the pocket that holds the due date slip. PROPERTY OF DC PUBLIC LIBRARY was stamped on it in crisp black ink.

"Here's the key," said the admiral.

He handed me a small bronze key. Engraved into it was USPS (for United States Postal Service), DO NOT DUPLICATE, and the numbers 32751. I studied it and passed it to the others.

"There's just a serial number," Margaret said, looking at it. "How could he know what it opened?"

"Because this was with the key," he said as he handed her a small piece of paper about the size of a postage stamp. She looked at it before passing it to Marcus and me. In dark pencil somebody had written:

PO BOX 1737
FRIENDSHIP
STATION
ХОРОШО

"Mr. Prothro assumed it was part of some sort of scavenger hunt or contest," the admiral continued. "He went to Friendship Station, which is located on Wisconsin, near the library, and discovered the binder in PO Box 1737."

"What's this at the bottom?" asked Margaret. "XOPOWO?"

"Some sort of code," he answered. "We haven't deciphered that yet."

I studied it closely and said, "I think this was written with a golf pencil."

"Why do you say that?" Marcus asked.

"Its writing is distinctive. My dad loves to play, and sometimes I ride along in his cart and keep score." I turned to Margaret. "Remember that time we played mini-golf?"

"I remember beating you by six strokes," she said with a proud smile. "But I don't recall anything significant about the pencils."

"They're small, and the lead in them is really thick and dark to make it easier to keep score while you walk around," I said. "The writing looks just like this."

"So you think the spy is a golfer?" asked the admiral.

"Not necessarily," I answered. "I just think he used a golf pencil. However, I'm pretty sure he's European. My guess is Russian."

Marcus gave me a look, and then he examined the scrap of paper. "What makes you say Russian?"

"The sevens are crossed," I pointed out. "That's how they write them in Europe. That's how I was taught when I was growing up there. I usually do it in the American style now, but sometimes I forget and do it this way out of habit."

"That points to Europe," said the admiral. "But why Russia in particular?"

"The code at the bottom," I said. "I don't think it's a code at all. I think it's Cyrillic." I pointed it out for the admiral.

"What's Cyrillic?" asked Margaret.

"The alphabet they use in Russia," I said. "A lot of the letters look like ours, but they're different. If that's English, then it's a code. But if it's Cyrillic, it's the Russian word for 'good.'"

Marcus and Admiral Douglas shared a look, and I could tell they were impressed.

"Well done, Florian," said Marcus. "That's really good."

Margaret was incredulous. "How do you know that? You speak French and Italian, not Russian."

"I speak a little Russian," I said, holding up my index finger and thumb. "I spent two weeks there with my parents visiting museums in Moscow and Saint Petersburg. The word means 'good,' but it's one of those words that has multiple meanings, like 'okay' or 'good luck.' They use it all the time."

"That's an interesting development," said the admiral. "Because there was one more item in the post office box."

He pulled out an antique purple book. The title was in Russian and stamped on the cover and spine in gold leaf. He gently placed it in front of Marcus, and it was obvious by the look they shared that the book had significance to them.

"Is it from the collection?" asked Marcus.

"You're the expert. You tell me."

When Marcus picked it up, he had the same expression

I've seen my mother make when she restores a painting. He was careful and deliberate. He cradled the book in his left hand and opened it to the second-to-last page. He held it closer to the light for a moment and smiled. Then he pointed to something as he showed it to Admiral Douglas.

"Someone's tried to erase it, but you can see where 'RIC' was once written right along the seam," Marcus said with a charge of excitement. "This book was stolen from the Russian Imperial Collection at the Library of Congress. That's amazing."

"First Florian speaks Russian, and now Marcus is a book expert," said Margaret. "I feel a little left out in the secret skills department. How do you know that it's from the Russian whatever collection?"

"The Russian *Imperial* Collection," he answered. "It was my first big case. I ran a sting operation that caught someone selling books stolen from the Library of Congress for tens of thousands of dollars."

"He didn't just catch *someone*," said the admiral. "He caught Alexander Petrov, a high-ranking official at the Russian embassy. That's when I realized that Marcus was a star on the rise. It was big news. Petrov was PNG-ed."

"What's that?" asked Florian.

"More alphabet soup," explained Douglas. "PNG stands

for 'persona non grata.' When someone gets PNG-ed, it means he's kicked out of the country for good. Petrov was expelled from the United States and sent back to Moscow in disgrace."

"Unfortunately, he left the country before I was able to wrap everything up," said Marcus with disappointment in his voice. "I knew he was the one selling the books, but I was never able to figure out how he got them from the library."

The admiral gave him a look as though he'd totally forgotten this piece of information. "That's right," he said with a sly grin. "You never did officially close that case, did you?"

"No," answered Marcus. "Once Petrov returned to Russia, all my leads dried up. I had to put everything in a box and ship it to cold-case storage."

Marcus glowered for a moment. The public might have viewed it as a victory, but he wasn't satisfied with the outcome. However, where he saw frustration, Margaret saw opportunity.

"Wait a second," she said gleefully. "If it's not officially closed, then you can still work on it."

The admiral smiled. "And there's your special skill for the day," he said. "Reading between the lines."

Marcus looked up at him and smiled. "I can do that?"

"Of course you can," said the admiral. "It's your case. You can do whatever you want without obtaining permission from anybody. And if, in the process of solving your book theft case, you just happened to figure out who was spying on the US government, that would be a bonus."

"This was your plan all along, wasn't it?" asked Margaret.

"I don't know what you're talking about," he said. "Although I do know that you're supposed to be at Texas Tony's eating ribs."

He couldn't officially put us on the case, but he'd gotten us as close to it as he could. There'd be no more formal acknowledgment. Where we went from here was up to us. We said our good-byes and went to the restaurant. The food was delicious, and we all had a great time.

Texas Tony's was filled with people who worked in the nearby government buildings, including many of the same faces we'd studied during our game of Toastbusters. The diners were laughing and having fun, and it dawned on me that in a city like Washington almost anyone could be leading a double life.

After all, even spies like barbecue.

And, it turned out, so did Dan Napoli, the mysterious agent from the reception. When I got up to get a second helping of beef brisket, I saw him at a table across the room.

He was seated with another man who had that crew cut, FBI look about him. For a moment our eyes locked.

Was he there for the same reason we were, because it was a good restaurant just a few blocks from work? Or was he there because he was spying on us?

We held the look until I turned to get my food. I tried to force the thought out of my mind, but I remembered the last thing he'd said to us. That he was certain our paths would cross again.

5.

An Open Book

DAN NAPOLI WAS STILL ON MY MIND THE NEXT DAY as Margaret and I rode our bikes along Nebraska Avenue. As we pedaled, my front wheel squeaked and wobbled, the result of an ill-advised attempt to jump over a curb onto a rain-slickened sidewalk earlier that week. The ensuing crash managed to injure my bike, my knee, and, most of all, my pride. Since the wheel limited our speed, we had plenty of time to discuss Napoli's sudden arrival on the scene.

"Could it have something to do with the new case?" Margaret asked.

"I don't see how," I said. "He was watching us before we

even found out about it. And I doubt Admiral Douglas told anybody we were part of his plan."

"Good point."

"Besides, Napoli works in the organized crime division. He shouldn't be anywhere near a spy case."

"True," she said. "But neither should we."

I flashed a guilty smile. "That's a good point too."

Officially, the Special Projects Team was only supposed to reopen Marcus's cold case about rare books stolen from the Library of Congress. But that evidence was in storage, which meant it was going to be a few days before we could start.

Unofficially, Margaret and I wanted to spend our Saturday finding out as much as we could about spies, libraries, and post office boxes. Luckily, the Capital City Cycle Shop was only a few blocks from the Tenley-Friendship Library. This meant I could get my bike fixed and we could check out the crime scene.

The library had a modern design with glass walls that made it bright and airy. There were vertical orange panels on the second floor that resembled the pages of an open book.

"It's pretty," Margaret said as we locked our bikes to the rack in front.

"It won a bunch of architecture awards."

She gave me a look. "And how do you know that?"

"Research," I said as if the answer were obvious. "I knew we were coming, so I looked it up. It has a special vegetative roof to absorb rainwater. The floors and countertops are all made from recycled materials. And because there are so many windows and natural sunlight, it needs less electricity for lighting. It's very environmentally friendly."

"What about espionage friendly," she joked. "Are there any special features designed to help spies?"

"None that they mentioned on the website, but I'm sure we can find a few."

We were almost to the front door when she saw him. "Uh-oh, we've been spotted."

"By whom?" I asked as I scanned the people nearby. "Dan Napoli?"

"Worse."

She took me by the shoulders and turned me so I was pointed at a concrete bench under a shade tree. Sitting there folding up a newspaper and staring directly at us was Marcus.

"Ooh, you're right. That is worse."

Even in black jeans and a Georgetown basketball shirt, he had "FBI agent" written all over him. I don't know if it was the short-cropped hair, the way he walked, or the fact that he looked like he wanted to arrest us.

"Florian, Margaret," he said, greeting us. "How very unsurprised I am to see you here."

"Hey, Marcus," said Margaret, trying to play it cool. "What brings you to the library? Looking for a good book?"

"No," he replied. "I was actually looking for a pair of seventh graders who can't follow directions. It turns out that I didn't even have to go inside to find them."

"This isn't what you think," I blurted.

"Really?" he replied. "Because I think you wanted to visit the library and study the crime scene in hopes of finding some little nugget of TOAST. I think you convinced yourselves that technically you're not treading on the other case because the library is a public place and you *aren't really* investigating. And I think you didn't tell me because you knew I'd say no."

"Well, if you put it that way," I said sheepishly, "it's exactly what you think."

"Guys, we are walking a fine line here," he said. "We cannot be seen as encroaching on an investigation run by a joint task force of the FBI, CIA, and NSA. Spy catchers don't mess around, and they don't have a sense of humor about these things. The admiral cracked the door open just a little bit for us. We can't go busting through it."

I knew he was right, but I also thought it was important for us to get a look inside.

"He wants us to work the cold case, right?" I said.

"Yes," said Marcus. "The cold case about rare books. Not the extremely hot case about Russian espionage."

"Well, something inside this library connects to that cold case. All we want to do is get a look so we can figure out what it is when the evidence arrives from storage. Besides, you're right. It is a public place. It's our local library, and we have every right to be in there. There's nothing suspicious or wrong about it. So I don't see how the joint task force can complain."

He took a deep breath and closed his eyes. I could tell he was tempted.

"You said the admiral cracked the door open," added Margaret. "We're not busting through it. We're just peeking through the crack."

"We even worked out a backstory," I said. "Margaret and I are doing a science project on Albert Einstein. While I look for books on the shelf, she's going to pretend she's texting someone, but what she'll really be doing is taking pictures. Nonfiction is upstairs in the back. We'll be in and out in less than ten minutes."

"You already know which part of the building it's in?" he asked, incredulous.

"He did research," Margaret said with a raised eyebrow. "Ask him about the vegetable roof?"

"Vege-*tative*, not vegetable," I corrected. "It's grass and dirt designed to absorb storm water. It's fascinating when you think about it."

"Tell him more," she said.

"What would you like to know?" I asked. "About recycled materials or the use of natural lighting?"

He chuckled. "You're going to bore me to death until I give up, aren't you?"

"That's the plan," said Margaret.

"Okay, okay," he said, resigned. "A quick in and out. Just a few minutes."

Margaret and I exchanged a low-key fist bump.

"If you two are doing a science project, then what's my role in this scam?" he asked. "Let me guess, I'm Margaret's uncle again."

She shook her head. "You don't usually have your uncle take you to the library. This time you should pretend to be my dad."

He gave her a surprised look. "I'm not sure I look old enough to be your dad."

"Seriously?" she replied, stifling a laugh. "Have you looked in a mirror lately?"

He chuckled, but he also looked a little wounded, and I noticed him checking his reflection in the glass door as we entered the library.

"One of those young, hip dads," I said.

He nodded confidently. "You got that right."

I took the lead and headed straight for the stairwell that wrapped around the edge of the atrium. "It's funny. You think of spies hiding in the shadows, but this place is filled with sunlight. It's the exact opposite of what you'd expect."

"That's because the spies you see in movies are nothing like the ones in real life," said Marcus. "They're experts at hiding in plain sight."

On the second floor, the main room was laid out with rows of bookcases in the middle and computer workstations along the windows. There was an area with overstuffed chairs where patrons sat reading and several study rooms along the far wall. Since all the walls were glass, you could see into everything. In this building, "in plain sight" was the only place to hide.

"Can I help you find something?" asked a librarian.

Margaret went to speak, but Marcus cut her off. "Yes, please. My daughter has a science project, and as usual she's put it off until the last moment. So we're scrambling to get it done this weekend." Because we were "undercover," Margaret had to play along.

"I said I was sorry, Dad," she replied, shooting him a dirty look.

"We're looking for books on Einstein's theory of relativity," continued Marcus.

"My kids do the same thing," replied the librarian with an understanding smile. "The theory of relativity is five thirty point eleven," she said, referring to its Dewey decimal number. "That's the second-to-last bookcase on this aisle, bottom shelf."

"Wow," said Marcus. "You really know your library."

She laughed. "Thanks, but I don't normally have it so well memorized. It's just you're not the first person to come looking for the theory of relativity this week."

Marcus shot us a quick look to make sure we caught this, but tried to keep the conversation flowing, hoping she might give us some information.

"Probably other parents from our class," he said. "We're always bumping into each other the weekend before a big project's due."

"Well, this man didn't have any kids with him, but he was frustrated, so maybe that explains it," she said. "I walked over with him and showed him that we had an entire shelf of books on the subject, but he was only interested in one specific book."

I was impressed at how Marcus dug for information without being obvious.

"I don't suppose he gave you his name," he said. "I can give him a hard time about it next time I see him in the carpool lane."

"No," she said, shaking her head. "I told him I could put a hold on the book, but he wouldn't do it. He just keeps coming back every day to see if it's been returned."

"Sounds stubborn?" said Marcus. "I bet it's Phil Anderson." He turned to Margaret. "Chloe's dad."

"Is he tall with red hair?" asked the librarian.

"That's him," said Marcus with a chuckle. "Tall with red hair."

"Funny," she said. "He didn't sound like an Anderson."

"What do you mean?" he asked.

"With an accent like that," she replied, "I would've guessed his last name was something Russian."

6.

Spasibo

IT TOOK EVERY BIT OF SELF-CONTROL I HAD NOT
to react when the librarian told us about the man who'd been
looking for the book. We'd only come to get a picture of the
dead drop where one spy had hidden the key for the other.
Now we had what may have been a partial description of one
of the two: tall, with red hair and a Russian accent.

Even more important: *He comes back every day to look for it.*

"Stay cool," Marcus whispered as we walked away from
the help desk. "And keep your eyes open."

Suddenly everyone in the library seemed suspicious. Any
one of them could've been an FBI agent or a spy. A woman
sitting in the reading area looked up from her book when we

passed her. A man standing by a table flipped through the pages of a George Washington biography but didn't seem to actually be reading it. Then there was the woman at the end of the aisle, just a few feet from where we were headed.

Young and athletic, she wore a white cap, exercise pants, and a shirt from the Marine Corps Marathon. She looked like she was about to go for a run. Except she was wearing basketball shoes. They didn't quite fit the picture. Was she an undercover agent who accidentally wore the wrong shoes? Or was she just a woman at the library?

Like I said, everyone seemed suspicious.

I took slow, steady breaths and focused on our cover story. As far as anyone was concerned, Margaret and I were students working on a project, and Marcus was her dad. I knelt down to look at the books on the bottom shelf and read off the titles to them. "*Physics of the Impossible*; *The Road to Reality*; *Big Science*."

"Those sound good," said Margaret. "Get all three."

I pulled them off the shelf. As I stood up, I tried to get a good look at the runner, but she'd turned away from us and was now deep in a book.

"There's an empty study room," Marcus suggested, pointing down the aisle. "Why don't we go in there?"

There were three study rooms side by side, each with

glass walls that let you see right into them. Two college students occupied the one on the far left. One was typing away at a laptop while the other was reading a book and writing notes on a legal pad. An older man with silver-gray hair was in the room on the far right. He had a stack of books on the desk and was intently reading. Judging by the titles, all the books were about the Civil War.

We took the study room in the middle.

Unlike the "box within a box" where we discussed secrets at FBI Headquarters, this room was completely exposed to outside eyes. "Not exactly a SCIF," I joked once we closed the door.

"No," Marcus replied. "But it's as close as we're going to find here. Everyone can see us, so act like we're discussing these books."

We sat down at the desk, and I handed them each one. We started to flip through the pages as we talked.

"Do you think the Russian with red hair is one of the spies?" I asked.

"My gut says yes," he replied. "It's significant that he was only interested in one particular book."

"But why would he come back?" asked Margaret. "The government's already confiscated the files."

"He may not know that," he said. "That's the weakness of a dead drop. Since they don't communicate directly, the two spies might not have a way of letting each other know that something went wrong. At least not right away."

"Spy number one hid the key, so he probably wouldn't come back," I said, piecing it together. "His part of the pass is over the moment he leaves the key."

"And spy number two can't be certain that the person who checked it out also discovered the key and found the post office box," he said. "He may be coming back hoping that it gets returned with the key still in it."

"That makes sense," said Margaret.

I looked out across the library as I considered all this. "So what do we do?"

"*We* do nothing," answered Marcus. "We've peeked through the door as far as we can. This belongs to the joint task force. They can set up surveillance and catch this guy when he comes back. I've got to get word to them and tell them what we've discovered."

"How?" I asked.

"What do you mean?"

"How do you let them know what we know without letting them know that we were poking around the edges of their case?"

"I think we'll have to come clean and tell them what we've done," he said. "I'll alert Admiral Douglas, and he can pass it along. They won't like it, but he's the director of the FBI, so they won't challenge him on it." Marcus stood up. "However, that's not exactly the kind of call you should place on a cell phone in a public library, so I'm going to have to find a secure location."

He moved toward the door but stopped and turned back to us. "I can't help but notice the two of you aren't getting up and leaving the active crime scene."

"We still need to get pictures," insisted Margaret.

He gave her an unpleasant look.

"She's right," I said. "And we need to get them now. Once the joint task force sets up surveillance, we won't be able to come in here without them seeing us."

He hesitated, and Margaret went in for the kill.

"You don't want a repeat of your first case."

"What do you mean?"

"You caught the guy who was selling the rare books. But you were never able to figure out who was helping him because, once he left the country, your case dried up. If the redhead is spy number two and they catch him, it might make it so we never find his partner."

This was obviously a sore spot for him. He was also in a hurry and didn't have time to debate with us. "Just be out of here in ten minutes."

He hurried out the door and disappeared down the stairwell. Despite our promises and good intentions, it took us longer to do what we needed because we were determined to be cautious and thorough. We moved around the second floor of the library pretending to look for different books while Margaret took pictures from every angle and I searched for pieces of TOAST. Since we didn't know exactly what we were after, we tried to get a little bit of everything.

One thing caught my eye when we were by a computer used for searching the catalog. There was a stack of scrap paper and a box of short yellow pencils so people could write down the call numbers of the books they were looking for. I nudged Margaret and pointed at the box.

It took her a moment, and then she smiled. "Golf pencils."

When we were in the SCIF, I'd said that the spy had used a golf pencil, but I'd forgotten that libraries used the same type.

"Think he wrote it here?" she asked.

"Seems a little out in the open," I said as I picked up one and pocketed it. "But we can compare them later."

I glanced at the clock on the wall. It had been twenty-five minutes since we'd promised we'd be gone in ten. "We better scram. We told Marcus we'd be out of here long before now."

"Oh my goodness," exclaimed Margaret. "Look over there."

I turned and saw a tall redheaded man bounding up the stairwell. He was dressed all in black with a sport coat. His hair was cropped short so that it stood straight up and gave him a tough-guy vibe. Most noticeable, even from this distance, were his ice-cold eyes.

"Is that him?" she asked.

"It could just be a guy with red hair."

He bypassed the help desk and went straight for the aisle marked "433–616."

"Although, he is going down the right aisle," I said. "Why don't you get a picture of him so we can show it to Marcus?"

"Easier said than done," she replied. "It's pretty crowded, and he's moving fast. I don't know how to get a good shot without him noticing."

His head turned slightly our way, and we got a quick glimpse of his scowling expression.

"It's got to be him."

"Then what do we do?" she asked.

"Go over by the circulation desk," I said. "I'll get in his way and slow him down long enough for you to get a clean shot."

"Are you sure?"

"We don't have time to figure out a better plan. He'll be in and out before anyone from counterintelligence arrives."

"Okay," she said. "But be careful."

She walked over to the circulation desk while I got in position. I was so focused on him that I almost ran into the woman dressed like a runner as she left to check out a book. I stood at the end of the aisle and tried to take up as much space as I could. In order to get past me, he'd have to slow down, which would give Margaret a clear shot.

By the time I got there, he was looking at the books on the bottom shelf and was obviously frustrated that the book he wanted wasn't there. This was definitely our guy.

I gave Margaret a slight nod, and she held up her phone to get ready. Everything was perfect . . . except that he didn't come back down the same aisle. Instead, he walked around the other end. Now I was completely out of position. He was moving quickly, so I had to hurry. I looked at where he was headed and tried to predict where our paths would cross. I had to practically run to get there in time. As a result, I didn't block him.

I slammed right into him.

"Uunnff!"

He was so muscular, it was like hitting a wall. I bounced off him, and my books fell to the floor.

"I'm sorry," I said apologetically. "I'm so sorry."

He looked right at me, and up close his eyes were even scarier. It was as if they had no color at all. I stood frozen in fear but hoped that Margaret had a clean angle.

Instead of responding, he just made a slight growling noise and bent down to pick up the books I'd dropped.

I was rattled, and when he handed them to me, I had to force myself to thank him. Except, in my nervousness, knowing who he really was, and trying to be calm, I thanked him . . . *in Russian.*

"*Spasibo*," I said.

"*Pozhaluysta*," he answered reflexively. Then he thought about it for a moment and gave me a curious look. "How do you know I'm Russian?"

I almost passed out, so I did what I always did when I was in over my head. I looked for TOAST and read him as quickly as possible.

"Th-the la-lapel pin on your jacket," I stammered. "It's the Russian flag."

He looked down and saw that I was right. "Smart boy," he said with his version of a smile. "Funny that you were able to see something so small but didn't see the large person you walked into."

I wasn't sure if this was an accusation or a joke until he laughed.

I was relieved both because he seemed satisfied with my reply and because I was certain Margaret had a chance to get a good picture.

That's when the librarian came by pushing a gray cart with books to reshelve.

"I see you found him," she said to me.

"N-n-n-no, no, no," I said nervously.

"What do you mean?" he asked her.

"They were asking about you earlier."

His eyes narrowed as he reexamined me. For the first time he actually looked at the books I was carrying. When he realized that they were all about the theory of relativity, his smile disappeared completely, and his expression became something very different.

Something terrifying.

7.

United Nations

I STOOD MOTIONLESS, TERRIFIED BY HOW HE might respond.

"What do you mean, *they* asked about me?" said the Russian spy.

"This boy, his friend, and her father," answered the librarian. "They said you had a daughter at their school." She turned to me, confused. "This is the man who wanted the book on the theory of relativity."

The situation was spinning out of control, and there was nothing I could do to stop it. The muscles tensed along his jaw, and he stared at me with those cold, colorless eyes.

"Who are you?" he demanded.

My lips opened, but nothing came out. Or at least no words did. There was a long whistling noise that sounded like the air coming out of a punctured tire.

"Who are you?" he repeated, leaning closer.

Finally, my mind was able to make my body move. I grabbed the librarian's book cart and rammed it into him with all my strength. When he staggered backward, I wedged the cart between two bookcases and ran as fast as I could.

I'd taken three full strides when I locked eyes with Margaret.

"Go, go, go," she said hurriedly. "Unlock the bikes."

Somehow I weaved my way through the crowd of people without knocking anybody over, although I almost fell twice on the stairs: First my foot slipped off the edge of the top step, and then my ankle rolled as I turned on the landing.

When I reached the ground floor, I heard a loud crash and looked back up to see the spy sprawled across the top few steps. My guess was that Margaret had tripped him. He had a stunned look on his face as she leaped over him, her feet quickly maneuvering around his tangle of arms and legs.

I hesitated, but she looked at me and barked, "Bikes!"

We'd locked our bikes to the rack with a single long

cable, so only one combination needed to be entered. I got there first, and my fingers fumbled with the dial.

"Hurry up!" she said as she rushed out of the library. "He's right behind me!"

I popped the lock and yanked the cable from the spokes just as she got there. We hopped on and started pedaling, and that's when I remembered my bent wheel.

It made a loud creaking noise as it wobbled to life. I looked back over my shoulder and saw that the man was now on the sidewalk hurrying toward us.

"Just pedal!"

My mind flashed back to watching the cyclists in the Olympics. They always lifted their butts in the air and leaned over the handlebars as they raced. I did the same as we hurried across Wisconsin Avenue.

"Where are we going?"

"There's a dirt path that connects the Metro station to the high school," she said as we pedaled furiously.

"Stop! Stop!" yelled the man as he chased after us. "I'm not going to hurt you."

I'd never once beaten Margaret in a bike race when my bicycle was in good working shape. But with my having a bent wheel, she really had to slow herself down to keep from pulling away.

"You got it, Florian," she said as I tried to pick up speed with him closing fast. "Just get to the path."

He got close enough that I heard his shoes slapping against the sidewalk, but once we got past all the people heading for the Metro station, I pulled away from him. When we reached the dirt path, he was fading, and I was at least six or seven yards ahead.

"Come back here!" he commanded, his voice halting as he tried to catch his breath.

I resisted the urge to look and just pedaled as fast as I could in my Olympic pose, leaning over the handlebars and focusing on Margaret up ahead of me. After about a minute, I saw her look back over her shoulder.

"I think he's gone," she said with a grin of relief.

I let out a deep breath and took a look for myself. There was no sign of him. I slowed slightly, and that's when the wheel finally gave way and locked up. The bike pitched forward and threw me over the handlebars.

I've heard that some people say time freezes during a crash and everything slows down into small distinct moments.

That wasn't my experience.

I was looking over my shoulder one instant and had a mouthful of dirt the next. There was no in-between, although

I did hear a loud thump that I'm pretty sure was my body hitting the ground.

The bicycle also landed on top of me with the pedal and chain scraping my leg and back.

"Florian! Are you okay?"

I pushed the bike off my body, hacked most of the dirt out of my mouth, and rolled over onto my back. Every muscle throbbed with pain, and instead of answering, I just let out a slow, steady groan.

She circled back and got off her bike to tend to me.

"What happened?"

I said, "My wheel locked up." But because of my discombobulated state, it sounded more like "Bly peal plogged scupt." And then more groans.

She turned back toward the Metro station, looking for any signs of the spy.

"Hist te bear?" ("Is he there?") I asked, still spitting out dirt.

"No," she answered. "But we shouldn't wait around to see if he comes back. Think you can get up?"

I closed my eyes for a second and nodded. Then I sat upright, still catching my breath. Finally I was able to breathe and use actual words.

"Not exactly rideable," I said, looking over at the mess that was my bike.

We were behind Wilson High School. There was a bicycle rack about fifty yards away.

"Why don't you lock it up and ride home on my handle-bars?"

I laughed. "Really? Lock it up? Think someone wants to steal a broken bike?"

"Someone might want the parts."

I brushed myself off the best I could, and we walked it over to the rack as pain throbbed through my body. As we walked, I tried to explain what went wrong at the library.

"I didn't mean to slam into him, and when I did, my brain malfunctioned," I said. "I answered him in Russian, and then the librarian told him that we'd been asking about him."

"On the plus side, I managed to get a couple of good pictures." She held up her phone for me to look. In the photo, the spy is handing me the book, and Margaret has a clear shot of his face.

"They should be able to run that through facial recognition software."

"That's good."

"And check out this one," she said, swiping through a couple. "Florian Bates, action hero."

In this image I was running from the man with a look of total panic on my face.

"More like action zero," I said.

"No. You did great. I'm proud of you."

"By the way," I said. "How'd he end up falling so spectacularly?"

"He was too focused on you to see my little foot sticking out," she said with a sly grin.

"It's a good thing," I said. "I needed every second."

We locked up the bike and sent a text to Marcus telling him to meet us at my house for important developments. We used a bunch of exclamation points rather than giving him a blow-by-blow of our near-death encounter with a killer spy. (What's the emoji for that?) Then I climbed up on her handlebars, and we started down Nebraska Avenue toward our neighborhood.

Apparently I was a little dramatic with my moans and groans because after half a block she said, "If you want, you can pedal, and I'll ride."

"No. It's just that every inch of my body is sore. So try to take it smooth."

"You mean like this?"

She swerved slightly to go over a bump in the road.

"Owww!" I wailed as I bounced on the handlebars.

"Just joking," she said.

"Well, it's not funny," I said as I laughed and winced at the same time.

She pedaled smoothly for a bit, but then she started picking up the pace.

"Okay, Margaret," I protested. "Once is funny, but take it easy."

She didn't answer. She just pedaled faster and veered over and popped up onto the sidewalk.

"I'm serious," I said as I reached down and clutched the handlebars to steady myself.

"So am I!" she said. "We're not alone."

I craned my neck to look without throwing off our balance and saw a black SUV about half a block behind us. The sunlight was reflecting off the windshield, so it was hard to see the driver's face, but I could tell it was him. I also recognized the license plate on the front of the vehicle. It was a diplomatic one, common in Washington and given to employees of various embassies.

"This is bad in so many ways."

She pedaled faster, and we zipped along the sidewalk. "We can't beat him home," she said. "It's all streets between here and there. He'd be right on top of us."

Luckily, we were on the left side of the road, so we were separated somewhat by the traffic heading in the opposite direction. But still, there was no way for us to outrun his car.

"Got any suggestions?" she asked.

My mind raced trying to come up with some plan that didn't end up with us getting run over by the SUV. Then I had a strange thought.

"Is Model UN today or next Saturday?"

"What?" she exclaimed.

"Josh was talking about it at lunch the other day," I said. "But I don't remember if it was today or next week."

"Seriously?" she complained. "We're being chased by a killer spy, I'm pedaling for two, and you're curious about the schedule for Model United Nations?"

"It's just that if they're meeting today . . ."

"Then the school's open," she said, finishing my thought.

"Exactly."

"That's brilliant," she said. "Just brilliant."

"Maybe," I offered. "But we won't be able to outrun him to Deal, either."

"Maybe not on the street," she said.

"Does your bike have wings that I'm not aware of?"

That's when I looked up and saw the small opening in the fence surrounding Fort Reno Park, which is located next to the school.

"You're going to ride through there?" I cried.

"No," she said. "*We're* going to ride through there. He can't fit through it, so he'll have to drive around."

"Are you sure *we* can fit through it?"

She laughed. "We'll know in about ten seconds."

I was much less confident than she was. Especially since I was on the front of the bike and would therefore bear the brunt of the impact if we couldn't. I held my knees and elbows in close and looked down at my feet, which were dangerously close to the spokes.

"Hold on!" she exclaimed, and I gripped the handlebars as tightly as I could.

It may have been my imagination, but it felt like my arms brushed against the posts on both sides of the opening. I was so relieved we made it through that I didn't mind the bumpiness once we started riding across the grass and dirt in the park.

The shortcut probably gave us only an extra thirty seconds, but that made all the difference. When we ditched the bike and ran up toward the entrance of the school, the SUV was just coming around the corner. We were on our turf, the one place we knew better than anywhere, and had enough of a lead that I thought we could lose him.

According to the signs in the front hall, Model UN was meeting in the cafeteria, but we decided to duck into the main office because it was closer.

"Mr. Albright?" I called out to the principal as we entered. "Are you here?"

There was no response, and through the window we could see the spy park his SUV and get out.

We ducked under the counter of the front desk, and my phone chirped to signal a text. It was Marcus saying he was almost at my house. I texted him, *Get to Deal!!!!* and put it on vibrate.

Things were quiet for a moment, and then we could hear footsteps in the distance. They weren't the steps of a student hurrying off to the cafeteria. They were slow and methodical. I was able to peek through a small crack in the desk and see into the hall.

The steps got closer, and we both tensed.

"If he makes a move toward us," whispered Margaret, "I'm going to get on the intercom and scream for help." She pointed toward the nearby microphone.

I nodded my agreement.

Finally the spy walked into view, and I could see him through the crack. He looked around for any sign of us and quickly realized there were just too many places where we could hide. He was momentarily frozen, and I was cautiously optimistic.

Then something caught his eye, and he walked over toward a trophy case. He put his hands on the top of the case so that he could lean over and examine a picture on the wall.

From my angle I had no idea what he was looking at. But he seemed pleased.

He snapped a picture of it and walked away.

We sat there silently for about ten minutes and were just about to get up when a foot stepped into view behind the desk.

We both screamed, only to see that it belonged to our principal, Mr. Albright.

"Florian? Margaret? Are you okay?" he asked.

We stood up, and I looked out the window to see that the SUV was gone. Margaret tried to make up some excuse for Mr. Albright while I walked over to the hall to look at the trophy case. I wanted to see what it was that had made him so happy.

There were nearly a dozen pictures on the wall above the case, but I instantly realized which one had attracted his attention. It was a picture of the girls' soccer team celebrating a big victory. Standing in the middle of the celebration was the team's star player.

The caption read, "The Vikings celebrate a hat trick by Margaret Campbell."

The spy now knew Margaret's name.

8.

Penalty Kicks

THERE WERE FOUR IMMEDIATE RESULTS OF OUR run-in with (and subsequent running away *from*) the red-headed Russian spy.

1. An FBI crime scene team was able to lift a complete set of fingerprints from the glass top of the trophy case. The fingerprints combined with the photos that Margaret took made Marcus confident that they'd have the spy identified within twenty-four hours.

2. Security details were assigned to keep an eye on Deal Middle during school hours and Margaret's

house in the evenings in the event that the spy
tried to track her down.

3. Margaret and I were enrolled in the Bureau's next
    available courses in self-defense and evasive
    tactics.

4. Marcus got yelled at for about an hour by the head
    of the joint task force on counterintelligence for
    intruding on their case.

Despite numbers two and three, Marcus assured us that
it was unlikely the spy would come back. This was something he reiterated numerous times the next day while we
were practicing soccer drills on the field behind the school.

"I'm sure it's just an instance of him getting surprised
and overreacting," he said as I passed the ball to Margaret
and she tried to volley it out of the air. "He didn't know what
to think of you guys, so he panicked. It makes no sense for
him to hurt you. He's not going to come back for you."

"You said that already," Margaret responded after she
curled the ball into the top right corner of the goal. "Multiple
times."

"I said it because it's true," Marcus replied defensively.

I passed her another ball. This time it bounced farther to her right than I intended, but she expertly adjusted and rocketed it just under the crossbar.

She stopped for a moment and gave him that great Margaret smile. "If you're not worried about me, then why are you here on a Sunday afternoon when you could be somewhere relaxing?"

"This *is* relaxing," he claimed. "Besides, it's my job to worry even when no one else should be worried. It's my natural state."

She laughed. "I appreciate it. But I think you're right. It doesn't make sense for him to come back."

"If you want to worry about someone, you should worry about me," I said. "I feel like one giant bruise after that bike accident."

"Yeah," she said. "Worry about Florian."

"Well, I worry about both of you," he replied, focusing on me. "And because of the dramatic nature of what happened, not to mention your bruises, I haven't really given you the appropriate amount of grief for staying in the library longer than you were supposed to or for making direct contact with a suspected spy."

"Why do you look at me when you say that?" I asked. "She was there too."

"She didn't bump into the man and start speaking Russian," he said.

Now they were both looking at me.

"I said I was sorry about that."

They let me stew in my embarrassment for a moment, and then Margaret mercifully changed the subject. "I love this new field," she said, bouncing up and down on the balls of her feet.

"What's new about it?" asked Marcus.

"They replaced the turf and upgraded the drainage system so it will be more forgiving," she said. "They put in metal bleachers, so you guys will be comfortable when you come watch me play, and they're installing a new scoreboard this week."

"What makes you think we're going to come watch you play?" I joked.

She gave me a look. "All right, smart aleck, it's time for penalty kicks. Get in goal."

I groaned. "Didn't you hear the part about how sore I am?"

"Come on, Gigi," she said. "You can do it."

"Who's Gigi?" asked Marcus.

"Gianluigi Buffon," I answered. "My favorite player and the greatest goalkeeper of all time. She calls me that because she wants to pummel me with soccer balls to the face."

"No," she said. "I call you that because you're going to try out for the boys' team as a keeper and I want you to get lots of practice"—then she laughed before she finished the thought—"getting pummeled with soccer balls to the face."

I took my position on the goal line as Margaret set the ball on the penalty spot twelve yards away. Stopping a penalty kick was difficult. Stopping one taken by a player as good as Margaret was almost impossible. In case there was any doubt about this, she proved it by putting eight straight balls into the net as I flailed and dived left and right, doing little to stop the shots but banging up my body even more.

"Time-out," Marcus called as she lined up to take number nine. "Can I offer a little coaching for Florian?"

"Fine with me," Margaret said confidently.

Marcus motioned me to the side, and we turned our backs to Margaret as he put his arm around me and started whispering.

"Why did you speak Russian to the spy?" he asked.

I slumped. "That's your coaching tip? I said I was sorry."

"It's applicable to the situation," he said. "So tell me. Why did you speak Russian to the spy?"

"Because I panicked," I replied.

"Exactly. Things were overwhelming, and you panicked. That's a completely normal reaction. But the problem is that when you panic, you stop doing the things you do well. All you do is react. And that's what's happening right now."

I gave him a curious look. "What do you mean?"

"A penalty kick is a panic situation. It's almost guaranteed to go in."

"Right," I said, not getting what he was going for.

"Which means there's no pressure on you," he explained. "It's supposed to go in. The pressure's on her because if it doesn't, then she's made the mistake."

"Okay, but how does that help me?"

"With the pressure off you, you can relax and do what you're best at," he said. "Something even Gianluigi Buffon can't do."

"What's that?" I asked.

"You can use TOAST."

I began to see where he was headed, and I smiled.

"You've been waiting for her to kick and reacting to where the ball is going," he continued. "But what you should do is dive toward where you think she's going to kick it. You should use TOAST to predict where she's going to kick it."

"And what if I guess wrong?"

"Then you miss it. No big deal, you've been missing them anyway. But if you guess right . . ."

"Okay," I said. "That makes sense."

I got back on the goal line and tried to disrupt her thought process. After all, he was right. The pressure was on her, and I wanted to increase it.

"I see it now," I said to Marcus as she lined up for the kick. "That's exactly what she does."

I was making this up, but it rattled her a little bit. "What's exactly what I do?" she asked.

"Nothing," I said with a smile. "Just talking to Marcus."

She leaned over and adjusted the ball on the penalty spot. As she did, I noticed her glance twice at the right side of the goal. She took three steps back, and right before she took the kick, she adjusted her shoulders slightly toward that side as well.

According to TOAST, it looked like she was going to my left and high. The instant she kicked the ball, I dived that way, and although I didn't stop the shot, I managed to get a couple fingers on the ball.

"Good one, Gigi," Marcus said. "You almost got it."

"But he didn't," Margaret reminded us.

"No," I said as confidently as I could muster. "But I'm going to get this one."

Marcus laughed, and Margaret gave me a look that she normally reserves for opposing players in actual games. "Game on."

I watched her set the ball again, and this time I was able to confirm something I'd wondered about before. When she placed it on the spot, she lined it up so that the logo was pointing in the direction she was aiming. She also glanced that way and once again adjusted her shoulders right before she kicked.

She was aiming lower left.

Suddenly the aches from my bruises disappeared as I focused on the ball and sprang into motion the instant she struck the ball. She smoked it, but I was already on the move and able to slap it wide of the goal post.

"Great save," Marcus said with an enthusiastic clap.

"Yeah," she mumbled. "*Good* save."

Margaret wasn't mad, but she wasn't happy, either. She was a tremendous competitor and one of the best goal scorers among the city's junior leagues. She didn't like having her shot stopped. She was deeply focused as she took the next ball and put it on the spot. I could see that she was feeling the pressure, so I was confident that I had her routine down.

Logo, glance, shoulders.

She took ten more shots. I saved four of them and came close on two more. More surprisingly, two shots completely missed the goal, something Margaret almost never did.

"Okay," she said after I saved the last one. "What am I doing wrong?"

And that's why she's such a great player. Instead of getting frustrated, she realized she needed to make adjustments and wanted help figuring them out. I explained how she was telegraphing where she was aiming, and after a couple of tweaks to her routine, there was no way for me to predict where her shots were headed. She scored on five in a row, and we called it quits.

We started putting the balls away in a big net bag, and she said, "Thanks. That really helps. I can't believe I was telegraphing like that." She stopped for a moment and added, "And those saves were epic. We're talking Gigi good."

I beamed. "You think so?"

"Yes," she said. "If you play like that in tryouts, you'll make the team for sure."

"I'd do the victory dance, but my body's too sore," I joked.

Marcus had moved toward the sideline to take a call a few minutes earlier, and now he was headed back toward us with a determined look on his face.

"We got him," he said.

"The spy?" asked Margaret.

"His name is Andrei Morozov, and he's a diplomat at the

Russian embassy," he said. "Officially he's an attaché on the fisheries committee."

"What does that mean?" I asked.

"He's one of the representatives for the Russian government in talks with the US about treaties and agreements regarding where and how much we fish the oceans."

I laughed. "No, I mean what does it mean in regard to the FBI and Morozov? Are they going to arrest him?"

He shook his head. "We don't have enough for that. Besides, we don't want him to know that we know who he is. They're looking for him now, and as soon as they locate him, we'll have a team follow him around the clock. That means they'll know if he's anywhere near you two."

"I thought you weren't worried about that," Margaret said.

"Well, now I'm even less worried," he replied.

We said good-bye to Marcus, and he headed over to the Hoover Building to find out all he could about Andrei Morozov. Once we'd bagged all the balls, Margaret locked them up in a storage shed by the field house (the coach had given her a spare key so that she could practice whenever she wanted), and we started walking home.

Despite Marcus's many assurances about our safety, I looked over my shoulder every thirty seconds or so to make sure no one was following us. At one point I was suspicious of an elderly man walking his dog, and I also gave the evil eye to a young mother pushing a stroller.

"You don't have to worry," Margaret said. "The FBI has a team following him."

"Actually," I pointed out, "they've got a team looking for him so that they can follow him. Which means, at the moment, he could be anywhere."

"This case is making you paranoid," Margaret said, reading my reaction.

"You know what they say," I responded. "Just because you're paranoid doesn't mean you're not being followed."

We were almost home when Margaret's phone buzzed. When she checked her message, she seemed surprised.

"What's that?" I asked.

She didn't respond. I don't think she was ignoring me so much as she was distracted and hadn't really heard me.

"Is it from Marcus?" I asked a bit louder. "Is something wrong?"

She hesitated before shaking her head. "No. Nothing."

We took a few more steps, and she just stared out into space as she walked.

"I'm a pretty good detective," I reminded her. "I even got an award from the FBI."

"I know," she said.

"Well, it doesn't take a detective to know that something's bothering you," I replied. "So why don't you tell me what it is?"

She stopped for a moment, trying to figure out how to answer.

She took a deep breath. "I just got an e-mail that surprised me. That's all."

"What does it say?"

"I don't know. I haven't opened it yet."

I was even more confused now.

"I just know it's about my parents," she continued. "My birth parents."

9.

Helix 23

"YOU GOT AN E-MAIL ABOUT YOUR *BIRTH PARENTS*?"
I asked, confused, assuming that I'd somehow misheard what
she said.

She nodded.

"How's that even possible?"

She looked around to make sure no one could hear us.
"I'll tell you in the Underground."

The Underground was the room in my basement that we'd
turned into the headquarters for Florian Bates Investigations.
It's where we went to brainstorm ideas, work on cases, and discuss things in private. I'm pretty sure it was the "discuss things
in private" feature that was appealing to her at the moment.

"We're all alone right now," I said.

She looked down the street toward her house and shook her head. "No. Not out here."

Margaret desperately wanted to find out whatever she could about the couple who left her—"abandoned" is the word she typically used—at a firehouse when she was only a few days old. She loved her adoptive parents and wouldn't have traded them for anything. But she still wanted to know her full story.

And that was a problem, because her full story wasn't a good one.

Margaret's birth father was Nicolae Nevrescu—a notorious criminal known as Nic the Knife. I had discovered this during an earlier case and had been sworn to secrecy. (Technically I'd been *threatened* to secrecy, but I agreed with him because we both wanted the same thing—to protect Margaret.)

Nic the Knife was determined to keep her sheltered from the life he inhabited. He felt that any connection between him and her was dangerous. That's why I was worried about the e-mail. What if someone from that world had found her? What if the e-mail was from someone willing to use Margaret as a way to hurt him?

Neither of us said a word as we entered my house. A note

inside my front door said that my parents were at the grocery store and would be back soon. We went down the stairs and into the Underground. Margaret plopped into an old, comfy chair that Florian Bates Investigations had inherited when we had gotten new living room furniture, and I sat at my computer, trying not to seem too nervous.

"Okay," I said, bracing myself for a revelation. "Who's it from?"

She handed me her phone, and there was an e-mail from Helix 23.

"What's Helix Twenty-Three?" I asked.

"It's a genetics laboratory. I read about them on a blog for adopted children and thought I'd give it a try. You put your saliva in a vial and send it in. Seven weeks later you get a full DNA report."

"You did this seven weeks ago?" I asked.

"Yes."

"And you didn't tell me anything about it?"

She gave me a funny look but didn't say anything.

"What?" I asked.

"You're a really great detective, Florian," she said. "And an amazing friend."

She paused for a moment, and I said, "Why do I feel like there's a 'but' coming in here?"

"But . . . I don't think you really want me to find my birth parents."

Her words stung because she was right. I didn't want her to find them even though I knew it meant more to her than almost anything. And the fact that I had a good reason didn't take the hurt out of what she said. I felt like a terrible friend.

"Why do you say that?" I asked her, careful not to deny something that we both knew was true.

"Mostly, it's a feeling," she said. "Whenever it comes up, you seem reluctant to work on it." She motioned to the caseboard we'd made on one wall trying to piece together the mystery of how she wound up at the firehouse. "We solve most of our cases pretty quickly, but this one has been stalled for a long time."

"True," I admitted. "But it's not because I'm reluctant. It's an incredibly difficult case, and we don't have much to go on. Besides, wasn't I the one who figured out that you were born at the hospital at Howard University?"

"Yes, you were," she said. "And I don't want to hurt your feelings. I'm not upset with you. I just don't think you're in love with the idea of me finding out the truth."

After a brief silence, I nodded. "I will admit that I'm worried you might find out something bad. I don't want you to be hurt."

"I understand," she replied, letting me off the hook a little.

"You're a detective and you're a friend, and sometimes those things are at odds with each other. But I'm going to find them, either with or without you. That's why I didn't tell you what I'd done."

"I didn't know you went on a blog for adopted children either," I said.

"Yeah, well, it's all kind of complicated," she replied.

I was tempted to tell her everything right then and there before she opened the e-mail. But I didn't. I knew Margaret well enough to know that she would want to talk to Nic the Knife, and that wouldn't be good. Her safety still outweighed my sense of guilt.

On the plus side, I was pretty certain DNA couldn't connect her directly to an organized crime family. In fact, part of me wondered (hoped unrealistically) if learning more about her ancestry might be enough to satisfy whatever it was she needed to learn.

"Well, I think it's a terrific idea," I said.

"Really?" she said.

"Of course," I answered. "Open it up and tell me what it says."

She looked at her phone and took a deep breath. Her finger almost touched the screen, but it wavered for a moment and she pulled it back.

"You do it," she said, thrusting her phone toward me. "I'm too nervous."

"Why?" I asked.

"We're talking TOAST here," she said. "My genes are the ultimate example of the Theory of All Small Things. This report has my smallest characteristics—the twenty-three pairs of chromosomes that make up my DNA."

"But there's no mystery," I said.

"What do you mean?"

"With TOAST you add up all the small things to get the answer," I said. "But the chromosomes add up to you, so they're great no matter what they are."

She smiled at that. "But they also point to where I come from, and that *is* a mystery."

The e-mail had a link that connected back to the Helix 23 website. I clicked it and opened a full rundown of Margaret's genetic history. On the first page was a map of the world with little blooms of color where her ancestors had come from. Next to it was a list with percentages of different ethnicities.

"Forty-two percent West African," I said, reading off one line. "Twenty-eight percent of that is from Ghana and fourteen from Cameroon."

"Ghana and Cameroon," she repeated as if committing it to her permanent memory.

"Eleven percent North African," I added. "Twenty-five percent Eastern European and twenty-two percent Southern European, probably from Italy."

She looked up at me, stunned. "Wait, what?" She snatched the phone from me to see for herself. "That means one of my parents is white."

This hadn't even occurred to me as being important. I was so concerned about who her father was—a ruthless criminal—that I'd forgotten to factor in what he wasn't: African-American. Margaret had grown up in a family with two black parents. This was a significant discovery.

"Did you ever consider that was a possibility?" I asked.

"I don't think so," she said. "I mean, I guess I knew it was possible, but I look a lot like my parents. People are always surprised to find out I'm adopted. So I just figured my birth parents looked like my parents too."

She sat there staring at her phone. Obviously, I'd known that Margaret was African-American since I met her. But despite everything we'd been through together, we'd never really talked much about race.

"Does that bother you?" I asked.

She thought about it for a moment. "I don't think 'bother' is the right word," she said. "But it does surprise me." There was a mirror in one corner of the room, and she got up to look at it. She studied her face for a moment, trying to rec-oncile the girl that she saw reflected with the information in her file.

"Does it change the way you think about yourself?"

She looked at her image for a moment more and then turned to face me.

"No," she replied. "When people see me, they see my skin color. I'm black. My parents are black. That's my identity. But it does change the story of the firehouse." She pointed to the caseboard where we'd laid out the information we knew about her. "When Captain Abraham told us about the night I was abandoned, he said that I was dropped off by a young man who was African-American."

"Right," I said.

She looked through the report. "But according to this, my African DNA comes through my mother's side, which means my father's white. So he wasn't the one who dropped me off."

"True," I said.

"There's another person in the mystery for us to find," she replied. "Maybe he was a friend."

"We should put it up on the board," I suggested.

"It also gives me a possible motive."

"In what way?" I asked.

"Not everybody's comfortable with white people and black people having babies together. That may have played a role in why they gave me up."

In this she was absolutely right. Nic the Knife had told me that this was exactly what happened. He wanted to marry Margaret's birth mother, but his family—the crime family—wouldn't have accepted the marriage or their daughter.

Now that the initial shock had worn off, Margaret started studying her report. We spent about twenty minutes going through it, and it was fascinating. Then she clicked a button sending a reply to the company.

"What's that?" I asked her.

"You click that if you want to be notified of any matches," she said.

"Matches?"

"If any relatives have submitted their DNA, they can tell," she explained. "And they'll send me an e-mail asking if I want to reach out to them."

Suddenly I was worried again.

"For all we know, my parents may be looking for me too," she said. "And if they use Helix Twenty-Three, I'll know."

I tried my best to be a good friend and smile, but I doubt it was very convincing.

10.

Operation Barbara Gordon

I HAD TROUBLE SLEEPING THAT NIGHT.

There were a lot of things on my mind, but mostly I was bothered by the fact that Margaret had kept her DNA test a secret. It hurt. Not because her reasoning was wrong but because she was absolutely right. It also made me think about how much it would upset her if she ever learned the secret I was keeping.

She might never forgive me.

The next day at school I was determined to prove that I was a good friend. No matter what she wanted to discuss, I'd be supportive and understanding. I was ready to do anything except tell her that her birth father was a notorious criminal. Our first chance to really talk came in the cafeteria at lunch.

"I'm going to ask you something, and I want you to be one hundred percent honest," she said as we sat at our usual table. "You've got to promise."

"Okay," I answered. "I promise."

She took a breath and looked me square in the eye. "Did you tell me everything I was doing wrong with my penalty kicks?"

"What?"

"You said I was pointing at the spot with the logo on the ball, taking a couple extra glances at my target, and adjusting my shoulders right before I took the kick. I just want to make sure that there wasn't anything else."

"You're serious?"

"Very," she said.

"After all that we went through this weekend, that's the thing that's been troubling you? Not Russian spies? Not your DNA?"

"The FBI's keeping an eye on the spy, and there's nothing I can do about my DNA. But if I'm telegraphing penalty kicks, that's a problem I can fix. So did you tell me everything?"

"Yes," I assured her. "Everything."

"Good." She took a few bites of her sandwich before

she spoke again. "Can I ask you another question?"

Once again I prepared for something important. "Anything."

"What's your favorite Serie A team?" she asked, referring to the top Italian soccer league.

I accepted that there would be no meaningful discussion. Soccer was apparently as deep as we were going to go.

"Juventus," I answered.

She considered this for a moment. "Their fans call them Juve, right?"

"Yes. Or the *bianconeri*, which means 'the white and blacks,' because of the stripes on their uniforms."

"Thanks," she replied as though this was important information.

Neither of us said anything for a moment until I asked, "Out of curiosity, why do you want to know?"

"I figure that if I'm a quarter Italian, then I should have a favorite Serie A team. And since you're my best friend, it should be the same team as yours."

And there it was. She turned soccer into something deep and meaningful. That's Margaret for you. I always seemed to get caught off guard with her. I hadn't even thought about the fact that we now had an additional connection with regard to our heritage.

"If you'd like, I can teach you a couple of the cheers in Italian."

She kept her focus on her sandwich but nodded. "I'd like that. Who knows? Maybe you and I are related."

"That would be *eccezionale*," I said.

"What does that mean?"

"Awesome."

She smiled, and we both ate quietly as the table filled with our classmates and conversation turned to normal seventh-grade topics.

After school we walked out the front entrance, and I scanned the rows of cars and parents to make sure Andrei Morozov wasn't hiding among them. He wasn't. There was, however, a black SUV parked across the street with an FBI agent keeping an eye on things. This was expected. What wasn't expected was the other FBI agent leaning against his maroon hybrid, wearing jeans and a Kansas City Monarchs baseball jersey.

"Marcus, what are you doing here?" asked Margaret, a bit annoyed, as we approached him. "You can't follow me everywhere to make sure I'm safe."

"That's not the reason I came."

"Oh, really," she said, disbelieving. "Then why? Did you suddenly want to catch up on the latest fashion trends among thirteen-year-olds? Are you thinking of enrolling in middle school?"

"Actually, I'm on my way to investigate some possible suspects in our case, and I thought you two might want to join me. But if you'd rather go and do your homework, I totally get that."

She momentarily slumped in embarrassment, and I took advantage of it by claiming the passenger seat.

"I vote for chasing suspects," I said as I quickly hopped in and buckled my seat belt.

"Margaret?" he asked.

"Sorry for snapping at you," she said. "I want to check out suspects too."

"Good," he replied. "And I'm sorry you feel like everybody's worried about you, but the truth is, we are. No matter what else is going on, we're going to do everything we can to keep you safe. We'd be crazy not to."

"I know," she said as she climbed in back. "And I appreciate it."

We started driving, and I asked, "Are we going to the Hoover Building to look at the evidence from your cold case?"

"I wish, but it's taking them forever," he said. "I got an e-mail today saying it won't be ready until later in the week."

"Can't you rush them?" I said. "This is an important case, isn't it?"

"Technically it isn't," he said. "Remember, as far as the Bureau's concerned, I'm reopening a nine-year-old rare-book-theft investigation that was already sort of solved. We are a very low priority."

"Then how are we checking out suspects?" asked Margaret.

"I don't have any of the physical evidence. But I still had a list of potential suspects on my computer. I spent most of the morning tracking down what they're up to now. Florian, get that blue folder sticking up out of my briefcase."

The briefcase was on the floor by my feet. I pulled out the folder to find two copies of the same list. I kept one and handed the other to Margaret.

"I was convinced Alexander Petrov had help from somebody inside the Library of Congress," explained Marcus. "I don't see how else he could've gotten those books. By the time he returned to Russia and the case went on life support, I'd narrowed it down to these four people."

"Why does it say 'Operation Barbara Gordon' on the folder?" I asked.

"Oh, ignore that," he said. "You know how the FBI is

with naming things. Every investigation needs some sort of code name."

"That's kind of a weird one, though," I said. "Who's Barbara Gordon?"

"It's not important. What's important is that list of names. If one of them—"

"Is she Batgirl?" asked Margaret.

I started to say, "That's ridiculous," but then I noticed Marcus's reaction. He cringed and kept his eyes focused on the road ahead. I turned to see that she'd looked it up on her phone.

"And when you say 'you know how the FBI is,' do you really mean something you read in a comic book?" she asked.

Marcus tried to keep a serious expression as he answered, "In addition to fighting crime alongside Batman and Robin, Barbara Gordon has a PhD in library science and is the head of the Gotham City Public Library. Since I was looking for a librarian with a secret identity, it just made sense at the time. Besides, the Library of Congress has the world's largest collection of comic books."

"Just when we thought you couldn't be any geekier," said Margaret.

He glanced at her in the rearview mirror and said, "I never claimed to be anything different."

This was the list:

Dr. Rose Brock
Was: Head of Reference and Reader Services for
Rare Book Reading Room
Now: Manuscripts curator and archivist at Folger
Shakespeare Library

Alistair Toombs
Was: Librarian for Rare Book Reading Room
Now: Head of Reference and Reader Services for
Rare Book Reading Room

Brooke King
Was: Book repair specialist in LOC Binding and
Collections Care
Now: Owner of Palace Books

Lucia Miller
Was: Rare Book digital conversion specialist
Now: Children's librarian at Petworth branch of the
DC Public Library

"What's our plan of attack?" I asked.

"We'll check out the first two today and the others tomorrow," said Marcus. "For the time being we're just trying to get a general picture of them to see if it's even possible that they're involved."

"How are we approaching it?" asked Margaret.

"Very low-key," he said. "If one of these four is a spy, I don't want them to know we're investigating."

"Don't you think they'll be suspicious when an FBI agent just pops up out of nowhere?" I asked.

"That's the funny thing—they won't think of me as an agent," he said. "I actually knew all four of them before I joined the FBI."

"How's that even possible?" I asked.

"The thesis for my PhD was about illustrations in nineteenth-century books," he said. "I spent a year in the Rare Book Reading Room doing research. That's how I got involved in the case in the first place. It was because of my expertise with books, not because I was an FBI agent."

"You're always full of surprises," said Margaret.

"You can just call me Mr. Mysterious."

"Wait a second!" said Margaret. "Isn't Mr. Mysterious the sworn enemy of Batgirl?"

Marcus laughed so hard, he started coughing.

Our first stop was the Folger Shakespeare Library, which is located two blocks from the Capitol and across the street from the Library of Congress. As we approached the building, Marcus gave us a quick rundown on our suspect.

"At the time of the first case, Rose Brock was in charge of the Rare Book and Special Collections Division," he said. "That means she had the most complete access to the collection. She could have easily stolen the books and covered her tracks afterward."

"But she's not there anymore, so why do you think she left?" I asked.

"She may have been fired," he said guiltily. "The unintended consequence of my investigation is that it embarrassed the library. I worry they may have blamed her because she was in charge of the department."

"So she might not be happy to see you?" suggested Margaret.

"Right," he said. "But it's also possible she left because she wasn't a great fit there. Most department heads tend to be academic and reserved, but that doesn't really describe Rose."

"What do you mean?"

"Here's a picture I got off social media today."

He showed us his phone, and the photo on the screen was of a woman with short-cropped, spiked hair dyed bright blue. She had multiple piercings along each ear as well as one in her nose. She was jokingly sticking her tongue out at the camera, and the caption beneath the picture read, "I Work Hard for the Bard!"

"I like her already," Margaret said.

"At least she should be easy to find," I added.

"Especially because she's scheduled to give the three o'clock tour," he said, checking his watch. "We made it with seven minutes to spare."

When we reached the door, he held up his hand for us to stop momentarily. "These four have been in Washington for a long time. If one of them actually is a spy, it means that person is under deep cover. They've created a whole separate identity that is innocent in every way. The key will be identifying something that gives away who they really are."

"You mean like a letter from Batman?" said Margaret.

"If only it were that easy," he said as we entered the library.

11.

The Shakespeare Cipher

THE OUTSIDE OF THE FOLGER SHAKESPEARE Library fit in perfectly with the imposing marble buildings of Capitol Hill, but once we walked through the doors, it was as if we'd traveled back in time. With oak paneling along the walls and banners hanging from the vaulted ceilings, it looked more like seventeenth-century England than present-day Washington.

We asked a security guard about the tour, and he directed us to the Founders' Room, which had a large wooden table, high-back chairs, floor-to-ceiling bookcases, and paintings on the wall.

Rose Brock was impossible to miss, although her bright

blue hair had now been dyed a deep purple. She had a friendly smile as she welcomed visitors, and she stopped everything the moment she saw Marcus. If there were any hard feelings about his investigation, she didn't show it.

"Marcus Rivers?" she exclaimed as she rushed over and gave him a big hug.

In keeping our cover, Marcus had to act surprised to see her.

"Rose?" he said. "What are you doing here?"

"This is home now," she answered. "What brings you by on a Monday afternoon?"

"Expanding the cultural horizons of my two young friends," he said. "I'd like you to meet Margaret and Florian."

"It's a pleasure," she said as she shook Margaret's hand. "Marcus and I go way back. In fact, I knew him when he actually had hair."

"That's very funny." He turned to us and added, "I knew her when her hair was its original color."

They both laughed, and it was great to see him joking around.

When she reached to shake my hand, I noticed an inscription tattooed along the inside of her right forearm: "R&J Act II, Scene II, Lines 47, 48."

She saw me look at it and explained. "*Romeo and Juliet.*

From the balcony scene." She instantly struck a pose as though she were performing Juliet. "What's in a name? That which we call a rose by any other name would smell as sweet."

It took me a second to piece it together. "Because your name is Rose."

"It's like the bard was sending me a secret message in the middle of his play," she said with a wink.

There were eleven people there for the tour, and she had us all gather around a portrait of Shakespeare to begin.

"Welcome to the Folger Shakespeare Library," she said. "We're home to the world's largest collection of materials related to William Shakespeare, the great English play-wright and poet who was born April twenty-third, 1564. In our collection, we have one hundred and sixty thousand books, sixty thousand manuscripts, and ninety thousand paintings, prints, drawings, and other works of art all relat-ing to the man known as the Bard of Avon."

"That's a lot," said Margaret.

"You're not kidding," replied Rose. "I always like to start the tour off with my favorite of those ninety thousand paint-ings, prints, and drawings. This portrait right here."

She motioned to a painting of Shakespeare as a middle-aged man.

"I like to start here because there's something wrong with this portrait," she said. "Can any of you find the mistake?"

Margaret flashed me the same competitive stare I'd seen when we played Toastbusters or she took penalty kicks.

"Game on," she whispered.

"Bring it," I replied.

I scanned the painting, determined to find the mistake before she did. Of course I had an advantage. My mother was an art conservator who'd quizzed me about paintings my whole life.

In the picture Shakespeare was balding and had a beard. His arm was resting on a skull, and he was holding some kind of document. Next to him was a coat of arms, and written in the upper left side of the painting was the phrase "*aetatis suae 47*" as well as the date the portrait was painted: 1612.

I looked at the skull and wondered why it was there. Then I remembered that there's a skull in the play *Hamlet*. Maybe the document he was holding was a copy of the play. Unfortunately, I didn't know enough about *Hamlet* to tell if either of these was somehow wrong.

I tried focusing on the technical aspects of painting that I'd learned from my mother. It was oil on canvas, and the brushstrokes were tight. Shakespeare was posed like all the aristocratic Englishmen I'd seen posed in countless portraits. Nothing seemed wrong.

"Does it have something to do with the skull?" Margaret asked.

"No," replied Rose.

"Is there something wrong with the brushstrokes?" I asked, hoping to luck into the answer.

"No," she said, chuckling. "It's nothing like that. The mistake is much bigger."

I was stumped. I looked at Margaret and watched her eyes dart around the painting. She'd already beaten me in Toastbusters. I didn't want to lose again.

Then Marcus spoke up. "It's a fake."

That's when I was reminded that he had a PhD in art history and was in charge of the Washington bureau of the FBI's Art Crime team.

"You mean it's a forgery?" I asked.

"No," he said. "It's a painting of someone who isn't Shakespeare."

"That's exactly right," said Rose.

"How'd you figure that out?"

"First of all, he's posed like a nobleman, but Shakespeare wasn't. He was a playwright, not a member of the aristocracy.

Secondly, the coat of arms in the painting does not match the Shakespeare family coat of arms hanging on the wall over there."

He pointed to a coat of arms that featured a yellow shield with a black stripe across it and looked nothing like the one in the picture.

"And finally, *'aetatis suae forty-seven'* is Latin for 'at the age of forty-seven,'" he said.

"What's wrong with that?" asked Margaret.

"Rose just told us Shakespeare was born in 1564," he said. "That means for most of 1612 he would've been forty-eight, not forty-seven."

"Still as sharp as ever," marveled Rose. "It's too bad you weren't around back in 1932 when they first hung it in the library. Mrs. Folger was certain it was the real deal. Of course, in her defense, someone had painted over the date and the coat of arms. They'd also changed some of his features to make him look more Shakespearean. Think of it as the eighteenth-century Photoshop."

"If it looked like that, then how did you find out the truth?" I asked.

"Someone questioned its authenticity," she said. "Like Marcus, he thought the pose was too aristocratic for a playwright. The painting was x-rayed, and that's when the hidden images were discovered. We had it restored to its original appearance, which is how it is now."

"But if it's not Shakespeare, then why do you keep it up on the wall of the Shakespeare library?" asked Margaret.

"Two reasons," she answered. "First, because it's a good story and Shakespeare was all about good stories. Second, it's a reminder that things are not always what they appear to be. We house the world's largest collection of his works, and we have to be careful not to be fooled by the phonies just because we want something to be real."

The tour was filled with unexpected bits of trivia like this. Rose was funny and irreverent and obviously loved all things Shakespeare. She quoted favorite lines in different voices and at one point pulled Marcus into a mini-performance of *Julius Caesar*. She had him pretend to stab her in the back as she dramatically gasped, "Et tu, Marcus?"

I got so wrapped up in how entertaining it all was that I had to remind myself to look for any small clues or tidbits of TOAST that might help with the case. By the halfway point, I'd decided she was probably too flamboyant to be a spy, but then something caught my eye while she was showing us the earliest collection of Shakespeare's works.

"It was published in 1623 and is called the First Folio," she explained as she pointed to the massive book inside a display case. "It contains eighteen plays that had never been printed before, and without it we might never have known about *Macbeth*, *The Tempest*, or *Antony and Cleopatra*."

She wore a loose-fitting sweater over a tank top, and when she excitedly gestured toward the book, the sweater slid down enough to expose a small circular scar just below her shoulder.

I glimpsed it for only an instant and couldn't be certain it was TOAST-worthy, so I spent the rest of the tour hoping to get a better look. I didn't get it until the very end when we reached an exhibit called *The Shakespeare Cipher*.

"Remember earlier when I said that it was like Shakespeare was sending me a secret message in the middle of his play?" she asked.

"Because of the line about the rose," I said.

"Exactly. Well, I'm not the only one. There's a theory by some scholars that a secret code really is hidden inside the text of some of his plays. Some people even think the code is a secret message that claims Shakespeare isn't the true author of the plays at all. They say he's as fake as that portrait in the Founders' Room."

As she said this, she pointed back toward the room where the tour began, and her sweater slid down her shoulder enough for me to finally see what I'd been looking for. The scar was round with a raised center. My eyes must've opened wide because I saw Margaret noticed me noticing it.

"What did you see?" she asked a few minutes later when the tour was over and we were walking around the exhibit while Marcus and Rose caught up with each other.

"A scar," I whispered. "It was from a tuberculosis vaccine."

"You been going to med school while I wasn't paying attention?" she joked. "How do you know what type of scar it is?"

"Because my mother has one just like it," I said.

"Okay? So what's the big deal?"

"I'll give you a hint: my father doesn't have one."

I gave her a moment to follow my logic, but she just gave me a blank look.

"I hate to sound repetitive, but what's the big deal?"

"My father doesn't have one because they didn't give that vaccine to American children."

A smile slowly formed on Margaret's lips. "But your mom got one because she grew up in Europe?"

"Exactly," I said.

"That means Rose Brock lived overseas when she was a kid."

"Just like my mom," I said.

"And just like spy number one. Do you think she's Russian?"

"I don't know," I said. "I couldn't pick out any accent during the tour."

"You know what Marcus said. Whoever it is has been under deep cover for a long time."

I looked across the room to where Marcus and Rose were talking and laughing and wondered if she really could be a spy. She didn't seem at all like what I thought one would be.

I reminded myself that the fact that she grew up overseas didn't make her guilty of anything. After all, my mother and I grew up overseas, and neither one of us was involved in espionage. According to the Theory of All Small Things, it was significant only if other details pointed in the same direction.

"Check this out," Margaret said, nodding toward one of the exhibit displays. "Look at who was in charge of the team that researched the Shakespeare cipher."

There was a photo of three people standing in front of a massive computer. Rose was in the middle, and in this picture her hair was pink.

"Dr. Rose Brock of the Folger Library led the team that developed the Shakespeare cipher," read the caption. "Here she is with specialists from the NSA in front of the agency's quantum decryption computer."

"She didn't mention that she was the one who came up with the theory," I said.

Margaret gave me a look. "She also didn't mention that she did work with the NSA."

12.

Mr. Jefferson's Library

"I DON'T WANT IT TO BE HER," MARGARET SAID AS we walked from the Folger to the Library of Congress. "I like her too much."

"I like her too," said Marcus. "Unfortunately that doesn't make her innocent. Did you guys pick up on anything?"

"I don't think she's from the United States," I said.

"Really? I always thought she grew up in Baltimore."

"Not according to the vaccine scar on her shoulder," I said. "It's not American."

"You're sure about that?" he asked.

"Positive. You can tell by the raised center. They used to

give a similar vaccine in the US, but the center from that one goes down."

"The things you know," he said.

"And according to the exhibit, she worked with code breakers from the NSA to develop the Shakespeare cipher," said Margaret. "So that gives her a connection to the intelligence community."

"Both of those fit with the idea of being a deep-cover spy," he said. "Ideally, you'd come to this country as a teenager, so you could establish a long history that looks traditionally American. Then, over time, you'd develop seemingly innocent relationships with people who might have access to top-secret information."

"What'd you learn when you guys were talking after the tour?" I asked.

"It turns out I was right about her being forced out of the library," he answered. "She had to leave about six months after my investigation."

"Does she blame you?" asked Margaret.

"Luckily, no. In her mind the villain of it all was Alistair Toombs."

"The guy we're checking out next?" said Margaret.

"Right. He was second in charge of the Rare Book Division, and the two of them butted heads all the time. They had totally different philosophies about how the department should be run."

"In what way?" I asked.

"Alistair's great with books but not so much with people. He'd prefer it if the collection were only accessible to a select few. But Rose thought the books were meant to be shared, so she was always looking for ways to get them into the hands of the public."

"And when some of those books disappeared . . . ," I said.

"He was able to convince the powers that be that his way was right, and she was out the door."

"Sounds like a jerk," said Margaret.

"To be fair, I don't think 'jerk' is a word I'd use to describe him," said Marcus. "He's more . . . *single-minded*. He sees the collection and nothing else."

Even though the library was across the street, we had to walk all the way around the building to reach the entrance. A large fountain with sculptures of Neptune and other mytho-logical creatures was in the front, and as we walked up the stairway that wrapped around it, Marcus acted as our tour guide.

"This is the largest library in the world with three build-ings here on Capitol Hill and a few more on a campus in Northern Virginia. Its main purpose is to provide research and information for members of Congress so they're properly informed as they debate issues of government."

We passed through security and entered a massive room with giant staircases, arches, and columns. The marble floors had intricate designs, and there were countless artistic details and elements like murals and mosaics. There were also statues and busts of famous leaders and literary figures.

"Here's the main man himself," he said as we walked past a bust of Thomas Jefferson.

"Why do you call him that?" I asked.

"Oh, I know," Margaret said gleefully. "Because all this started as his personal book collection."

"Very good. The original library was destroyed during the War of 1812 when the British burned Washington. Luckily, Jefferson had nearly seven thousand books of his own that he'd collected from around the world. Congress bought them and started over."

We had to snake our way through a pair of large school groups as we followed Marcus up a staircase to the second floor. When we reached the door to room 239, he stopped and turned to us.

"This is the Rare Book Reading Room," he said. "It's only supposed to be used by people who are doing research, so there's no telling how much time we're going to get in there."

"In other words, look around quickly and make lots of mental notes," said Margaret.

"Exactly," he said.

The room was pretty but not ornate. A handful of readers were sitting at long wooden tables, and a chandelier hung in the middle of the room. Two librarians worked silently behind a reference desk, and a third was organizing books on a small wooden cart. It was so quiet, my first instinct was to hold my breath to keep from making any noise.

"The room was designed to look like the one in Independence Hall where the Declaration of Independence was signed," Marcus whispered.

Alistair Toombs was the librarian sitting to our right. He wore a crisp short-sleeved white shirt with a blue-and-red-striped tie. Wire-framed glasses sat low on his nose and wispy blond hair had been combed over in a failed attempt to cover a bald spot at the top of his head. Nothing about him seemed remarkable except his right arm.

It was sunburned.

His left arm and face were pasty white, but his right arm looked like the center of a medium-rare steak. It was beyond strange.

He was meticulously sketching a diagram when Marcus

cleared his throat to get his attention. He seemed perturbed as he looked up and said, "Yes?"

"Hi, Alistair," Marcus said warmly. "Long time no see."

The librarian studied him for a moment, but his eyes registered no recognition. "Do I know you?"

"You're breaking my heart," Marcus said jokingly. "I'm Marcus Rivers. I spent about a year here researching my PhD dissertation on illustrations in nineteenth-century books. We must've seen each other at least three or four times a week."

"We get many researchers," he said coolly.

"True, but I bet most of them don't go on to work for the FBI and catch someone who'd been stealing books from the Russian Imperial Collection."

He adjusted his glasses and looked at Marcus again. "Oh," he said with a tart face. "That I remember."

I noticed Marcus had blurred the facts of the story by saying he'd caught the person who'd been stealing books as opposed to only catching the one who'd been selling them. No doubt he wanted Toombs to think that case was long ago solved and closed.

"How can I help you?" asked the librarian with no hint of helpfulness in his voice.

"This is my niece Margaret and her best friend, Florian.

I was just giving them a tour of the library and wanted to show them around the area where I toiled for a year of my life. I don't suppose we can get a peek behind the scenes."

Toombs pursed his lips for a moment and said, "This is a research library not a tourist attraction."

"Yes, but . . ."

"No buts," said Alistair. He went to say something else that I assumed would end with us being asked to leave, so I decided to interrupt their conversation.

"I like your idea for the new design."

"I beg your pardon," Toombs replied.

"Your new design for the reading room. That's what you were sketching out, isn't it? Changing the orientation of furniture will really open things up."

He looked down at the diagram and then at me, uncertain how I'd made the connection.

"You know, I think we can help you," I said, pressing forward.

"Help me with what?" he asked.

"Well, obviously you have big plans."

"I do? And how is that obvious?"

"There are indentations in the carpet from when you moved the tables to try different configurations, like the one you're drawing right there. Also, the chairs at five of the tables are identical, but all of the chairs around this table are different."

I pointed to the table closest to the reference desk.

"The four chairs that are supposed to go there are lined up against a wall in the hallway," I continued. "These are the ones you're considering, and you want to try them out. And those fabric swatches behind your desk are probably what you want to use to cover the armchairs right where you walk in. All very nice."

His eyes traced through my observations starting with the indentations in the rug, then the mismatched chairs, and finally the fabric swatches. When he was done, he looked back at me.

"And in what way do you think I need help?" he asked imperiously.

"Well, none of those things are possible if the library's budget gets slashed. And according to what I read online last week, that's exactly what's being proposed in the congressional budget. Someone needs to convince the president to tell Congress not to do it."

"And who's that someone?" he asked. "You?"

"No," I said. "Thomas Jefferson."

He gave me a blank stare.

"You need to come up with a creative way to remind

President Mays that this library is first and foremost Thomas Jefferson's personal book collection," I continued. "Maybe you can invite him to stop by after hours and look at the books that actually belonged to Jefferson. He's obsessed with Jefferson."

"Let me guess. You read that online too."

I ignored the statement and pulled up a picture on my phone. When I found what I was looking for, I handed it to him.

"This is him with a peace medal that belonged to Jefferson. You can tell how much he loves it just by his expression."

The picture had been taken the first time I went to the White House. The president had me use TOAST to find the medal, which had been lost for more than seventy-five years. Of course, I didn't actually say any of this to Toombs. I just let him connect the dots himself.

At first he barely glanced at the picture. But then his eyes opened wide, and I knew I had him. "Wait a second," he said, suddenly flustered. "Is that *you* with President Mays?"

I looked at the picture and said, "You know, I think that is me with the president. How about that?"

"Florian's a close friend of the first family's," said Margaret, vastly overstating my relationship. "Lucy Mays even came to see him perform in our school talent show."

"Actually, she came to see both of us," I corrected.

"She's really thoughtful that way," Margaret said as if the three of us were BFFs.

Toombs was flabbergasted and didn't know how to react. He looked at me and then at Marcus. Finally he did some mental calculations and said, "Would you like a tour of the Rare Book collection? I can take you into the stacks."

"The stacks?" asked Margaret.

"Where we keep all the books," he explained.

"Are you sure?" I asked. "After all, it's a research library, not a tourist attraction."

"Yes, yes, about that," he said. "I clearly misspoke. It is in fact a research library, but it's also a national treasure owned by the American people."

Marcus gave me a nod, and Alistair Toombs tried to smile like it had all been his idea. We were going into the Rare Book collection. This is where the books had been stolen from the Russian Imperial Collection. We were finally headed to the scene of the crime.

13.

Our National DNA

ALISTAIR TOOMBS PRESSED A BUTTON UNDER his desktop, and the door behind him clicked open. We followed him into a vestibule that had a wall of lockers on one side and the door to his office on the other.

"There are over eight hundred thousand items in this department, and most of them are one of a kind, which makes them impossible to replace," he said as he waved his ID badge in front of a magnetic card reader to unlock the door marked RARE BOOK AND SPECIAL COLLECTIONS STACKS.

He opened the door, and we entered a darkened room that extended farther than we could see. Lights above us flickered to life, revealing a seemingly endless maze of bookshelves.

"Those are new," Marcus said, referring to the lights.

"I had them installed a couple years ago," he said. "Now all lighting in the stacks is motion activated. If there's no movement in an area for three and a half minutes, the lights in that zone turn off. It protects the collection from unnecessary exposure to ultraviolet rays."

"Is the darkness what makes it colder?" Margaret asked as she crossed her arms in a shiver.

"No, that's the climate control," he said. "Temperature and humidity are kept at optimal preservation levels, which is seven degrees cooler than the reading room."

"That's got to be expensive," said Marcus.

"It is," said Toombs. "But I'll do whatever it takes to protect the collection."

The shelves were filled with books and containers that looked like cereal boxes lined up with the narrow sides out. I pointed to one and asked, "What are these?"

"We make custom boxes to provide an extra layer of protection for items that are particularly vulnerable," he said. "Like this one."

He scanned the shelf for a moment and pulled out a tan box with the number 158 written on the top corner. He placed it on the empty portion of the shelf and opened it like a clamshell to reveal a small brown book tattered with age.

Margaret and I shared a look of anticipation, and he pulled it out for us to see.

"This is Thomas Jefferson's personal copy of *The Federalist Papers*."

"What are *The Federalist Papers*?" I asked.

"Essays written by Alexander Hamilton, James Madison, and John Jay in support of the Constitution."

"Hamilton?" said Margaret. "Like the musical?"

"Exactly. In fact, Alexander Hamilton's wife, Eliza, gave this copy to her sister Angelica, who then gave it to Jefferson. You can see the note she wrote."

He opened the book to show us a note from Eliza to Angelica on the title page.

"That's pretty cool," said Margaret.

"And this is even cooler." He turned to the inside cover, where there was a series of notations. "These were written by Jefferson himself. It's very rare. He almost never made notations in any of his books."

"That's Thomas Jefferson's actual writing?" I asked, stunned.

"Yes, it is," he said.

"That's exactly the kind of thing that will impress President Mays," I said.

The three of us stared at it in awe.

"You see, these aren't just books in here," he said. "They're the genetic code of who we are and where we're from. They make up our national DNA."

I began to understand what Marcus meant about Alistair's single-mindedness. He may not have been friendly, but he wasn't really a jerk. He was just completely devoted to the books in his collection. And if that made him socially awkward, it also made him a little noble.

"Marcus, which books were part of your investigation?" I asked, trying to get us to the crime scene.

"The Russian Imperial Collection," he answered.

"That's right over here," said Toombs.

I was impressed by how rapidly he navigated the stacks, making quick turns as the lights above us turned on and illuminated our path. It was obvious he knew every inch of it. The books of the Russian Imperial Collection filled an entire aisle of shelving on both sides. Most of them were protected in boxes like the one that held Jefferson's copy of *The Federalist Papers*.

"These items all belonged to Czar Nicholas II," he said. "There are documents from the eighteenth and nineteenth centuries, biographies, military histories, and works of great literature. The Romanovs, the Russian royal family, kept them at the Winter Palace in Saint Petersburg."

"Then how did they end up here?" asked Margaret.

"When the Russian Revolution overthrew the Romanovs in 1917, the books were taken out of the country," he answered. "Twenty years later they were sold to the library by a book dealer in New York."

"Aren't they part of Russia's DNA?" Margaret asked. "Shouldn't they be in a library over there?"

"That's a great question," he said. "They'd certainly love to get their hands on the entire collection. They've even told me so. I think they have a fair argument to make, but it's not my place to decide which books should be . . ."

He stopped midsentence when something caught his eye. He looked toward the opposite corner of the stacks.

"Why are those lights on?" he wondered aloud. "No one should be over there."

He seemed torn, unsure if he should check on it and, if so, unsure what he should do with us.

"We'll wait right here," Marcus volunteered.

"Thank you," he said. He started to walk away, but then he hesitated and looked at Margaret and me.

Marcus, sensing his unease, said, "I'm a special agent with the Federal Bureau of Investigation. I'll keep an eye on everything."

"Of course," he said as he walked away. "I'll be right back."

We could follow his progress through the stacks by watching the lights turn on automatically as he walked. Once he was far enough away, Margaret whispered, "He has trust issues."

"He has reason to," said Marcus. "All of these valuable objects are his responsibility."

I took some quick pictures of the shelves and the aisle.

"Just don't touch anything," said Marcus.

"I won't," I replied. "I just want to get some shots of the crime scene."

"I think it has to be him," said Margaret. "He's guilty."

"Based on what?" asked Marcus.

"Look at the security," she said. "Buzzers. Key cards. Motion detectors. I don't see how someone can sneak in from the outside, and he's the only suspect who still works here."

"That's a good point," said Marcus. "But the truth is, we don't know when the books were taken. Maybe they were all stolen nine or ten years ago and one just happened to turn up this week. And back then all of the suspects worked here."

"Wouldn't someone notice if a book has been missing for that long?" I asked.

"Not necessarily," said Marcus. "Books in the special collections don't get circulated much. I remember looking at some that hadn't been checked out in fifteen years, and I wouldn't be surprised if no one's looked at them since."

"What do you make of the sunburn?" asked Margaret.

Marcus laughed. "I have no idea. But that's Alistair for you."

We all quieted when we heard his footsteps approaching.

"What was it?" asked Marcus when he returned.

"A lost intern," he said, shaking his head.

"I think everything you've done back here is really impressive," said Marcus.

"You haven't even seen it all," he said proudly. "Down in the server room there's a computer that tracks every single entry and exit from the stacks as well as every time a light turns on or off. I can literally go down there and see who was in the stacks and where they went."

"That's amazing," he said. "Good for you, Alistair."

"We should probably head back. It's nearly closing time," said the librarian.

"Of course," said Marcus.

As we started to follow Alistair, I noticed something about the wall. Normally the paint on a wall will fade due to sunlight and other factors, but because there were no windows and so much was done to protect the books from temperature and humidity, the walls looked almost freshly painted, which is why it was so easy to spot the discoloration in one area. There was a spot about two feet by two feet that had been repainted a slightly different shade of brown.

"What was here?" I asked.

"Aren't you the eagle eye," he said. "That was an entrance to a book tunnel."

"What's a book tunnel?" asked Margaret.

"They're throughout the library and connect to the different committee rooms in the Capitol," he explained. "Our first responsibility is serving the Congress. When this building opened, it featured a conveyor belt system that carried books back and forth. You'd load them on in here, and some congressional staffer would take them off in there."

"Why don't they still use it?" she asked.

"What was a technical marvel in 1897 is no longer state-of-the-art," he answered. "And as the library continued to grow and the collections spread, it became more efficient to have a staff of workers who bring the books back and forth in carts."

"What did they do with the tunnels?" I asked.

"They just plastered over the entrances," he explained.

The tour ended at his office, where he showed us some renderings of what the redecorated reading room might look like. They didn't look all that different from the current layout, but we oohed and aahed like they were major improvements. I also used the time to scan his desk and shelves for any deeper clues to his personality.

Everything about the room was neat and orderly. The desk was practically spotless, and I realized all the books on the shelves were organized alphabetically. Even the pictures on the wall were arranged following a careful geometric pattern. The only thing that seemed out of place was the tube of sunburn cream next to his computer, no doubt to ease the pain of his right arm.

What was interesting about the pictures, though, was that they showed a different side to his personality. They were striking images of landmarks and landscapes that had been taken around the world. They were all outdoors and served as such a contrast to the interior nature of books and libraries.

"Did you take these?" I asked.

"Yes. I've played around with photography ever since I was a kid."

"They're beautiful," said Margaret.

"Yes, they're really terrific," added Marcus.

There were photos of famous locations, such as the Eiffel Tower and the Golden Gate Bridge. And there were images of places like a waterfall and a mountaintop. But one picture in particular attracted my attention.

"Have you been to Saint Petersburg?" I said, pointing

toward a photo of the Hermitage Museum, which I'd visited with my parents on our tour of Russia.

"Several times," he replied. "That picture was taken two years ago when I was there on an exchange with the National Library of Russia. I took that because, before it was a museum, that was the Winter Palace."

"Where the books in the Russian Imperial Collection were kept?" I said.

"Exactly," he responded. "Have you been?"

"With my parents," I answered. "They work in museums, and we went there on a vacation."

"*Eto krasivyy gorod,*" he said in Russian. "It's a beautiful city."

"Yes, it is," I said.

I was so focused on this connection to Russia that I didn't notice something else about the wall. But just like she did when we played Toastbusters, Margaret picked up on what I overlooked.

"What picture's missing?" she asked.

"What's that?" he said.

"There used to be a picture here, and now it's gone," she said, pointing to the wall.

She was absolutely right. There was a gap in the pattern, and if you looked closely, you could see a small hole where the nail had been.

"A lighthouse," he said. "I took it down because I just took one I like better. Sunrise at the Bodie Island Lighthouse in Nags Head."

He opened the bottom drawer of his desk and took out an expensive-looking camera. He turned it on and flipped through some images until he found what he was looking for.

"This is it," he said proudly.

The picture was spectacular. The black-and-white lighthouse was in the foreground in the early dawn, and beyond it you could see the sun peeking out of the ocean, the sky a brilliant mix of purple and orange.

"It's amazing," I said. "Absolutely amazing."

"I had a print made, and they're mounting it in the frame that was already here."

He handed us each one of his business cards and said, "If there's anything I can do for any of you, please don't hesitate to contact me."

I could see the hopeful look in his eyes, so I said, "And I'll make sure to tell the president how helpful you've been."

He beamed. "Thank you. I'll check with the Librarian of Congress to see about giving him a special invitation to look at the Jefferson collection."

Once we left the library, we sat on the edge of the big fountain with Neptune to compare notes.

"I still say it's got to be him," said Margaret. "And you think so too, Florian. That's why you put him on the spot about the picture from Russia."

"I know," I said. "But he loves that collection. Do you really think he'd steal from it?"

Marcus nodded his head. "You know, I think he might."

"Why do you say that?" I asked.

"Money. Not for himself but for the books. The department has a special fund that people can donate to. That may be how he paid for the motion lights, the high-tech climate control, and the computer that keeps track of who uses the stacks."

"So if he sold one of the books, he could take the money and make an anonymous donation to the department," I said.

"And if he were going to steal from it," said Margaret, "he wouldn't take something that was part of our national DNA like a book that belonged to Thomas Jefferson. He'd take something that was valuable but didn't necessarily belong in the Library of Congress."

I nodded at her reasoning.

"And remember what he told us," concluded Margaret. "He'd do whatever it takes to protect the collection."

14.

Palace Books

THAT NIGHT MARGARET AND I WENT INTO THE Underground and started making a caseboard. We began with pictures of the Tenley-Friendship Library and Andrei Morozov, which we taped to the center of the wall because we knew for certain they were part of the case. I wrote "Fisheries Attaché" on his picture and put a sticky note on one of the library that read, "Relativity—530.11."

"We need to get some photos of the Friendship Station Post Office," said Margaret.

"And a map of Wisconsin Avenue showing what's between them. But until we do that, we'll use this."

I wrote out an index card to look like the message that

had been discovered with the key, making sure to cross the sevens and add the Russian word at the bottom.

PO BOX 1737
FRIENDSHIP
STATION
ХОРОШО

Next to that Margaret put up the pictures I'd taken of the shelves that held the Russian Imperial Collection as well as photos of Rose Brock and Alistair Toombs that we'd found online.

"What do we need to find out about Rose?" she asked.

"Where she's actually from," I said. "If the person who wrote that note is Russian and she turns out to be Russian, that's important."

"We also have to determine what kind of relationship she has with the NSA. If she's close to someone who works there, that could explain how she got the secrets."

She wrote "Russian?" and "NSA?" on an index card and taped it beneath Rose's picture.

"And Alistair Toombs?" I asked.

"He has full access to the Russian Imperial Collection, and it would be easier for him to steal the books than anyone else. He also speaks Russian and said he'd do anything for the collection."

She wrote out another index card, which said, "Access to collection," "Speaks Russian," and "Would do ANYTHING."

"I can't stop thinking about that weird sunburn," I said. "I mean, how do you burn only one arm?"

"I know. It's not like there's a shirt that has one long sleeve and one short one. But is it relevant to the case? Or is it just strange?"

"I'm going to throw out a crazy idea," I said.

"Those are my favorites," said Margaret.

"Is there some chance that the thief is accessing the books by using—"

"The book tunnel?!" said Margaret, completing my thought. "That's exactly what I was thinking."

"I don't know how they'd do it, but it belongs on the caseboard."

We found some articles about the tunnel online and printed a picture that we put up on the board. Margaret had to go home, but I stayed up researching whatever I could think of, including the Shakespeare cipher and the Rare Book Reading Room.

I must've stayed up too late because I was tired the whole

next day in school. After classes were over, Marcus picked us up, and we drove over to Palace Books near Dupont Circle. Brooke King, the third name on our list of potential suspects, owned the store.

"I'm not sure how long she's been in the bookstore business," he said. "Back then she worked as a repair specialist in the conservation department."

"Like my mom, except with books instead of paintings," I said.

"Exactly. She's really good, too. One time my parents' basement flooded, and the water damaged a bunch of books, including a Bible that'd been in our family for generations and some old high school yearbooks. My mom was heart-broken, but Brooke fixed them up better than ever."

"She's the only one of the suspects who didn't work in the Rare Book Reading Room," Margaret pointed out. "Why'd you suspect her?"

"As a conservationist she had access to all departments," he said. "She'd also repaired a number of books in the Russian Imperial Collection, so she knew it extremely well."

We parked in front of a row of town houses that had been converted into businesses. The bookstore was the downstairs of one that also had an artist's loft.

PALACE BOOKS was painted in bright blue letters on the

front window. Underneath it in smaller print it said, RARE AND ANTIQUE BOOKS, APPRAISALS & CONSERVATION.

A bell above the door announced our arrival.

The inside of the store could best be described as organized clutter. Bookcases filled the walls, and their shelves were stuffed to capacity. There were two display cases in the middle of the room. One had old maps and the other antique books. Books were stacked in piles of various heights on a table that also had a cash register, a computer, and a half-empty package of blueberry muffins from a bakery called Orville and Wilbur's. (The muffins looked especially delicious.)

There was, however, no sign of anyone who worked there.

"Hello," Marcus called out.

He waited a moment, and when there was no answer, he called out again a bit louder. "Hello? Are you open?"

"Coming!" a voice called from a back room. "Are you Huckleberry Finn?"

We all shared a confused look.

"What?" asked Marcus.

"Huckleberry Finn?" came the reply, making no more sense than the first time.

Just then a woman entered dressed in jeans and a yellow sweater. Her black hair was pulled back in a ponytail, and she was wearing gray socks but no shoes.

"Somebody is supposed to bring by an early edition of *Adventures of Huckleberry Finn* to be appraised," she continued. "Is that you?"

"No," said Marcus. "My name is—"

"Special Agent Marcus Rivers," she said with a big smile as she recognized him. "What a lovely surprise."

Marcus did an excellent job of "recognizing" her, making sure it wasn't too quick or practiced.

"Wait a second," he said, trying to place her face. "Brooke?"

"That's right."

"Brooke . . . Prince?"

She laughed. "Close but wrong royalty. *King*, not Prince."

"That's it, Brooke King," he said with an enthusiastic nod. "I can't believe you remember me."

"How could I forget the man who got Alexander Petrov kicked out of the country?" She cackled with delight.

"What are you doing here?" asked Marcus.

"About three years ago I'd saved up enough money and decided to go out on my own," she said. "Welcome to Palace Books, for all your rare and antiquarian book needs."

"That's fantastic," he said. "Congratulations."

"I almost called it Brooke's Books, but I thought that was too cutesy. Besides, I figured my name is King, and a king belongs in a palace, so I went with that."

"It's perfect," replied Marcus. "I love it."

"Thank you." She gestured to Margaret and me. "Are they with you?"

"Yes," he said. "They're friends from my neighborhood. Margaret and I are helping Florian find the perfect gift for his mother's birthday."

She gave me a playful look as though she were examining me carefully. "Is that so? And your mother likes rare books?"

I shrugged. "I don't know about *rare* books in particular, but she loves books. In fact, she loves anything artistic or creative."

"She reminds me of you," Marcus told her. "His mother is an art conservator at the National Gallery of Art."

"A fellow conservationist?"

"That's what Brooke used to do," explained Marcus, because we had to pretend like we didn't know anything about her.

"I still do," she said. "I've got my own workshop set up in back and do freelance repair work for libraries and collectors. It helps offset the costs of the bookstore."

"Best of both worlds?" he said.

"And the worst," she joked. "That's why you'll have to pardon my mess. The last few days have been crazy. I drove down to North Carolina for an estate sale and purchased all of these." She motioned to the stacks of books on the table. "And then I had car trouble. I've been sorting books and dealing with mechanics ever since I got home."

"What kind of car trouble?" he asked.

"I understand books not engines," she said. "All I know is that I had to drive three hundred miles without air-conditioning."

"Ugh," said Marcus. "That's not fun."

"No, but I think it was worth it," she said. "They were selling a great collection of nineteenth-century books. I'm going to give them a little love and attention in my repair shop, and they should sell well."

"Very nice."

She turned her attention toward me.

"Now, for your mother's birthday present," she said. "Tell me about her."

"Like Marcus said, she's an art conservator. She was born and raised in Italy."

Brooke smiled. "Stop right there. I know the perfect book."

"Already?"

"I'm good at what I do," she said playfully.

Even though the shelves had no discernable organization I could understand, she knew exactly where to go. She walked straight to a bookcase and carefully pulled out a thin white volume, which she handed to me. It was a children's picture book, and on the cover was a line of marching bears. The title read, *La famosa invasione degli orsi in Sicilia.*

"*The Bears' Famous Invasion of Sicily*?" I said, translating.

"You speak Italian?" she asked, delighted.

"We lived there until last summer," I said.

"Then you understand how important it is to have connections to where you come from," she said. "I guarantee your mother read that book when she was a little girl. It's very famous in Italy."

Even though it wasn't really my mom's birthday, I wanted to buy her the book. But I also thought that it might be useful to have an excuse to come back to the store once we knew more about the case.

"It's really nice," I told her. "Can I think about it?"

"Of course," she said. "I'll hold it for you, and if you decide you want it, you can just come back."

Just then the bell rang, and an older man entered the store carrying a book wrapped in plastic. Brooke's eyes lit up.

"Huckleberry Finn?" she asked.

"Yes," he said.

She looked like a kid about to open her birthday presents. "I have to take this," she said to us.

"We'll get going," said Marcus.

"Come back if you decide you want the book," she told me.

"I will," I answered.

Since there were people on the sidewalk, we waited until we got in the car before we talked about anything.

"So, what did you all think of Brooke?" asked Marcus.

"I think she's another suspect who I don't want to be guilty," answered Margaret. "She's funny and nice."

"It also took her less than thirty seconds to find the perfect birthday present for my mother," I added. "I like her too."

"This case must have been so hard on you," Margaret said to him.

"In what way?"

"These people were your friends, but you had to consider them suspects in a crime," she said. "Even Alistair Toombs has some likable traits."

"That part was harder than you can imagine. I was new to the Bureau, and it was such a big investigation. I told myself I had to ignore my personal feelings and follow the clues no matter where they led. Even if it meant I hurt someone."

"Did you?" I asked.

"Did I what?" asked Marcus. "Follow the clues?"

"No," I answered. "Did you hurt someone?"

He was quiet for a moment and then softly said, "Yes. Very much." He didn't speak for nearly a block before he added, "That's why I'm going to need you to check out the last suspect on your own."

We waited some more, but that's all he said. He just continued driving, deep in thought.

15.

Lucia

THE LAST SUSPECT ON OUR LIST WAS LUCIA MILLER, a children's librarian at the Petworth branch of the DC Public Library. For some reason, Marcus was sending us on this surveillance by ourselves.

"Is this some kind of test?" I asked.

"It's nothing like that," he assured us. "It's just that the situation with Lucia is . . . *complicated*. When I was working on my PhD, she'd just gotten out of college and was new to the library. We were both young, so we started to hang out. And hanging out turned into going out."

"Wait a second," Margaret said excitedly. "Was she your girlfriend?"

He hesitated before answering, "Yes."

"Does Kayla know?" she asked.

"Why would Kayla care about an old girlfriend?"

"Seriously?" I said. "We're consulting detectives for the FBI. You think we can't put clues together?"

"Yeah," said Margaret. "I think the two of us knew you were a couple before the two of you did."

He laughed as he realized it was pointless to try to dodge this.

"Okay, yes, Kayla and I are a couple," he admitted. "And yes, she knows that I was engaged to Lucia."

"What?" said Margaret. "You were going to marry her?"

"That is what 'engaged' means. We were planning on getting married, but then we didn't. And now we haven't spoken in nine years. So you can imagine how ineffective it would be if I went into her current workplace under false pretenses to investigate her. We wouldn't get any clues, and there might be some books thrown at me."

Margaret shook her head. "Every day a new surprise."

"What was her job at the Library of Congress?" I asked.

"She scanned the pages of various books in the collection to create digital versions that the public could access online."

"Did she work with the Russian Imperial Collection?" I asked.

"Extensively," said Marcus.

"What do you want us to find out?" I asked.

"Just the basics. See if you can get an idea of what she's been up to and if it's connected to anything having to do with government secrets. The goal at this point is to eliminate suspects so we can narrow the scope of the investigation."

"Don't you want us to find out what's going on in her life?" asked Margaret.

"No," he said. "Only information that might pertain to the case. Beyond that, it's none of my business, and she deserves her privacy."

He parked at a diner across the street from the library.

"Can you tell us what she looks like?" I asked.

He reached into his briefcase and pulled out a photograph. "This picture's nine years old, but it should give you a start. We took it on a trip to San Francisco. She was there for a library conference, and I tagged along."

In the picture Marcus and an African-American woman were standing in front of a cable car. They were in their twenties and looked happy. He had his arm around her, and they were smiling.

"It can't be her!" exclaimed Margaret.

"Why not?" I asked.

"Because she's African-American. We're looking for a deep-cover spy from Russia. Do they even have black people in Russia?"

"That's a good point," I said.

"It would be a great point if it weren't for Lucia's father," said Marcus. "He was a foreign service officer with the State Department and was stationed in Moscow for two years while she was in high school. She's fluent in the language and has Russian friends both here and there. Believe me. I wouldn't have made her a suspect if I didn't have reasons."

There were so many questions I wanted to ask, but I got the sense he'd already told us more than he was comfortable with, so I remained quiet.

"What are you going to do while we're in there?" asked Margaret.

"This diner serves breakfast all day," he said. "I'm thinking pancakes and bacon would hit the spot."

The Petworth Library resembled an old-fashioned schoolhouse with red brick walls, white-framed windows, and a cupola on the roof. It reminded me of Alice Deal Middle. Not that Margaret and I were concerned with architecture as we approached the entrance. We were still in a state of shock from Marcus's revelation.

"How is it that we've never heard about this woman before?" asked Margaret.

"Well, it ended nine years ago, when the two of us were only three."

"You know what I mean. It's Marcus we're talking about. And he was engaged? To a suspect?"

"I wonder what that was like for him," I said. "You're pursuing a case, and the evidence points to someone that close to you."

"I think you got that backward," said Margaret. "What was it like for her? The man you plan to spend the rest of your life with thinks you may be a criminal. I bet that's why they broke up. She felt betrayed."

The first thing I noticed when we stepped inside was that the floor in the main room was actually a giant map of Northwest Washington with a gold marker indicating the location of the library. A librarian at the front desk directed us upstairs to find the children's department.

Almost the entire second floor was devoted to children's books. There was an area for little kids, a separate story time room, and a large reading room with big wooden bookcases, seating and tables, and a large fireplace.

"There she is," said Margaret.

Lucia Miller was tall with thick curly hair. Her dress had a flower-print design, and she wore red-framed glasses. She was helping a girl decide between two books. We pretended to browse at a nearby bookcase and watched her.

"She's beautiful," said Margaret. "She looks the same as she did nine years ago."

"She certainly doesn't look like a spy," I said. "But I guess that's the point, right? It's not like spies really lurk around in trench coats."

"There's no way she's a spy," said Margaret.

After helping the girl, Lucia circled the room, going from person to person and offering assistance. She was moving counterclockwise, which gave me an idea.

"Go to the nine hundreds and find a couple books on Russia," I said. "When you do, meet me at the table by the fireplace."

"What are you going to do?" she asked.

"I'm looking for cookbooks."

She gave me a funny look, but I didn't wait around to explain. I kept my eye on Lucia, trying to time out how long it would take her to reach the table. My goal was that we'd get there right before she did. I found two books designed to teach kids how to cook simple recipes and plucked them off the shelf.

I sat at the end of the table, and a minute later Margaret sat directly across from me.

"What's the plan?" she whispered.

In the window I could see a reflection of Lucia walking straight toward us. "Just follow my lead," I whispered.

"Good afternoon," Lucia said, flashing an easy smile. "Are you two finding what you need?"

"Not exactly," I said.

"Maybe I can help."

"We're having a culture day in our social studies class, and everyone is supposed to bring in food from a different country."

"We got Russia," Margaret said, picking up on my plan. She held up one of her Russia books for emphasis.

"But we can't figure out what to cook," I said. "And these cookbooks don't have those kind of recipes."

"Well, today is your lucky day," said Lucia.

"What do you mean?"

"At this library, we just happen to have a resource that can tell you all about Russian food and even the best place in town to get the ingredients."

"Really?" I said. "Is it over in the cookbooks?"

"No." She laughed. "It's me. I lived in Moscow for two years. I can help you figure it all out."

"That's awesome. How'd you end up living in Russia?"

"My dad worked in the embassy," she explained. "I went to high school there."

"This is our lucky day," said Margaret. "Do you have any suggestions about food we should make?"

"Borscht is famous there, but I think you want to stay away from that."

"Why? What's borscht?"

"Sour soup made with beets," she said.

Margaret laughed. "We definitely want to stay away from that."

"My favorite Russian food is piroshki. They're little buns with baked-in fillings like meat and vegetables."

"And they're good?" asked Margaret.

"Dee-lish," she said, drawing out the word. "There was a bakery around the corner from where we lived that made the most amazing piroshki. They got me through the cold Moscow winter."

She humorously put her hand over her heart at the memory, and when she did, I noticed she was wearing a wedding ring.

"Where can we find a recipe?" I asked.

"Not up here in the kids' section. You were right about that. Come with me."

She led us over to her desk and sat down at a computer. "I'll go online and find a good one that has straightforward directions."

As she did the computer search, I scanned her desk for any signs of TOAST. There was a framed picture of her with two small children who looked to be twins and a coffee mug with pictures of the characters from *Where the Wild Things Are*. Her nameplate read, MS. LUCRETIA MILLER— LIBRARIAN. (Apparently, Lucia is short for Lucretia.) She also had a small plaque that read, THANK YOU FOR YOUR DEDICATION AS A LIBRARY OF CONGRESS VOLUNTEER.

"You work at the Library of Congress, too?" I asked, pointing at the plaque.

"I used to, but now I just volunteer in the Young Readers Center," she said.

I looked over at Margaret, and she seemed deep in thought.

"This one looks good," Lucia said. "I'll just print this up for you."

"Thank you so much. You mentioned something about a store to buy the ingredients."

"Yes. Gorky's is a deli and market over on Wisconsin Avenue. I go there when I have a craving. Ask for Natalia. She's the owner. Tell her I sent you, and she'll take good care of you."

She reached over to her printer and pulled off the recipe. Then she did a quick search for Gorky's to get the address for us.

"Here you go," she said as she wrote the address on the top of the paper. "Forty-two thirty-seven Wisconsin."

She handed me the paper, which I folded and put in my pocket.

"Thank you so much," I said.

"My pleasure."

I started to walk away, but I noticed that Margaret was lingering. She still had that expression of deep thought.

"Can I ask you something a little personal?" she said.

I was panicked as to where this was going, but there was nothing I could do about it. My worry was that she was somehow going to ask about Marcus and their relationship. It would totally blow our cover.

"I guess so," said Lucia uncertainly.

"When did you go natural?"

The librarian smiled and answered, "Why? Are you thinking of getting the big chop?"

Margaret nodded, and I don't think I'd ever been so confused in my life. I had absolutely no idea what they were talking about.

"I did it eight years ago. I was at a point in my life

when I needed a fresh start. I needed to say, 'This is who I am.'"

Margaret beamed. "I totally get that."

The more they talked, the more confused I was.

"Look at him," said Lucia, referring to me. "It's like we're speaking Latin."

"Actually, I might understand a little Latin. This is much more complicated than that."

"We're talking hair," she said.

I nodded like I knew what she meant, but I was still pretty confused.

"I think yours looks amazing," said Margaret. "Thanks for all your help."

"Thank you," said Lucia. "You two have a great day."

We walked away, and I asked, "What's the big chop?"

"I'll explain it later," said Margaret, who seemed to be in a hurry.

"What's the matter?" I asked.

"I just feel bad about it all," she said. "She was supposed to end up with Marcus, and now she's married with kids."

"That's not all," I said.

"What else?"

I waited until we entered the stairwell to pull the paper out of my pocket. I held it up for Margaret to see.

"Check out the seven in the address she wrote."

"I don't have to," she said. "I noticed she crossed it when she wrote it out."

"And you know what that means?" I said.

"She's our new prime suspect."

16.

Evasive Tactics

THERE WERE ONLY A HANDFUL OF PEOPLE IN THE diner as we slid into the booth across from Marcus. He'd almost finished his pancakes and was midchew when Margaret started talking in her signature "I'm going to tell you everything I'm thinking really fast" kind of way.

"Before we talk about the case, I need to say something," she said. "First of all, I absolutely love Kayla. She's a hero, a role model, a total rock star. I adore her, and what I'm about to say has nothing to do with her."

Marcus swallowed his bite and flashed me a wry smile. "Here it comes."

"How in the world did you let that woman get away

from you? You're a smart man who went to Harvard and Georgetown."

"I take it you met Lucia," he said.

"The second she agreed to marry you, you should have rushed to the nearest church and had the ceremony," she continued. "You realize that, don't you?"

"This sounds remarkably like a conversation I once had with my mother," he said. "I know. I was an idiot. Lucia's amazing."

"Yes, she is. She's smart. . . . She's kind. . . . She's—"

"Our prime suspect," I said, interrupting.

This brought Margaret's rant to a screeching halt. She scrunched up her face for a second and let out a long sigh. "That too."

Marcus looked crestfallen. "Really?"

"I'm afraid so," I said.

He started to take another bite but seemingly lost his appetite on the spot and put his fork down instead. He looked through the window toward the library and then back to us and said, "Let's talk about it in the car."

No one said a word until he pulled out onto Kansas Avenue and I asked, "Can you take us to the forty-two hundred block of Wisconsin Northwest?"

"What'll we find there?" asked Marcus.

"Lucia's favorite Russian market."

"You weren't even in there long enough for me to finish my pancakes. How'd you get the name of her favorite Russian market?"

"We're good at this," I answered with more than a little pride. "We told her we were struggling with a class project on Russia and had to cook some food from there. She said it was our lucky day because she used to live in Moscow. After that it was easy."

"Well played," he said. "Now, what makes you think she's the prime suspect?"

"We already know that she has a connection to Russia and speaks the language. And you said she worked extensively with the Imperial Collection."

"She got the job because of her language skills," he said. "When you're making digital versions and scanning all those pages, it helps to be able to understand what's actually on them."

"And we have two crime scenes so far," I said. "The Rare Book stacks and the Tenley-Friendship Library."

"Lucia has easy access and familiarity with both," said Margaret, jumping in. "She works for the DC Public Library system, and she volunteers at the Library of Congress."

"There's a third location," Marcus reminded us. "The Friendship Station Post Office."

"Anybody has access to that," I said. "But I think we're going to find out something when we get to Gorky's."

"What's that?" asked Margaret.

"I saw the map when she pulled it up on her computer, and I think Gorky's is just a few blocks from the post office. If she goes there enough that she knows the owner by name, it makes sense that she'd pick that one for the dead drop."

"Plus she crosses her sevens," added Margaret.

Marcus thought about this for a few moments. "That's all circumstantial."

"That's how TOAST works," I said. "You start adding little things up until they become big things. So far she's got the most little things."

"How'd she act?"

"She was great," I said. "She had no reason to suspect we were up to anything. She was going around to all the kids, checking on them."

"Did you know that she's married and has a couple kids?" asked Margaret.

"Yes," he said. "Twin girls."

"I thought you hadn't talked to her in nine years," I said.

"My mom told me," he answered. "Lucia and she were always close and have stayed in touch. She still stops by my parents' house a couple times a year."

"You don't mind that?" asked Margaret.

"I don't have a right to mind," he said. "I'm the one that screwed things up. Neither of them did anything wrong, so why should they stop being friends?"

Margaret and I shared a look, and she nodded at me as if I should be the one to ask the obvious follow-up question.

"How'd you screw things up?"

He didn't answer right away, but he knew it was something we needed to hear.

"I was working the case and following the evidence. I had my list of possible suspects—there were probably about eight or nine names on it at the time—and I accidentally left it out on my kitchen table. She came by my apartment, saw the list, and confronted me about it."

"What'd she say?"

"She said I had to know in my heart that she couldn't have done something like that."

"And what did you tell her?"

"That it didn't matter what my heart told me. All that mattered was what the evidence told me. And the evidence told me that she had to be considered a suspect."

"Ouch," said Margaret.

"Yeah, that didn't go over well," he said. "She called off

the engagement about a week later. Looking back, I can't blame her."

I went to ask another question but could tell he didn't really want to talk about it anymore. So we just rode quietly along Piney Branch Parkway, a two-lane road that wound through a heavily wooded section of the city. The late-afternoon sun and the changing color of the leaves gave everything a brown-and-orange glow.

Some seventies funk was playing on the radio, and when Marcus reached for the dial, I thought he was going to turn it up to cut down on the conversation, but instead he turned it off and adjusted his rearview mirror.

"You know that evasive-tactics class you're scheduled to take in a couple weeks?" he asked us.

"What about it?"

"Consider this a preview."

He steadily began to increase our speed, and I felt a surge of adrenaline race through my body.

"Someone's following us?" asked Margaret.

"That's what I'm trying to figure out. There's a silver SUV four cars behind us, and it always seems to stay exactly four cars behind. Like it's trying to keep close but not too close. It looks like one I noticed earlier when we left Palace Books."

Marcus passed a car and said, "Don't turn around to

look. I don't want the driver to know we've seen him."

I was sitting in the back, so I tried to watch in the rear-view mirror. Sure enough the silver SUV sped up and passed the car in front of it. The sunlight reflecting off the windshield made it so I couldn't get a look at the driver.

"Here's the lesson," he said. "Step one is to identify if you're actually being followed. We don't want to do anything drastic that'll scare him off. But we want to check our theory. We're going to turn up ahead on Beach, and once we're out of his view, I'm going to speed up. If he's following, he'll be surprised by the sudden increased distance between us, and he'll try to make that up in a hurry."

Marcus turned left at the intersection, and the instant we were beyond the corner, he accelerated for about thirty seconds, passing several cars along the way. Then he slowed down to a normal speed.

We were far enough away that it was safe to look back without fear of the other driver noticing. Once the SUV reached the intersection, he instantly sped up and started passing cars like we had.

"Got him," said Marcus.

"Do you think it's Andrei Morozov?" asked Margaret.

"If so, he's changed cars," I pointed out. "The other day he was in a black SUV, and this one's silver."

"Does it have diplomatic license plates?" she asked.

"It's too far for me to tell."

"So now what?" Margaret asked Marcus.

"Now we let him catch us."

"What?!" Margaret yelped.

"It's the only way we can find out who it is," he said. "And as soon as we know that, then we'll lose him."

He clicked the hands-free button on his steering wheel, activating the phone. There was a beep, and he said, "Call Agent Cross."

Moments later we could hear the phone ringing, and then Kayla answered.

"Hey there."

Her friendly tone was immediately counteracted by Marcus's no-nonsense manner. "I'm in the car with Florian and Margaret, and we're being pursued."

"Are you in danger?"

"No, it looks like it's just surveillance," he responded. "How soon can you be at the Connecticut Avenue entrance to the National Zoo?"

"Twenty-five minutes."

"Excellent. Wait there and keep your engine running."

"Be safe," she said as she clicked off the call.

Marcus had a calm focus as he checked his mirrors. My

heart was racing, but he just seemed completely relaxed.

"We're in the middle of something, so I'm not going to make a big deal about it," Margaret said. "But Kayla *is* your girlfriend."

"I believe we covered that earlier."

"But on your phone she's 'Agent Cross'? Isn't that a little formal? Don't you have a cute nickname for her like Honey Pie or Kay-Kay?"

He laughed. "It's an FBI phone, and we try to keep things professional at work. Besides, I programmed that before we were dating, back when we were just colleagues."

"Why are we going to the zoo?" I asked.

"Because if he wants to follow us when we get there, he's going to have to get out of his car and walk," he answered. "That should give us a chance to see him."

It took me a second to figure out his plan. "And if we park on one side and Kayla picks us up on the other . . ."

"He'll be too far from his car to follow us when she does."

"That's brilliant," I said. "Did you just come up with that on the spot?"

"Yeah," he said, and almost seemed embarrassed by the compliment.

"You're really smart with the investigation stuff," Margaret said. "It's the figuring-out-women part that I think you still need help with."

Marcus laughed. "That sounds like another conversation I had with my mother."

The National Zoo is built on a hill next to Rock Creek Park. The Connecticut Avenue entrance is at the top of the hill, and we parked a little more than halfway down and entered near the Great Ape House.

"Don't look for him," Marcus instructed us. "We don't want him to know we're suspicious. Just move fast so he doesn't have much time to consider options. He's either got to follow us or he's going to lose us."

We didn't stop to look at any animals until we reached the elephant house. First we lingered at the fence and watched one playing in the water. Then we walked inside, where a keeper was giving an educational talk.

"He won't follow us in here," explained Marcus. "It would be too risky. He'll wait on the outside."

We listened as the keeper explained some of the zoo's conservation efforts in Asia. When she was done, a large tour group headed out the door.

"We've got fifteen minutes until we meet our bus," said the tour guide, who was holding up a red pennant. "Just follow me."

"Perfect," Marcus said to us. "Let's follow him."

The group walked outside and started heading back to

the main entrance. We followed behind them but left a gap so we weren't quite with the group.

"Let's give him time to spot us so that he can follow," he said. "Then move around the right side of the group so they'll block his view."

It's amazing how tense it all felt considering how slowly we were moving. We were in a crowd of tourists tired from a long day of sightseeing and walking uphill. After a few minutes, we started moving around the group. And when we turned the corner, Marcus caught us with a surprise.

"You keep with them all the way to the entrance," he said. "And when you reach the street, you should see Kayla's car. Hop in and tell her to take you home."

"What about you?" I asked, confused.

"I'm going to peel off so I can watch him watching you," he said. "He'll think I'm in the crowd, so he won't notice I'm gone. At least not for a while."

And before we could ask anything else, he slipped behind a wall near the zebra exhibit and disappeared.

Five minutes later we reached the exit to Connecticut Avenue and saw Kayla's car.

"Marcus texted me the plan," she said as we hopped in. "Lie down on the seats until we've pulled away."

We did as she said, and in an instant we were headed down the street. I closed my eyes for a second to catch my breath.

"You can get up now," she told us when we were a few blocks away. "I'm guessing you guys had an interesting day."

"You could say that," answered Margaret.

"So what do you think Marcus is going to do?" I asked.

"He's probably going to try to give him a taste of his own medicine," she answered. "As soon as the person following you realizes he's lost you guys, he's going to return to his car, and that's when Marcus will follow him."

"That sounds fair," I said.

"By the way," she added, "what are you guys doing tomorrow after school?"

"I've got a soccer game," said Margaret.

"I'm going to go to the game, and then we're going to pick up my bike from the shop," I answered.

"How about Thursday?"

"We're all free," said Margaret.

"Great," said Kayla. "I want to give you your self-defense lesson."

"Are you going to throw me through the air again?" I asked, remembering how much it hurt the first time we met at Quantico.

"There's always that chance."

"Are we driving down to Quantico for the lesson?" asked Margaret.

"No, I've got a place here I like better," she said.

The great thing about Kayla is that when you're just hanging out, she seems like one of the kids. We listened to music and joked around the rest of the way home. We even mentioned that we got Marcus to finally admit to us that they were a couple, which she thought was hilarious.

"I've told him you guys have known for ages," she said, laughing.

When we reached Margaret's house, she parked on the street and checked her phone.

"Any word from Marcus?" I asked.

"Yes, there's a text," she said. She opened it and seemed surprised. "That's interesting. He spotted the tail and sent me a picture."

"Is it Andrei Morozov?" asked Margaret.

"No. It's not."

She held it up for us to see the picture.

It was Dan Napoli.

17.

Hat Trick

MARGARET LIVED FOUR DOORS DOWN AND ACROSS the street from me in a two-story yellow house with a big porch on the front. After Kayla dropped us off, we sat on the porch with our feet on the steps and looked out at the neighborhood in the autumn twilight.

"Why would Dan Napoli follow us?" she asked.

"I don't know. Maybe it's a mistake? Could he be part of the protection detail that's keeping an eye on you?"

"No," she said. "Those guys are only supposed to watch my house in the evening and school during the day. Besides, they're all members of the joint task force on counterintelligence. Napoli's part of the organized crime division. He should be tailing mob bosses and criminals."

I had a momentary panic flash as I worried that Napoli might have somehow figured out the connection between Margaret and Nic the Knife. Apparently, this caused me to make an expression.

"What?" asked Margaret.

"I didn't say anything."

"No, but you made that face."

"What face?"

"That 'I just thought of something' face."

"No, that was just my regular face." Then I quickly changed the subject. "By the way, what was all that talk about hair? What's the 'big chop'?"

"I've been thinking of going natural."

I gave her a blank look. "You say that like you think I know what it means."

"I forgot," she joked. "The great Florian Bates can speak multiple languages and identify the origin of vaccine scars but knows absolutely nothing about girls' hair."

"I'm thinking of making that my official slogan. Or maybe I'll shorten it to: good with clues, bad with 'dos."

"Catchy," she said. "African-American hair is naturally coily or kinky. To straighten it, you have to apply a chemical to relax the hair."

"Seriously? You put chemicals on your hair?"

"That's just the half of it," she said. "But lately I've been thinking of going natural by letting it grow thick and curly like Lucia's."

"And the big chop?"

She flashed a nervous expression. "To go natural, you have to cut off all the hair that's been treated. They call that the big chop, and if you're like me and have always had long straight hair, just the thought of it's overwhelming."

I looked at her for a moment, her head haloed by the yellow porch light. "If it's overwhelming, then why do it? I think your hair always looks great."

"That's because my hair *does* always look great," she said with pride. "But it's not just the style; it's the statement. You heard what she said."

"That she chopped hers eight years ago."

"Exactly. Do the math. That's right after she broke up with Marcus. She was looking for a fresh start. She wanted to feel strong."

"Then what's your statement?" I asked.

"A few months ago my parents and I went to the Smithsonian's African-American history museum. I was blown away by the stories of these amazing people doing everything they could for civil rights. I was just so proud to be black, and I thought I should show that pride. So I stopped using relaxer and started letting my hair grow out."

"That's another thing you didn't tell me."

"You see me and my hair every day. I was hardly keeping it a secret."

"But I can't tell," I said. "It doesn't look any different to me."

"That's because I know all the tricks. I keep it up in a bun, or sometimes I'll wear a hat. But as it grows out, it gets harder to hide."

"So when's this big chop?" I asked. "I want to be there."

"I'm still deciding whether or not I'm going to go through with it. Besides, it's not a spectator sport. I'm not going to have you come watch."

"No?"

"But you do get to watch me play soccer tomorrow," she said. "First home game of the season. We're playing Columbia Heights on the new field."

"I saw that they got the scoreboard up. It looks sharp."

"It really does." She paused for a second. "Can I admit something that's embarrassing?"

"That's what I'm here for."

"I'm kind of obsessed with scoring the first goal on that field. I want to be the first player to ever have a point show up on that scoreboard."

It was classic Margaret.

"And how much have you been thinking about this?"

"Only way too much. It's silly. I know that. It doesn't really matter, but if I'm the first one to do it, then I'll always be first. Forever. Even if no one remembers it but me."

"I'll remember," I said. "Just like I remember the goal you scored to win the city championship. And the header on the goal line that saved the game."

She grinned. "Those were both pretty good plays, weren't they?"

"No," I said. "They were *amazing* plays."

I usually expected to see some amazing plays whenever I watched Margaret on a soccer field. I certainly did the next afternoon when I sat in the new bleachers ready to cheer for her and the rest of the Deal Vikings. What I wasn't expecting to see, however, was Nicolae Nevrescu. He wore a shirt and tie and was sitting three rows behind me along the center aisle.

"Hello, Florian," he said as I walked up and took a seat next to him. "Nice to see you."

"What are you doing here?" I asked under my breath.

"I came to watch the game. Just like you did."

"That's not a good idea," I replied. "If you keep popping up in Margaret's life, she'll start to get suspicious. Besides, there are going to be FBI agents here."

He chuckled. "There are FBI agents everywhere I go. They watch my office and my home. They follow me into the grocery store, and they come to all my construction sites. I don't pay attention to them."

"No, but they pay attention to you. And how can you explain what you're doing at a girls' middle school soccer match on a Wednesday afternoon?"

"You worry too much, Little Sherlock," he said. "I have a perfectly good explanation."

"You do? What is it?"

"I can't tell you right now because they're signaling me to come down to the sideline. I'll be right back."

I was completely baffled as he got up and walked down to where the game announcer was standing with a microphone. Moments later the principal came over and talked to them both.

"Good afternoon, everyone, and welcome to Alice Deal Middle School," said the announcer. "Before we kick off the game, we'd like to acknowledge the generous support of the Nevrescu Construction company for donating the money and labor to upgrade our field and install our new bleachers and scoreboard. As a small token of our appreciation, Principal Albright is presenting a Deal Vikings jersey to the company's CEO, Nicolae Nevrescu."

The small crowd applauded as the principal handed Nic a maroon Deal jersey and he slipped it on over his shirt and tie. I looked onto the field to see if Margaret caught any of this, but she was already in full game mode. When she had that kind of focus, UFOs full of aliens could land on the sideline, and she wouldn't notice.

Nic shook some hands and came back up the bleachers and sat next to me.

"Satisfied?" he asked with a smile.

"You donated all this to Deal?" I said, stunned.

"No," he answered. "I donated all of this to each middle school in the district."

"Why all of them?" I asked.

"Because it might have been suspicious if I only donated to one," he said. "Besides, Margaret will play on all of those fields during the season, and she deserves the best."

"Yes, she does," I said. "Yes, she does."

The ref blew his whistle, and the game was under way. It took Margaret only six and a half minutes to create her first scoring opportunity. It started when she stole the ball near midfield and tore off for a breakaway. Two defenders closed in on her, but she was simply too fast for them. The only Columbia Heights player who had a chance to stop her was the opposing keeper, who charged out from her goal.

I expected Margaret to chip the ball over her head, but instead she ran right at her. Just as they were about to collide, Margaret drilled the ball. It came off her foot like a rocket. The keeper managed to deflect it straight up into the air as she dived to the ground.

Margaret was undeterred. She hurdled the keeper, took a step, and volleyed the ball into the back of the net. The fans went wild, none louder than Nic the Knife. It was (at least as far as I know) the first time I ever high-fived a mob boss.

"That alone was worth every penny," he said, catching his breath. "Every single one."

"It was unbelievable," I added.

I looked down at the field as Margaret plucked the ball out of the net and jogged with it back toward the center spot. The entire way, her eyes were glued to the scoreboard waiting to see the zero turn to one.

"And you know what?" Nic said, leaning over toward me. "It will always be the first goal scored on this field. It will always be the first goal registered on that scoreboard."

Now there were three of us who would remember.

"I should warn you about something," I said after the game resumed. "She had a DNA test run to learn what she can about her background. She's determined to find her parents, and you just got a glimpse of what Margaret's like when she's determined to do something."

He kept his eyes focused on the game, but he listened intently as I continued.

"If any other blood relative uses Helix Twenty-Three, then she'll receive an alert and will have the opportunity to contact that person by e-mail."

"I don't have many relatives in this country," he said. "So that shouldn't be a problem."

"What about her mother?"

For the first time he turned his attention from the game to me. "There's not much I can do about that. I'll tell her and let her decide what to do."

"You still have contact with Margaret's mother?" I asked.

He raised his eyebrows as he answered. "You already know too much. Let's leave some things a mystery."

"Good idea."

Margaret scored again right before halftime. It was on a long shot taken from outside the penalty box that caught the keeper out of position. By that point Nic just seemed like any other family member in the crowd. I almost forgot that he was a criminal until there were about twenty minutes left in the game. That's when I saw the tall man with red hair take a place on the opposite sideline.

It was Andrei Morozov.

"Oh no," I said. "This is not good."

"What's the matter?" asked Nevrescu.

"That man over there with the red hair," I said. "He's come looking for Margaret."

Nic's eyes narrowed as he stared at him. "Who is he?"

"You wouldn't believe me if I told you," I said.

"Who is he?"

"His name's Andrei Morozov. He's a Russian spy."

"Seriously?"

"Unfortunately, yes."

Nic thought about this for a moment and nodded. "I'll take care of it."

"Wait," I said, surprised by his answer. "What do you mean?"

"Exactly what I said. I'll take care of it."

"No, you can't do that. You can't . . ."

"Don't worry, Florian," he said as he stood up. "I'm not going to hurt him. I'm just going to talk to him."

"I don't think that's a good idea," I said. "He can be pretty scary."

"That's all right," Nevrescu said with a grin. "So can I."

Even from behind I could see a transformation in the way he carried himself. By the time he reached the bottom of the bleachers, he'd gone from birth father to godfather. Morozov didn't see it coming because he was too busy looking for Margaret. Luckily, she was on the opposite end, which made her harder to find. He was so focused that he didn't even notice Nevrescu until he was right on top of him.

At first the spy wasn't interested in talking to him at all. But Nic was persistent. He handed him one of his business cards, and then after talking for a moment Morozov made a phone call.

The call lasted only about forty-five seconds, but when it was over, the Russian's body language had changed dramatically. It looked like he was apologizing, and when he was done, Nic leaned closer and whispered something in his ear.

Morozov nodded and then scurried back toward the parking lot, Margaret now a distant worry. Nic walked back to the bleachers, and by the time he sat next to me, he was all smiles.

"Well?" I asked, unsure what had happened.

"Margaret will not have any problems with that man. Neither will you. You have my word."

"What did you say to him?"

"You know too much," he said. "Let's leave some things a mystery."

I kept looking toward the parking lot to see if Morozov

was coming back, but he never did. Late in the second half Margaret scored again to close out the hat trick. A few minutes later Nic got up to leave.

"Aren't you going to stay to the end?" I asked.

"No, I have some things to follow up on," he said.

I worried that it might have something to do with Morozov. "You promise you're not going to hurt him?"

"There is no need," he said. "The danger is gone. But I'm disappointed in you, Florian."

"Me? What did I do?"

"I thought we had an agreement about looking out for Margaret. She was in danger, but I didn't know. The next time, you tell me right away." He handed me his business card. "That has my direct phone number. Let me know if there is trouble, okay?"

"Okay," I said.

"You are a good friend to her. Thank you."

I watched him walk away and get into his car. He was pulling out of the parking lot just as the final whistle was blown. Fifteen seconds later a black sedan pulled out and started to follow him. It was no doubt one of the FBI agents who kept him under constant surveillance.

18.

Diplomatic Immunity

DEAL BEAT COLUMBIA HEIGHTS 4–2, AND AFTERWARD
Margaret and I went to the Capital City Cycle Shop to
pick up my newly repaired bike. Before heading home, we
decided to ride over to the Friendship Station Post Office
and Gorky's. We also discussed Nicolae Nevrescu's surprise
appearance at the game. (Although I left out the part about
him intimidating Andrei Morozov.)

"You're not making this up?" she asked. "Nic the Knife
paid for the bleachers? The scoreboard? Everything?"

"There was even a big announcement before kickoff,"
I told her. "Principal Albright presented him with a jersey.
People clapped. It was a thing."

"How'd I miss that?" she asked, perplexed.

"You were already in game mode," I said. "You looked like a cheetah about to take down a gazelle."

"That does sound like me. Any idea why he suddenly become a fan of middle school soccer?"

"He said something about getting a tax write-off for his construction company. It's probably like those scholarships he gives out."

"I guess so. But I still think it's strange."

I was worried she'd keep asking questions, but luckily, we reached the post office, and she dropped the conversation to focus on the case. We took photos of the front of the building as well as the area around PO Box 1737. We tried to walk around the back to see where they loaded the mail onto trucks, but that area was fenced off, and there was a security guard who seemed unhappy that we were poking around.

"I think it's time we left," I said when I saw him looking at us and calling someone on a walkie-talkie.

Our stop at Gorky's was more productive.

"Check it out," Margaret said as we locked our bikes to the rack behind the store. "Diplomatic plates."

Sure enough, two of the cars in the small parking lot had diplomatic license plates like the one we'd seen on Morozov's SUV.

"They probably work at the Russian embassy," I said. "It's less than a mile from here."

The inside of the store had two distinct sections. One half looked like a small Moscow market with shelves full of Russian groceries, and the other was a deli with five tables, all of which were in use. Virtually no one was speaking English.

"Do you understand what they're saying?" Margaret whispered after we passed two men in an animated discussion.

"Not a word," I said. "I only know how to say a few phrases, and I can't keep up with anyone speaking that fast."

We pretended to browse through a display of colorfully wrapped chocolates while I tried to take some pictures for the caseboard. Unfortunately, this attracted the attention of the store clerk, who walked over to us. She had a sour expression on her face.

"Are you looking for something in particular?" she asked in a thick accent.

"Yes," I said. "We're . . . umm . . . we're . . ."

"Looking for Natalia," said Margaret, coming to the rescue.

The woman seemed both surprised and suspicious. "*I* am Natalia. What do you want with me?"

"Lucia Miller sent us," Margaret answered. "She said you could help with our school project. My name's Margaret, and this is Florian."

Suddenly her entire demeanor changed. "Any friend of Lucia's is a friend of mine. What do you need?"

Over the next ten minutes Natalia was incredibly helpful as we talked about our fictional school project and the store. Five things we learned during our conversation:

1. Gorky's was popular with the staff from the Russian embassy. Including the ambassador, who sometimes stopped by for lunch.

2. Lucia had been a regular since the store opened ten years earlier.

3. Gorky's was part of a small chain of three stores. The first two were located in Baltimore, where there was a large Russian immigrant community.

4. When she still worked at the Library of Congress, Lucia helped Natalia's son Josef get a job there as a security guard.

5. Natalia had a tuberculosis vaccine scar that looked exactly like Rose Brock's.

Before we left, she gave us each a piece of imported Alyonka candy.

"We can't just take this," I said.

"It's my pleasure," she insisted. "Besides, after you taste it, I guarantee you'll come back and buy plenty more."

The candy had two wafers with a nougat filling and was dipped in chocolate. It was delicious.

"She's right," I said as we rode home down Wisconsin Avenue. "I already want to go back and buy more."

"It's incredible," said Margaret. "Next time you screw up and need to apologize to me, I recommend starting with a box of these."

"Good to know," I said with a laugh.

We rode some more, and she said, "By the way, I'm proud of you."

"Why?"

"Because for the first time since he chased us, I haven't noticed you looking over your shoulder for Andrei Morozov."

It's not like I could tell her the real reason I was no longer concerned, so I tried to sound as if it were no big deal. "Like you said, the FBI's following him so we shouldn't be worried."

"No we shouldn't."

We were about a block and a half from my house when I

said, "But there is someone who's following me. Or rather, is about to be following me."

"Who?"

I started pedaling as fast as I could, and once I zipped past her, I called back, "You, because now that my bike's fixed, I'm faster."

"Do not even think you can beat me," she said as she began her pursuit. "It will only lead to disappointment."

Despite the fact that I had a head start and she'd just played an entire soccer match, she passed me as we turned the corner onto our street. I'd never beaten her, so I resorted to a desperate maneuver and called out, "Wait, wait, wait!"

"What's wrong?" she asked, slowing down.

"Nothing," I replied as I sprinted past. "Except that you're a sucker."

I beat her to my driveway by only about three feet, but that was more than enough for me. When I got off my bike, I did a ridiculous version of the victory dance she'd done after winning Toastbusters.

"You're counting that as a win?" she said incredulously.

"You bet I am," I responded.

"Even with the head start and the fake emergency?"

"I'm sorry," I replied, holding my hand to my ear. "I

can't hear you over the awesomeness of my triumph."

I exaggerated the dance moves even more until I finally got her to laugh out loud. My good mood got even better when we walked through the front door and were greeted by the irresistible aroma of my mother's pasta sauce.

"Hey, Florian," Mom called out from the kitchen. "How was the game?"

"Amazing! Margaret scored a hat trick."

"Hi, Mrs. Bates," Margaret said. "It was good. We won four to two."

"Congratulations."

We reached the kitchen and were surprised to discover Marcus there chopping peppers and onions.

"Hey, Marcus," I said. "What are you doing here?"

"I was waiting for you guys to get home, and your mom put me to work."

"He agreed to help chop in exchange for rigatoni Bolognese," said Mom.

"Easiest decision of my life," he replied.

"Why were you waiting for us?" Margaret asked eagerly. "Has there been a development in the case?"

"We're about to find out," he answered. "I got tired of waiting, so I drove out to FBI Central Records in Winchester and got that." He pointed over to the table, where there was a white evidence box. "I thought you guys might like to go over it in the Underground."

"Really?" I said. "Here, and not in the Hoover Building? Is that even allowed?"

"Until I figure out what's going on with Dan Napoli, I'd rather keep you guys away from headquarters. Besides, since I drove out there to pick everything up, the file's technically in transit right now. I think we're fine."

"How long do we have until dinner?" I asked my mother.

"At least forty-five minutes," she said. "By the way, you're welcome to join us, Margaret."

"Let me call my parents and check," she said happily.

While Margaret was on the phone, Marcus and I headed to the basement. When we had a moment alone, I told him about running into Nic the Knife. Marcus was the only other person who knew about Nic being Margaret's birth father, and when I told him about his confrontation with Andrei Morozov, he was stunned.

"I don't even know where to begin with that," he said.

He was about to ask me a follow-up question when Margaret came bopping into the room and we had to shut down the conversation.

"Let's get started," he said.

First we asked him to walk us through the basics of what

happened nine years ago. As he did, I wrote up a time line of events on a yellow legal pad.

"I spent a year researching my PhD in the Rare Book Reading Room," he said. "That's when I got to know everyone and became familiar with the Russian Imperial Collection."

"And when did you get engaged to Lucia?" asked Margaret.

He gave her a skeptical look. "I don't know that it's relevant, but about a year later. It was after I'd gotten my degree and right before I started at the FBI."

"You started in Art Crime?" I asked.

"Yes. And one Saturday afternoon I was in an antique bookstore in Georgetown—"

"Was this part of an investigation?" interrupted Margaret. "Or are antique bookstores your idea of a fun Saturday afternoon?"

"Purely fun."

She looked like she was going to make a snarky remark, but she managed to keep it to herself.

"I was browsing when I saw a book that looked like it belonged in the Russian Imperial Collection. So much so that I checked for the mark."

"Like the one in the book the other day in the SCIF," I said.

"Exactly. When the Library of Congress brings in a one-of-a-kind item, it typically places a small mark on a particular page. For each book in the Russian Imperial Collection the letters *RIC* were written in pencil along the seam of the fifth page from the end. Someone had tried to erase it from this book, but I could still see the indentation on the page, so I knew. I asked the bookseller about the book, and he said that he'd recently gotten it from a collector. Back at the Bureau, I told my boss about it, and we set up a sting."

"How did the sting work?" asked Margaret.

"I told the bookseller that I knew someone very interested in purchasing antique Russian books and asked if he could put me in touch with the collector to see if he had any others to sell."

"And the collector turned out to be Alexander Petrov?" I asked.

"Yes. But when I spoke to him on the phone, he used a fake name and claimed to be a Russian literature professor," answered Marcus. "He said he didn't have any books at the moment but expected to get some soon. Five days later he called and said he'd acquired two more books. We agreed to meet at a café in Georgetown so I could authenticate them and negotiate a price."

"And these books were also from the Russian Imperial Collection?" asked Margaret.

"Yes, they were," he said. "The moment I verified that, I

signaled the surveillance team that was watching us, and we arrested him on the spot." He smiled at the memory of it all. "That's when things got interesting."

"What do you mean?" asked Margaret.

"Do you know what diplomatic immunity is?"

"Not exactly," she said.

"Basically, it means if you're in one country representing the government of another country you can't be arrested."

"That doesn't make sense," said Margaret.

"It's supposed to protect people from being arrested for make-believe charges," he said. "As soon as the handcuffs went on, Petrov told us that he was not a professor but rather a cultural attaché. He claimed diplomatic immunity and alerted his embassy. They sent a pair of security officers to come get him."

"Did he deny he stole the books?"

"He didn't say a single word after he'd called for the officers. But the next day the embassy released a statement saying that he took full responsibility for what happened. As punishment he was forced to leave the country and return to Russia. It was a big deal on the news for a little while, and it ruined his career as a diplomat."

"So you never got to question him?"

"No. And we weren't allowed to search his apartment or

his car. We were blocked from all our standard investigative techniques."

"Then what's in there?" I asked, pointing at the white evidence box that Marcus had placed on the table.

"His one mistake," said Marcus.

19.

Mrs. Hoover Speaks Mandarin and Other Fun Facts about the First Ladies

ALEXANDER PETROV'S MISTAKE HAD BEEN A SIMPLE one. When he came to meet Marcus at the café, he'd brought the two rare books in a briefcase. But in the chaos of being arrested and then waiting for the embassy's security officers to arrive, he'd forgotten about it and left it behind.

"I just saw it sitting there, and before he had a chance to send someone back to get it, I drove it down to the Hoover Building and entered it as evidence," said Marcus.

"Did he ever realize his mistake?" I asked.

"Oh yeah. The embassy threw a fit and said the FBI was withholding property of the Russian government. But the

TRAPPED!

director wouldn't budge an inch. He told them that if he wanted his briefcase back, Petrov had to come into the office and answer questions."

"So what's in the box?" I asked.

"Yeah," said Margaret. "We want to run it through the Toaster."

There were eight items listed on the evidence inventory:

A brown leather briefcase.

Eleven business cards identifying Alexander
Petrov as a cultural attaché with the embassy.

A letter to Petrov from an artist in Birmingham,
Alabama, named Jarrett Underhill.

Two unopened Russian candies in purple wrappers.

A ticket stub from the Baltimore Museum of Art.

Four unpaid parking tickets.

A receipt for an ATM withdrawal of two hundred
dollars.

A kid's library book called *Mrs. Hoover Speaks Mandarin and Other Fun Facts about the First Ladies.*

We went through them one by one, and Margaret made sure to take pictures of each so we'd have them for reference in the Underground.

We quickly dismissed the briefcase, business cards, and candy. None of them seemed important to the case, although we briefly debated how the candy might taste after nine years in storage and decided it would probably be something like an old tennis shoe.

"What about the ticket stub to the museum?" asked Margaret. "According to Natalia, Baltimore has a large Russian immigrant community."

"Who's Natalia?" asked Marcus.

"She runs Gorky's."

"And didn't you say that you thought Rose Brock was from Baltimore?" I asked.

"Yes," he said. "But so are a million other people. There's nothing suspicious about a cultural attaché going to an art museum. That's part of his job."

"And is reading picture books about the first ladies part of his job too?" asked Margaret as she held up the evidence bag with the book. "It doesn't really seem like normal reading material for a spy."

"You're absolutely right," said Marcus. "It's a library book. That didn't seem significant nine years ago, but now with what we know about the recent case, it might have been used to pass a message or hide a post office box key."

"So you're thinking this library/post office dead drop has been going on for the whole time?" I asked.

"It's a definite possibility."

"Then answer this," said Margaret. "Of all the books in the library, why use this one?"

"That's an excellent question," said Marcus. "First thing tomorrow morning I'm going to have it run for fingerprints."

"You think the prints are still good?" she asked.

"The book hasn't been touched in nine years," he said. "They should be perfect."

"Except a library book gets handled by lots of people," I said. "How will you know which prints are the right ones?"

"Think about it," he said.

It took me a moment to get it. "You're looking for one that matches prints on the new book. That's perfect."

"He sure does have a lot of parking tickets," Margaret said.

"That's because he didn't have to pay them," said Marcus.

"Parking tickets are also covered by diplomatic immunity. These were just the four he was carrying. I checked with the Metropolitan Police, and he'd had more than twenty during the previous year."

"Is it just me, or does this guy sound like a jerk?" asked Margaret.

"It's not just you," Marcus said with a laugh. "I remember checking them to see if he ever got ticketed near the Library of Congress. That was the hole in my case. I could never make a connection of any kind between him and the library."

I started reading off the locations of the tickets. "He's got them for Massachusetts Avenue, Alabama Avenue, U Street, and Dupont Circle."

"All over town but nowhere near the library," said Margaret.

"What was the date of the arrest?" I asked.

Marcus checked in a spiral notebook. "November twentieth."

I looked at the dates on the tickets. "He got these on November third, eighth, seventeenth, and nineteenth." I picked up the ATM receipt and checked the date on it. "This was the nineteenth too."

"Why's that important?"

"I don't know that it is," I said. "I just know that the day before he was arrested he got a parking ticket and withdrew two hundred dollars from the bank."

"You said you could never place him in the Library of Congress?" asked Margaret.

"That's right," he said.

"Isn't that odd?" she asked. "I'm not exactly sure what a cultural attaché does, but it sounds like the kind of job that takes you to the Library of Congress at least every now and then."

"That's exactly what I thought," said Marcus. "But I went through the guest lists of every official event. I checked phone records. I did everything I could to place him in that building and came up empty each time."

"Which is why you knew he had to have help from someone on the inside."

"Exactly."

"How'd you narrow the list of suspects down to four?" I asked.

"Originally, I identified nine people who had access to the books in the collection," he said. "But then I thought about the first call to Petrov. When we talked, he said he didn't have any books he could sell."

"But five days later he had two," I said.

"Exactly. That meant whomever it was had access during

that week. That narrowed it down to the four. By the way, there's more new evidence as of today."

"What's that?"

"I had the financials pulled on our four suspects," he said, taking out a folder with a dozen or so pages in it. "After all, each of these books should sell for thousands of dollars, so I was wondering who had large sums of money pop into their accounts at unusual times."

"What'd you find?"

"Not much, unfortunately. A couple years ago Lucia started depositing money in larger amounts, but it was right as she was buying a new house. I dug a little deeper and found out that she cashed out some investments and received some money from her parents. Likewise, Brooke King had a lot of money flowing through her account three years ago."

"Which is when she was buying her bookstore," I said.

"Exactly," he replied. "I looked into it and saw that money went to purchase things for the store like"—he picked up an invoice and read—"'fourteen wooden library shelf units, a barcoding inventory machine, and a Worldwide Super Fortress Safe.'"

"What about Alistair Toombs and Rose Brock?"

"Not surprisingly Alistair has the most boring financial records in the history of the world. There are no spikes or aberrations. Rose Brock, however, occasionally deposits large sums, which she typically spends on trips to Europe."

"Any of those to Russia?"

"At least three trips to Saint Petersburg."

None of us liked thinking that Rose was guilty, so this was not particularly good news.

The last piece of evidence in the cold case file was the letter. Technically, it was two pieces of evidence. The letter itself was in one baggie while the envelope was in another. Margaret looked at the envelope and asked, "Do we know who Jarrett Underhill is and why he was writing Petrov?"

"Actually, at the time, I thought that was the most interesting clue of all," said Marcus. "Underhill is a sculptor who lived in Birmingham, Alabama. He wrote Petrov hoping to arrange some kind of cultural exchange between artists in the United States and Russia."

"What's interesting about that?" I asked.

"Underhill claims he never heard of Petrov and insists he never sent the letter."

Margaret and I shared a look.

"Did he know that you had the actual letter?" I asked.

"I went down to Alabama and interviewed him myself," he said. "I showed him the letter, and he denied that it was his."

"Maybe he was lying," said Margaret.

"If so, he was really good at it," said Marcus. "I believed him."

I picked up the bag with the letter and read it. Underhill, or at least the person claiming to be Underhill, wanted to start a program where artists from Russia and the United States could work together on projects in each other's studios. He thought it would strengthen the cultural relationship between the countries.

"This is actually a cool idea," I said. "There's certainly nothing scandalous or spy-worthy about it. More importantly, there doesn't seem to be any reason to lie about it."

"Here's something," Margaret said, looking at the envelope. "The stamp's upside down."

"I remember that," said Marcus. "I spent an entire afternoon trying to figure out how that might be important."

"And what'd you get?"

"A headache," he said. "I finally decided that it was a simple mistake."

I took the envelope from her and studied it. The upside-down stamp had a picture of the Statue of Liberty. It seemed pretty obvious, but I didn't know how that might be important. Then I noticed something that was much less obvious.

"I don't think Jarrett Underhill was lying," I said.

"Why do you say that?" asked Marcus.

"The return address on this envelope says it was mailed from Birmingham, Alabama," I told him.

"Right. That's where Underhill lived."

I held the envelope up for them to see.

"Then why does the postmark say Harrisonburg, Virginia?"

20.

Self-Defense

MARCUS STARED AT THE POSTMARK AND SHOOK his head. "How could I have missed that?"

"It's easy to overlook," I said. "You assume the postmark matches the return address. Besides, you were probably focused on the letter and not the envelope. Anyone would have missed it."

He looked up at me and said, "Anyone but you."

I didn't know what to say, so I didn't say anything at all.

"What could the explanation be?" asked Margaret.

"Either Jarrett Underhill drove six hundred miles to mail a letter he claims he never wrote," said Marcus, "or someone went to a lot of trouble to involve him in this."

"I don't know why anyone would do that," I said. "But the second explanation seems more likely."

"Where's Harrisonburg?" asked Margaret.

"About two hours southwest of here in the Shenandoah Valley," said Marcus. "It's home to James Madison University."

"Maybe Underhill has a connection to the school?" she asked.

"We can check that," said Marcus. "But I doubt it."

"And he had no connection to Russia or the embassy?" I asked.

"None," said Marcus. "But this part's odd. He did have one to the Library of Congress."

"Really?"

"He sculpted a bust of Mark Twain that's on display in the John Adams Building."

"Did any of our suspects have anything to do with that sculpture?" asked Margaret.

"Not a one," he said. "I spent a lot of time investigating that and couldn't find any place where they overlapped."

Soon after that, it was time for dinner, and we went upstairs. Rather than discuss the case, we mostly talked about the soccer game. The food was delicious, and when we were done, Marcus left for the Hoover Building, and Margaret went home. I spent about an hour doing homework, and then I went back into the Underground to study the case-board.

I added some new details from the day, including a map of Harrisonburg and a picture of *Mrs. Hoover Speaks Mandarin and Other Fun Facts about the First Ladies*. I went online to a website devoted to the artwork of Jarrett Underhill. I even got a map of the city and marked the locations of Alexander Petrov's parking tickets.

I kept thinking I was on the verge of figuring something out, but the clues never snapped together. The idea behind TOAST is that you add up the small things in order to find the big ones. But these small things didn't seem like they were part of the same equation.

The next day after school Kayla picked us up for self-defense class.

"Have you heard anything from Marcus today?" I asked when we got into her car.

"Just a text canceling our lunch date," she said. "He said he was busy with the case and needed to keep working."

"Hopefully that means he's on the verge of a break-through," said Margaret. "Maybe he's been able to match the fingerprints."

"Are you guys ready for your lesson?" she asked us.

The first time I had a training session with Kayla was the

day we met, and I mistakenly assumed that since she was petite and had a perpetual smile, she was more kindergarten teacher than martial artist. After fifty minutes of her tossing me around the gym, I swore I'd never underestimate someone again.

"Where're we going?" asked Margaret.

"Julie's Gym," she said. "You're going to love it."

When I heard the name Julie's Gym, I imagined it was one of those fitness clubs with rows of treadmills and a juice bar. Or maybe a yoga studio with a lot of moms doing crazy pretzel stretches.

The first hint I was wrong was when we drove down a street with abandoned warehouses and boarded-up windows. Then Kayla parked in a small lot surrounded by a rusted fence topped with razor wire.

"Get your gym bags," she said as she turned off the car. "We're here."

Margaret and I shared a look. "We are?"

Julie's turned out to be a hard-core gymnasium for boxers and mixed martial arts fighters. There was no air-conditioning or carpeting, and the closest thing to a juice bar was a water fountain that looked like it hadn't worked in years. For some reason, opera blared over the speakers.

Everything reeked of dirt and sweat, and when Margaret took a whiff, she recoiled. "That smell!"

"I know," said Kayla. "Isn't it great?"

I scanned the assortment of tough guys who populated the gym and asked, "Which one of them is Julie?"

"This one," she said, nodding toward an African-American man in his sixties who'd started walking toward us. He was massive, at least six foot four, with a pudgy face and gray hair. "Hey, Julie."

"Miss Kayla," he replied with a friendly baritone. "Always a pleasure. I see you've brought friends."

"Teaching a little self-defense class," she told him.

"Your name's *Julie*?" I asked, confused but trying not to sound rude.

"*Julius* Rucker," he said, shaking my hand. "But Julie to my friends."

"Back in the day, Big Julius was one of the top heavyweights on the East Coast," said Kayla.

"They used to call me the DC Destroyer," he added with a proud smile.

"What was your record again?" asked Kayla.

"Officially, it was thirty-three and eight, but you know three of those . . ."

"Yeah, yeah, yeah," she joked. "Julius feels strongly that three of those decisions were incorrect."

"Very strongly," he said.

"And the music?" I asked.

"Opera is all about murder, betrayal, and deception," he said. "It's the perfect music to fight to." Then he leaned over and added, "Besides, it classes up the joint, don't you think?"

Both Kayla and Big Julius laughed hard at that.

"What do you need?" he asked her.

"Just the mat next to the ring," she said.

"It's all yours." He turned to Margaret and me. "You listen to her, all right? This woman knows what she's talking about."

It was obvious by the reaction she received that Kayla was not only well known but also well liked around the gym. A boxer working the speed bag nodded and flashed a smile without missing a beat, and two guys stopped jumping rope long enough to say hello.

"Okay, limber up," she instructed us when we got to the mat.

"Do we have to?" I asked.

"Pre-exercise stretching is essential," she said. "These guys know it, and you know it too."

We could not have looked more out of place. Everyone else wore black and gray with the occasional splash of blood red, and the only things more prevalent than muscles were tattoos. Meanwhile, Margaret and I were in PE uniforms that said, ALICE DEAL MIDDLE SCHOOL PHYS. ED., and Kayla was wearing bright blue exercise pants and a Gryffindor T-shirt.

"Okay," she said once we were suitably limber. "Today I'm going to teach you both the art of WAR."

"That sounds ominous," I said.

"It's not ominous; it's a memory tool I designed to help you think fast in a crisis," she said. "The *W* is for Weakness. Identify your opponent's weakness and exploit it. *A* is for Anticipate. Anticipate your opponent's next move and disrupt it. And *R* is for Redirect. Redirect your opponent's energy and use it against them."

We practiced each phase for about twenty minutes. For Weakness, she taught us how to break out of different holds and demonstrated how a sudden kick or well-placed elbow could impede an attacker.

Anticipate was more about strategy than maneuvers.

"Your attacker has a plan," she said. "And as long as you're reacting to that plan, you're giving him control. But if you can anticipate what he's going to do, then you might be able to disrupt that plan and take away some of that control."

To demonstrate this, she walked us through various scenarios and asked us to predict her next move. When we did, she told us to come up with actions that could disrupt the plan.

"Be ingenious," she said. "He may be stronger, but I bet

you're both smarter and more creative. Use TOAST. Let your brain be your strongest muscle."

We ended with Redirect.

"What do you mean by that?" I asked her.

"It means using someone's strength and energy against him," she said. "If you hit a tennis ball against a wall, it bounces because the wall redirects the energy off the ball in the opposite direction."

"Yeah," I said. "But I'm guessing in most situations, I'm more tennis ball than wall."

She laughed. "Well, you don't have to be a wall to redirect it. Let me demonstrate."

There was a fighter who'd taken a break and was watching our lesson. He was at least eight inches taller and a hundred pounds heavier than her. "Would you be willing to attack me for my demonstration? I need it to be someone big like you so that I can teach the kids not to be intimidated by size."

"Aren't you worried about injuries?" he asked.

"Oh, I promise not to hurt you," she said. "I'll go easy."

He laughed. "I wasn't worried about me."

"Great, then you'll do it?" she said. "What's your name?"

"Tyson," he said.

"Nice to meet you, Tyson," she said. "I'm Kayla. Come over here and let me introduce you to Florian and Margaret."

I noticed that Big Julius and a couple of the other fighters were moving over to get a look. I think they had an idea that Tyson might not know what he was in store for.

"All right," she said, setting the scenario. "This is Tyson. He's much bigger than I am. He's much stronger than I am. So if I try to fight him head-on, I'm going to lose. That's why I need to use his own strength and size against him."

"How do you do that?" asked Margaret.

"Just watch," she said. "Imagine that I'm walking down the street in the middle of the night and Tyson runs up from behind and tries to grab me."

He was reluctant at first, but she encouraged him. Finally he charged at her, and just as he reached her, Kayla turned to her side, twisted her body, and grabbed him by the arm. Using all of his momentum, she was able to flip him in the air and body slam him onto the mat.

There was a whooshing sound as the air was forced out of his body.

"See, it's as simple as that," she told us. "I redirected his strength and speed up and over so in effect he did this to himself." She looked down at him. "You okay, Tyson?"

He didn't answer so much as moan.

"Thanks for your help," she said cheerily.

I looked over at Big Julius and the others, who were all snickering.

For the rest of the lesson, Margaret and I took turns getting tossed, flipped, and thrown around the mat. At one point, Kayla was demonstrating how to escape a two-handed hold on her arm. My grip was tight, and I really thought I had her. But in less than three seconds, she'd reached between my arms, pulled herself out, and somehow left me twisted like a pretzel with my face down against the mat.

Margaret didn't fare any better. She had Kayla wrapped in a bear hug from behind, and since she's a lot taller, she thought she had the upper hand. She thought wrong. In a sudden move Kayla snapped forward and flipped her over her head and against the mat.

An hour later Margaret and I were sitting on the stoop in front of her house laughing and moaning as we recounted the lesson. The weather was perfect, and although our muscles ached, at least the breeze was nice. We also talked about school and the case. Margaret even tried to figure out how Kayla's WAR principles might apply to soccer.

"You know, I read up on natural hair last night after you left," I said.

"Really?" She seemed touched.

"Of course," I said. "I want to know everything that's on your mind."

"So, what do you think?" she asked.

"I think it would look great," I said. "But more importantly, I think it would be absolutely Margaret in every way."

She talked a little bit more about what the big chop would entail, and then Marcus arrived. He parked on the street and seemed lost in thought as he came up the walkway to her house.

"Marcus, you missed it," Margaret said. "Kayla took us to this gym, and then she flipped this huge guy in the air. . . ." She stopped when she saw his expression. "Is everything all right?"

"Yes," he said.

"Did you find out anything new about the case?" I asked. "Did the fingerprints match?"

He didn't answer the questions. Instead, he asked Margaret, "Are your parents home?"

"Yes, they're both inside. What's the matter, Marcus? Am I in trouble of some sort?"

"No, no," he said absently. "It's not about you at all. I just need to talk to your parents."

"Why do you need to talk to my parents if it's not about me?"

He closed his eyes for a moment and took a deep breath. Then he looked at us and said, "Because I need a lawyer."

21.

Back to the SCIF

MARGARET'S PARENTS WERE BOTH ATTORNEYS who specialized in cases that involved government agencies. This included everything from representing an employee who'd been unjustly fired by the Department of Agriculture to negotiating the sale of a historic building to the National Park Service. They were partners in a law firm located downtown but also had an office next to their living room so they could sometimes work from home.

This is where they talked with Marcus behind a closed door for five minutes while Margaret and I tried to figure out what was going on. We were nervously pacing back and forth when Mrs. Campbell came out to talk to us.

"Margaret, I just spoke with Florian's mom, and you're going to have dinner at their house tonight," she said. "Take your books so you can do your homework there too. We're going to be with Marcus for a while."

"Mom, what's going on?"

"You know I can't tell you that, sweetie," she said. "Just go."

My mind raced all through dinner trying to figure out what could be happening. I assumed that it somehow involved Dan Napoli following us, but that didn't really make sense because he was an agent with the organized crime division and we were working on a case that involved stolen books and spies.

"It's a mistake," I blurted out at one point. "It just has to be a mistake."

"Don't worry," Margaret said calmly as she looked across the table at me. "You know how you are with mysteries? And how Kayla is with beating up bad guys?"

"Yes," I said.

She smiled proudly. "That's how my parents are with the law. They're the best. They'll take care of him."

It was another hour and a half before Margaret's dad came over to get her. He had a concerned expression that he tried to hide behind a smile, but I could tell the situation was serious.

"Is Marcus okay?" she asked.

"He just went home," he said, without answering the question. "He wanted me to tell you both not to worry about him."

"But is he okay?" asked Margaret.

"Come on," said her father. "You've got to get ready for bed."

I went down into the Underground and stared at the caseboard, trying to figure out what was happening. First, I focused on the four suspects we'd checked on. Next, I thought about the evidence we'd seen in the cold case file.

Finally, I went through everything I knew about Dan Napoli, which admittedly wasn't much. He'd transferred from New York six months earlier. He worked organized crime. He spied on us at the awards reception and Texas Tony's. He followed us on the day we went to see Brooke King at Palace Books and Lucia Miller at the Petworth Library. We lost him at the zoo.

"What am I missing?" I said to myself.

The next morning I met up with Margaret before school, and we sat on one of the aluminum benches behind the building.

"What'd you find out?" I asked.

"Not much," she said. "Mom and Dad won't tell me

anything. That's what makes me think it's serious. If he'd just come over to ask for advice, they'd tell me that without any of the specifics. I did, however, have some toast for breakfast."

"I don't know why that's important but okay," I said. "I had cereal."

"No, I mean TOAST," she replied. "A little Theory of All Small Things around the breakfast table."

"Oh, I get it," I said as I flashed a grin. "What did you find out?"

"First of all, my father called his secretary and cancelled all his meetings for the day," she said. "Then he reserved the Federal Room."

"What's that?"

"It's a really nice conference room at the firm. It has top-level security features and a private entrance. They use it when they have to talk to a high-ranking government official without letting the whole world know what they're doing."

"You mean someone like Admiral Douglas?"

"That's just the name that I thought of."

"What time did he book it for?"

"One o'clock."

"Anything else?" I asked.

"I got onto the computer in his office and checked his search history," she said. "He was looking up names for private investigators in two cities."

"Which ones?"

"Birmingham, Alabama, and Harrisonburg, Virginia."

"Jarrett Underhill?" I said.

"Jarrett Underhill."

The warning bell rang, telling us we had five minutes to get to class.

We planned to talk about it more during lunch, but we never got that far. Our second-period English class was discussing *A Wrinkle in Time* when the teacher, Ms. White, got a call and told us to report to the front office. The two of us shared a confused look as we stood up.

"And bring all your books," she added.

Ms. White's classroom was on the second floor, and as we walked down the stairs toward the office, I asked Margaret, "Do you have any idea what's going on?"

"No," she said simply. "But I have a feeling it isn't good."

For the second time in a week we walked into a room and were surprised to see our parents. (Although in the SCIF it had been all four, and here it was only our mothers.)

"Is everything okay?" Margaret asked, suddenly panicked. "Did something happen to Dad?"

"No, no, everything's fine," she said. "We just had to come down here to check you out of school."

"Why are you checking us out of school?" I asked.

"It's complicated," said Mom. "We'll talk about it in the car."

As we walked to the car, I noticed both were dressed professionally. That wasn't unusual for Margaret's mother because she was a lawyer. But my mom worked in an art restoration studio and usually wore clothes that were nice but less formal.

"Where are we going?" I asked.

"The Hoover Building," answered Mom.

They didn't tell us anything more until we were in the car and headed downtown.

"We're going to FBI Headquarters because the two of you need to answer some questions," said Mrs. Campbell.

"Are we in trouble?" asked Margaret.

"Not at all," said her mother.

"Then why did we have to leave school? And why did you have to come with us?"

"Because you're both minors, and you can't be questioned about a crime without a parent present," she explained.

"But we talk about crimes there all the time," said Margaret.

"Yes, sweetie," she said. "But those are crimes you're trying to solve. This time you're being called in as witnesses."

"Who's going to be asking the questions?" I asked.

"There's a joint task force on counterintelligence," she explained. "And the director of that task force is going to ask the questions."

"Is Dad going to be there?" asked Margaret.

"No," said Mrs. Campbell.

Margaret thought for a moment and then said, "That's because he's representing Marcus, and they don't want him to be there when they ask us questions."

Her mother didn't answer, but it was obvious by her expression that Margaret was right.

Every other time we'd been to the Hoover Building, we'd been with some combination of Marcus, Kayla, and Admiral Douglas. They always prearranged our visits so that we could go straight to Marcus's office. But this time we had to check in like regular guests. Our pictures were taken and put on little badges, and we waited in the lobby until a female agent came to get us. When we got on the elevator, she pushed the button for subbasement four.

Margaret leaned over and whispered, "We're going back to the SCIF."

As we walked down the hallway, I couldn't help but think

how much things had changed in a week. The previous Friday we'd walked down the same hall on the way to receive medals from the director of the FBI. Now we were headed into the unknown, and even though our mothers stressed that we weren't in any trouble, I felt like we needed to defend ourselves.

"Remember what Kayla taught us," I whispered to Margaret. "Remember WAR."

She nodded.

When we reached the SCIF's waiting room, there was already a group there, three men and a woman. We had to wait as they signed in on a visitor's log and handed over their cell phones to the guard behind the desk. We didn't really speak to them other than to say hello. They seemed polite enough with one exception. There was a tall man with dark brown hair who studied us without expression. He had a thin scar partially hidden by his right eyebrow, and it looked as though it had been years since he last smiled. He was the last one to sign in, and rather than hand one of us the pen, he dropped it on the desk and went inside the SCIF.

That's when the guard turned his attention to us and said, "I need everyone to sign in and give me any cell phones."

A week earlier the admiral had skipped the signing-in part. No doubt because he wanted no record that he'd brought us into the SCIF. This time we each had to fill in our name, address, and phone number on the visitor's log.

I looked up at the last name on the list above us, Michael J. Moretti. He was the one who'd given us the evil eye. When we entered the room, he was also the only one who wasn't sitting at the table. He was behind the others in a chair with his back against the wall, more like an observer than a participant.

The woman was sitting in the middle of the trio at the table, and she took charge of the meeting. "Thank you all for coming down on such short notice. Please sit down."

She wore a dark blue suit and had black hair with flecks of gray. She looked to be in her mid-fifties.

"Hello, Florian, Margaret. I'm sorry we had to interrupt you at school, but we're dealing with a time-sensitive issue of great importance, and it's urgent that we talk to you."

I started to ask a question. "Can you tell—"

She cut me off and said, "If you'll please hold your questions for now, things will move smoothly. You'll have a chance to ask whatever you want later."

I nodded. "Okay."

"This is not a formal deposition, and we are not recording the conversation," she said. "However, we are going to take notes. It's my understanding that Mrs. Campbell is an exceptional attorney, so if any legal questions arise, I'm sure she can assist you."

One thing that struck me as odd was that none of them introduced themselves. She'd skipped over that part when she started talking. I tried to remember the names from the sign-in sheet in the anteroom as she continued. I also wondered if they had her do the talking because they thought we'd feel less threatened by a woman.

"Earlier today we spoke to Admiral Douglas, and he implied that you two do some kind of work for the FBI. Could you please explain the nature of that work?"

"No," said Margaret.

"No, you don't work for the FBI?"

"No, we're not allowed to tell you about it," she said. "The work we do is secret."

Moretti scoffed and shook his head, but he still let the woman run the meeting.

"I assure you that our security clearance is more than high enough for you to share any 'secrets' you may have," said the woman.

I looked to Mrs. Campbell, who nodded that it was okay for us to talk.

"We're classified as covert assets and work on the Special Projects Team with Special Agent Marcus Rivers."

She paused for a moment. "You do understand why that's virtually impossible for us to believe?"

"Yes, I do," I answered. "But your lack of understanding doesn't make it untrue."

She smiled at this, and I began to get a sense that she somehow liked us, although that may have just been a technique she'd been trained to develop. The skill of making the people you're questioning think you're a friend or ally.

"Well, Admiral Douglas says it's true, and so does my boss, so I guess I'm just going to have to accept that for now and move on to more pressing issues."

"Fine," I said.

"I also want to assure you that neither of you is in trouble. Nobody thinks you've done anything wrong. We just need some questions answered, and the important thing is for you to be honest with us."

"How honest?" I asked.

"I beg your pardon," she said, thrown by the question.

"How honest would you like us to be?"

"You're either honest or you're not," she said. "There aren't varying levels of truthfulness. The best thing for you to do is tell us the complete unfiltered truth. I'm certain that's what Special Agent Rivers would want you to do."

"If you want us to be honest, then how come you lied to

our parents?" I asked with just the right level of accusation in my voice.

"I'm sorry, Florian," she said, confused. "I don't have any idea what you're talking about. None of us have lied to your parents."

"Really?" I said.

"Really," she answered firmly.

"You told them that we were being questioned by the joint task force," I said.

"That's exactly what's happening," she said. "I am the leader of that task force."

"I don't doubt that," I answered. "But the task force is made up of representatives of three agencies: the National Security Agency, the Central Intelligence Agency, and the FBI's Counterintelligence Division. You're with the CIA. He's with the NSA," I said, pointing to the man to her right. "And he's FBI," I said, motioning to the third agent at the table.

"And how do you know that?" she asked.

"It's pretty easy," I said, not so much to show off as to disrupt her flow. "He's the only one of the three of you that doesn't have a visitor's badge. That's because his office is here in the building. Which means he's FBI."

"And the two of us?" she asked.

"When you signed in, you had to list your address," I said. "You live in Virginia. He's from Maryland. The CIA is based in Langley, Virginia, and the NSA at Fort Meade, Maryland."

She smiled. "And how do you know that I don't live in Virginia and drive to work in Maryland? They're right next to each other."

"You said that Admiral Douglas told you that we consulted for the FBI and that your boss confirmed this," I said. "We haven't done any work for the NSA, but earlier this year I uncovered a spy ring that was operating out of a Chinese restaurant and spying on CIA employees. Your boss would certainly know about that."

Now she was truly impressed. "That was you?" she said, stunned.

"So, when you told our parents that we were being questioned by the joint task force, you were only talking about the three of you," I said. Then I pointed at Moretti, who was still sitting with his back against the wall. "Why did you leave him out?"

Moretti adjusted his chair and leaned forward.

"I'm also with the FBI's counterintelligence team," he said.

"You're a terrible liar, Agent Moretti," I told him. "You're with the organized crime division. If you want us to be honest on this side of the table, then you should be honest on that side. Don't you agree?"

The woman across the table smiled at me. "I'm beginning to see how it's possible that you consult with the FBI."

"Why don't we start over?" I suggested. "My name is Florian Bates. This is my best friend, Margaret Campbell. We're seventh graders at Alice Deal Middle School, and we consult for the FBI. Who are you?"

22.

Gordian Knot

THE MOOD IN THE ROOM CHANGED SIGNIFICANTLY after my little TOAST display. The four people across the table introduced themselves and gave their agency affiliations, including CIA agent Melinda Dawkins, who was in charge of the joint task force, and Michael Moretti, who was the SAC, or special agent in charge, of the FBI's Balkan transnational organized crime department. He made a point of saying the full name, and I assumed that was his way of trying to rattle me.

"So that means you investigate crime families with connections to that region of Europe?" I asked, even though I was fairly certain of the answer.

"That's correct," he said. "Which among others includes Albania, Bulgaria, Kosovo, and Romania."

He stretched out the last one for emphasis, and now I knew why we were there. In some form or another, this involved Nic the Knife.

"Before we continue, I would like to know how you knew my name and identified me as part of the organized crime division," said Moretti. "I want to make sure that no one outside this room has provided you with information about what we're doing in an attempt to influence your answers."

"You mean Marcus?" I said.

"Yes, I mean Agent Rivers," he said.

"*Special* Agent Rivers," corrected Margaret.

"You two sure seem to know a lot for a pair of twelve-year-olds who just walked into the room."

My guess was that he suspected Marcus was somehow involved in organized crime. How he reached that conclusion baffled me, but it was the only thing that made sense. According to Kayla's WAR technique, the second option for defending yourself was to anticipate your attacker's plan so that you could disrupt it. I saw where he was going, and I decided to change the direction of the conversation.

It was time for a little showing off.

"First of all, your name was written above mine on the

visitor's log for this room, so it doesn't exactly take Sherlock Holmes to figure that out," I said. "As for your accusation about Marcus giving us information about you, I don't need him to tell me anything to know that, even though you have an Italian last name, you're Irish. That you grew up in Boston playing hockey and worshipping the Bruins. Or that you miss your kids, who are back in New York with your ex-wife. So, I certainly didn't need him to tell me that you were with the organized crime division. We do this because we're good at it. Not because we're kids playing a game."

"Boom," Margaret added as an exclamation point.

"You see, I know that you're Irish because you're wearing a claddagh ring," I said, pointing at his hand. "The heart's pointed outward, which means you're single, but when you handed your cell phone to the guard, the wallpaper was a picture of you with your kids. That's how I knew you were divorced. Your Boston accent's a dead giveaway, especially the way you pronounce Kosovo. My dad's from Boston, and you sound like my uncles. The puck-sized scar above your eye and the four false teeth give away the hockey in your background."

He instinctively reached up to his mouth to check his teeth.

"Your phone number has a 212 area code, which is how

I knew you'd lived in New York. And when I thought about that, it reminded me where I'd seen you before. Last Friday night you were at Texas Tony's with Dan Napoli, who also transferred from New York and is a member of the organized crime division."

The room was quiet for a moment while everyone waited for Moretti to respond, but he didn't say a word.

"Okay, then," said Dawkins, trying to suppress a smile. "That was very impressive, Florian. Now that we've got that out of the way, let's get started. Are you familiar with the term 'Gordian knot'?"

"Yes," I said. "It's a legend from ancient Greece. The knot was so tangled and intertwined that it was virtually impossible to untie. It was prophesized that whoever could undo it would one day rule all of Asia. After unsuccessfully attempting to untie the knot, Alexander the Great realized there was a much simpler solution and chopped it in half with his sword."

"Very good," she said. "And I believe we have several different cases that have become entangled and need to be undone. Hopefully, you and Margaret can use some of that brainpower you just displayed and play the role of Alexander for us."

The first thing they wanted to know was about our

encounter with Andrei Morozov. We told them about running into him at the library and recounted how he chased us to the school. When we were done, Dawkins asked, "Was that the last time you saw him?"

Margaret and I answered at the same time, but while Margaret said, "Yes," I said, "No."

Margaret gave me a confused look.

"Which one is it?" asked Dawkins.

"Margaret never saw him again," I explained. "But I did."

"What are you talking about?" asked Margaret.

"He showed up briefly at the soccer game on Wednesday afternoon," I said. "He was only there for a few minutes, and then he left."

"Yes, he did," said Dawkins.

"Why didn't you tell me?" asked Margaret under her breath.

"I didn't want to worry you," I said to her. "I'm sorry. I should have said something."

"As you are aware, the task force had someone following Morozov," she continued. "Would you be surprised to know that in addition to that day at the soccer game, he also drove by the Campbell house at least three times, or that on Tuesday he parked by your school and spent twenty minutes watching while you were both in PE class?"

"Really?" said Margaret with a flash of panic.

"Needless to say, we were a bit worried about him and your safety," she said. "So imagine our surprise last night when the embassy sent Morozov home to Russia. No warning or announcement. Just a simple notification to the State Department that he was being permanently recalled."

"So I don't have to worry about him anymore?" Margaret said, relieved.

"Not unless you find yourself in Moscow sometime soon," said Dawkins. "The problem magically took care of itself." She looked at me. "The soccer game is one of the places where our cases began to get entangled. You see, we on the special task force are very interested in Mr. Morozov, while Agent Moretti and his colleagues on organized crime are very interested in another man who was at the game named Nicolae Nevrescu. Do you two know him?"

"He's a gangster," said Margaret. "A member of EEL, which stands for the Eastern European League. Earlier this year he kidnapped Florian."

"Which is why we found it surprising that Florian and he sat together at your soccer game talking like old friends," she said.

All eyes were on me, and I had to be careful how I answered. I knew that the FBI followed Nic the Knife everywhere he went and would be able to tell if I lied. I just had to make sure I didn't tell them everything.

"Yes, he abducted me, but it was a misguided attempt to find out information about a case we were working on," I said. "He'd been mistakenly identified as the mastermind of a robbery at the National Gallery of Art. Eventually, he wound up working with the Bureau and helped us solve the case."

"And that day at the soccer game?"

"I was surprised to see him," I said. "He was there because he'd donated the money to improve the field and install new bleachers and a scoreboard. We were talking when Andrei Morozov showed up. When I saw him, I was worried, and Nevrescu asked why I was worried. I told him that Morozov had been following Margaret and I was concerned about what he might do."

"And that's when Mr. Nevrescu walked over and talked to Morozov?" she asked.

"Yes," I answered.

"What did he tell him?"

"I have no idea," I said. "He didn't tell me."

"Well, it must have been something," she said. "Because Morozov instantly left the field, went straight to the embassy, and a day later was on a plane for Moscow."

"Like I said. I have no idea what Mr. Nevrescu said to him."

Moretti interrupted and said, "May I ask a question?"

"Of course," said Dawkins.

"Are there any other times that you've interacted with Mr. Nevrescu?"

At first I didn't know what he was talking about, but when I remembered, things started to make a lot more sense. "About a month ago Margaret and I went to his office."

"Why did you do that?"

"We were working undercover, and a friend of ours named Yin Yae had been kidnapped," said Margaret. "We asked him to help us solve the case."

"I'm sorry," said Moretti. "You've lost me."

"We were trying to figure out how the kidnapping may have been executed, and we went to him for his expertise."

"And did you solve the case?"

"Yes, we did," Margaret said proudly. "Along with Marcus."

"You see, this is the part that interests me," Moretti replied. "Marcus has closed so many cases that he was just given a Director's Award for Excellence. But it seems like all the cases he solves involve getting help from Nic the Knife and a pair of twelve-year-olds. So far you've already mentioned the National Gallery case and a kidnapping. It's almost like he's building his career with the help of a notorious criminal. Almost like organized crime wants to see to it that Marcus is promoted to a position of power."

"You couldn't be more wrong," I said. "Marcus is the most honest person I've ever met. He wouldn't break a rule, much less a law."

Moretti flashed a smile that was unnerving. "Agent Dawkins, why don't you take it from here?"

Dawkins got up and walked over to the cabinet, which she unlocked. She brought back two books, which were in evidence bags.

"Do you recognize this book?" she asked, holding one up. It was antique with a dark blue cover.

Margaret and I both said no.

"It was delivered to my office by special courier. Turned in anonymously. And it has been identified as having been stolen from the Russian Imperial Collection of the Library of Congress."

"Okay," I said. "I know about the collection, but I don't recognize that book in particular."

"Me neither," said Margaret.

"On Monday, did Marcus take you to the Rare Book Reading Room at the Library of Congress?"

"Yes."

"Did Alistair Toombs show you around the stacks, including the bookcases that held the Russian Imperial Collection?"

"Yes."

"At one point did he leave you alone with those books?"

It took me a moment to remember because it hadn't seemed significant. "Yes."

"Why was that?"

"Lights came on in a different part of the stacks, and he wanted to see who was there," said Margaret. "It turned out to be an intern."

"Okay," she said. "This is where I need total honesty. This next question is the whole ball game. At any point did Marcus touch any of the books in the collection?"

"No," Margaret and I both said definitively.

"Are you certain?" she asked. "Not even to point something out or show you one of the books?"

"I'm certain," I answered.

"Cross my heart," said Margaret.

She held up the book again. "Then how do you explain how this book has his fingerprints on it?"

Margaret and I recoiled. We had been certain we were providing him with an alibi, but in fact, we'd done the opposite. We'd made him look guiltier.

23.

Two Books

MARGARET AND I SAT THERE AND STARED AT THE book in the evidence bag. It had a blue cover, red spine, and apparently Marcus's fingerprints.

"There's an easy explanation," said Margaret. "He picked up the book."

"But you just said he didn't," responded Melinda Dawkins. "In fact, you were adamant that he didn't."

"He didn't pick it up when we were there on Monday," she said. "He did ten years ago when he was researching his PhD project."

"Don't be ridiculous," said Mike Moretti. "You think his fingerprints are that pristine ten years after the fact?"

"Yes," said Margaret. "Those books are kept in ideal conditions and virtually never handled. How many people do you think have checked that book out in the last ten years?"

"Special Agent Rivers offered the same explanation," said Dawkins. "But he had no explanation for this."

She held up the other book, which was also in an evidence bag. This one was smaller and had a green cover.

"Let me guess, it has his fingerprints, too," I said.

"Actually, no," she replied. "It's also from the Russian Imperial Collection, but it has been thoroughly wiped clean and has no fingerprints at all."

"Then what connection does it have to Marcus?" I asked.

"It was found last night during the execution of a search warrant at the home of William and Anntionette Rivers."

It took me a moment to place the names. "Marcus's parents?"

"Yes," she said. "It was on a bookcase in their basement."

Margaret and I slumped in our chairs.

"Do you have any knowledge of either of these books?"

"No," I said.

"Me neither," offered Margaret.

"You're both very smart. Can you think of any plausible explanation?"

"He's obviously being set up by the real criminal," said Margaret.

"I don't suppose you have any proof that might back that up?"

"I don't need any," she replied. "I know it in my heart."

The CIA agent smiled. "Unfortunately, we work in a world where evidence matters more than emotion."

I instantly thought back to Marcus and his breakup with Lucia. He had said virtually the same thing to her. I also remembered how Marcus said she still came by his parents' house sometimes. Maybe she had hidden the book in the basement the last time she visited.

"What are you thinking, Florian?" asked Dawkins.

I didn't feel like it was fair to throw the blame on Lucia, so I didn't bring it up. Instead, I said, "I'm confused about jurisdiction. You're running a joint task force on counter-intelligence, and Agent Moretti's with organized crime. Even if Marcus did steal those books, which I'm certain he didn't, it shouldn't involve anyone in this room."

"You're right," she said. "The theft of rare books should be handled by the Art Crime team. The only problem is that the agent in charge of the Art Crime team happens to be the prime suspect. But since a similar rare book was found with the government secrets, we think these books may be an element of our case. And because of Nicolae Nevrescu's conversation with Andrei Morozov, organized crime is also involved. Like I said, Florian, we've got quite a tangled knot that needs to be untied."

"So you think he may somehow be involved in espionage?" I said, looking at her. "And you think he's been closing cases by getting help from the Romanian mafia?" I said to Moretti.

"We have to follow the evidence," said Dawkins. "Which brings us to our final question." She reached into a file and pulled out a pair of photographs of Marcus entering and exiting our house holding the cold case evidence box. "On Wednesday night, did Marcus bring a sealed evidence box to your house?"

I had worried at the time that he wasn't supposed to do that. "Yes. It was evidence from a case involving a former Russian diplomat named Alexander Petrov."

"And why did he bring it to your house?"

"So Margaret and I could look at it and try to help him solve the case."

She shook her head. "He really shouldn't have done that," she replied.

"Well, the reason he did it was because he was worried about us coming here," said Margaret. "Dan Napoli and who knows who else from organized crime had been following us around town. Just like Andrei Morozov."

This caught Dawkins by surprise. "Is that true?" she asked Moretti.

"Of course not."

"We lost him in the zoo," Margaret said.

"And you saw him?" asked Dawkins.

"Well, no," said Margaret. "We saw the car, and we went into the zoo to lose him, but only Marcus saw him. There is a picture, though. He texted it to Kayla—I mean Agent Cross."

We might as well have said that it was all made up based on their reactions.

The questioning was over, and Dawkins thanked us for our help. I could tell that she felt bad about the situation. When I went into the waiting room and signed out, I looked up at her line on the visitor's log and memorized her telephone number long enough so I could type it into my phone when we walked down the hall.

All of us were quiet as we rode the elevator back up to the main floor. Margaret looked like she was about to cry, and her mother placed a tender hand on her shoulder. She fought the emotion all the way until we walked out of the Hoover Building and were standing on Pennsylvania Avenue. That's when tears started to stream down her cheeks. I couldn't remember ever seeing her that upset.

"Why didn't you tell me that Andrei Morozov was at the soccer game?" she said, shooting me an angry look. "Why didn't you tell me that Nic the Knife threatened him?"

"I didn't tell you because he was only there for a minute and I didn't want you to worry," I said. "And when Nic came back and told me that he'd taken care of it, I didn't know what to think."

"But why would he do that?" she asked, her voice rising. "Why would he do that for me?"

"I think he likes us," I said. "He's got this weird sense of right and wrong, and for whatever reason he wants to look out for us. He even gave me his cell number. He told me to call him if there were any more problems."

She shook her head in total confusion. "That doesn't make sense."

"Maybe it doesn't, but that's what happened," I said. "If you want to be mad at me, you can be mad at me later, but right now we have to focus on helping Marcus."

She took a deep breath. "Okay, how do we do that?"

"I need you to stop right there," said Mrs. Campbell. "As an officer of the court and as cocounsel for Marcus, I cannot have any knowledge of what I think you're about to do. You can't have this discussion in front of me."

"No," said my mom. "But I'm an art restorer who took no such oath. So why don't we get in the car and see if we can fix this?"

Mrs. Campbell gave Margaret a hug and then walked toward her law office, which was just a few blocks away, while we headed for the car.

"What's the plan?" asked my mom.

Margaret and I looked at each other for a moment.

"Whoever is setting Marcus up is also the spy," said Margaret. "So we need to figure out who could've stolen the books after we were there on Monday and also been able to hide one of them in the basement at Marcus's parents' house."

"So where do we go first?" asked Mom.

"His parents' house," I said. "That's the scene of the most recent crime."

"What about lunch?" she said.

"We can't just stop and eat," I said. "We have to solve the case."

"But you missed lunch, and I know how you get when you don't eat," she said. "You might think better on a full stomach."

"I am kind of hungry," Margaret said.

We compromised and ended up grabbing burgers and eating in the car as we drove. Mr. and Mrs. Rivers lived in Northeast Washington in the same house where Marcus grew up. The neighborhood was quiet and peaceful looking, and they lived in a two-story town house with a big stoop on the front. We'd met Marcus's parents a few times but had been to their house only once.

"Florian, Margaret, what are you doing here?" asked Mrs. Rivers when she answered the door.

"We're here to help Marcus," said Margaret.

She smiled. "Well then, I guess you better come right in."

24.

Bella Donna

THE LIVING ROOM AT THE RIVERSES' HOUSE WAS practically a shrine to Marcus and his sister. Just by looking at the pictures in the room, you could follow the arcs of their entire lives. There were baby photos, a picture of Marcus in a high school football uniform, and a collage from his sister's wedding. The most prominent pictures, though, were of graduations. Marcus once told me that he'd been the first person in his family to go to college, and he earned degrees at Harvard and Georgetown. His sister followed him by graduating from the University of Virginia and now worked as a researcher for the National Institutes of Health.

Mr. and Mrs. Rivers were proud of their children and

had every reason to be. I could only imagine how upsetting it had been for them the night before when FBI agents scoured their home.

"My Marcus did nothing wrong," said Mrs. Rivers as she brought out a tray of iced tea and little lemon cookies that had powdered sugar on them.

"We know that," said Margaret. "That's why we're trying to figure out what happened."

She told us that the previous night she and her husband had been watching television when there was a knock on the door. There were six agents with a warrant, and they instantly started searching the house.

"They began upstairs with the bedrooms and worked their way down," she said. "I called Marcus, and he was over here in a flash, but they wouldn't let him inside. He even got into an argument on the stoop with the agent in charge."

"Did you get his name?" asked Margaret.

"Napoli," she said. "Dan Napoli."

Margaret and I shared a look.

"And when did they find the book?" I asked.

"About an hour after they arrived," she said, tears welling in her eyes. "I don't know how it got in there, but it wasn't Marcus."

Everyone was quiet for a moment while she composed herself.

"Can you tell us the last time that Lucia Miller came to visit?" I asked.

Mrs. Rivers shook her head. "Lucia has nothing to do with this. I don't know why Marcus ever got that in his head in the first place, but it wasn't her."

"Yes, but . . ."

"She hasn't been here for at least three months."

I wanted to push some more but didn't want to upset her so I let it go.

"Can we look in the basement?" asked Margaret.

"Yes," she said. "My husband spent half the night cleaning up down there. I told him to wait, but he can't sleep when he's upset, so at least it gave him something to do."

We followed a narrow set of stairs down into their basement, which had been turned into a large room with a couch, two comfy chairs, and floor-to-ceiling bookcases on three walls.

"I love this room," said my mom.

"Thank you," replied Mrs. Rivers. "William knows carpentry, and he built all the bookcases for me because I love to read."

"They're beautiful," she said.

"Where was the book the FBI found?" I asked.

"Right over here," she said as she led me to the spot.

I reached up to touch it and accidentally got powdered sugar from the lemon cookies on some of the books.

"Florian," my mom said. "Try not to make a mess in their house."

"It comes right off," said Mrs. Rivers, shooting me a wink. She reached up and brushed it off with the back of her hand.

I took a couple of pictures of the room and of the cellar door that led to the backyard.

"If someone broke in, this would be the way," I said.

We unlocked the door and opened it. There were no signs of anyone trying to break in or pick the lock.

"Do you know how old this lock is?" I asked.

Mrs. Rivers laughed. "I imagine it's as old as the house, Florian."

"Just checking," I said. "Can I see what the key looks like?"

"I'll show it to you when we go back upstairs."

I didn't say anything about it, but I made a mental note that it meant if Lucia had had a key when she was engaged to Marcus, it would still work. We walked out into the backyard to see if there was anything noteworthy out there.

"Did the agents look around here?" asked Margaret.

"No, they didn't go outside at all."

"I wonder why?" asked Margaret.

"Because they assumed Marcus was guilty," I said. "And he wouldn't have had to break in."

We looked around for a few more minutes, and when we went upstairs, Mrs. Rivers showed me the key to the basement door, and I took a picture of it. The last thing I saw as we walked out the door was the FBI Director's Award that Admiral Douglas had presented to Marcus the week before.

His parents had put it on a table in the entryway.

When we got into the car, my mom turned to me and said, "I don't care how you do it, Florian. But you solve this. We're not helping Marcus anymore. Now we're helping that woman's baby boy."

"Yes, ma'am," I said.

"And I'm not just a driver," she said. "I've got many hidden talents. Put me to use. What would Marcus or Kayla be doing if they were with you?"

I thought about it for a moment and said, "You know, you might be able to help some more."

"Great," she replied. "What are we looking for?"

"A deep-cover spy," I said. "Someone who probably came

to this country when he or she was only a teenager and then, when they grew up, started spying for Russia."

"Unless it's Lucia," Margaret said reluctantly. "We know that she grew up in the United States, but she lived in Moscow during high school."

"Got it," said Mom. "I know just what to do."

She started driving the car.

"Where are you going?" I asked. "You don't know where any of the suspects are."

"That doesn't matter right now," she said. "Because first I have to go home and change."

"Mom," I said with a touch of whine in my voice. "We don't have time."

"I know," she said. "That's why I'm driving faster than usual."

"I mean, we don't have time to go home and change."

She flashed me a smile. "Sure we do. Now tell me everything about the four suspects."

Margaret and I filled her in on everything that we'd discovered during the week and offered her our different theories and suspicions.

"If you had to put one suspect at the top of your list, who would it be?" she asked.

"I'm leaning toward either Rose or Lucia," I said.

Margaret laughed. "That's funny because I'm thinking Alistair or Brooke."

"So you're telling me you really don't know," she said.

"I guess so," I admitted.

"Then it's good that you have me along to break the tie."

She pulled into our driveway, and we hurried up the steps to the house.

"Mom, we really don't have time," I said.

"This will only take a moment," she said. "And it's necessary."

"I don't understand what's wrong with what you're wearing," I said.

Mom smiled and said, "And you call yourself Italian." She gestured to the suit she'd worn. "This is what you wear when your son is being questioned by the FBI. It's not what you wear when you're going undercover."

She bounded up the steps, and I shook my head.

"I think we've created a monster."

When my mother was in her early twenties, she lived in Milan, where she developed a strong sense of pride when it came to Italian fashion and style. Of all the things she missed about living in Italy, I think clothes were at the top of the list.

Five minutes after heading upstairs, she came back down

and looked like a totally different woman. Her style was always simple and elegant. She wore a long gray skirt with a large black belt and black turtleneck. She also wore black leather boots.

"Wow, Mrs. Bates!" said Margaret. "You look amazing."

"*Grazie mille*," she said, using the Italian expression for "thank you very much." "Now we are ready."

"Seriously, Mom," I complained. "What are you dressing for? A spy movie?"

"No," she said. "I'm dressing for a spy."

"What do you mean?" asked Margaret.

"If you want to identify which of these people grew up in Europe, then you need to throw a little Europe their way," she said. "This necklace and these earrings are Russian. When they see them, they'll recognize them, and I'll be able to tell."

"Except a deep-cover spy will have spent almost all their life in America," I countered. "They're not European anymore."

My mother laughed and said, "*Puoi portare lat donna fuori dall'Europa, ma no puoi portare Europafuori dalla donna.*"

Then she put on a pair of oversized sunglasses and walked out of the house with dramatic flair.

"What did she say?" asked Margaret.

"'You can take the girl out of Europe, but you can't take Europe out of the girl.'"

25.

Library Games

OUR FIRST STOP WAS THE FOLGER SHAKESPEARE
Library. On the drive over we told Mom all about Rose
Brock, with her ever-changing hair color and the *Romeo and
Juliet* tattoo on the inside of her arm.

"Why do we suspect her?" asked Mom.

"Well, she says that she grew up in Baltimore, but she has
a European vaccine scar," I said.

"And she made frequent trips back to Europe including at
least three to Russia," said Margaret. "She's also worked on a
project with the NSA, which as far as we know is the only connection any of the suspects have to an intelligence organization."

"Got it," she said. "And what are we looking for?"

"We don't know if she has any access to the Library of Congress," I said. "She used to work there, but she got forced out. And if she doesn't have a way to get back in there, then she couldn't have stolen the books from the Russian Imperial Collection."

Mom smiled as she took it all in. "This is fun," she said. "I see why you like it so much."

"It's not a game," I said to her. "We're not actors playing parts. You need to just be yourself."

"I understand," she said. "Why don't you trust your mother just this once."

Because we weren't certain what we were looking for, we had to be careful not to appear as if we were just wandering around. A skilled spy would instantly see through that. We needed to have a "reason" to be in each place, and our reason at the Folger was to show my mom the fake portrait.

"This library holds the world's largest collection of Shakespearean works and items," I told her as we walked through the building. "But the thing I really want to show you is this portrait."

I led her to the Founders' Room and showed her the painting that Rose Brock had shown us on the tour.

"Who's this?" she asked when she looked at the picture.

"What do you mean?" I asked.

"Well, it's not Shakespeare," she said.

I couldn't believe it. "How did you know that?"

"Florian, what do you think I do for a living?"

"You restore paintings at the National Gallery," I said.

"Yes, and the reason I can do that is I have a fair amount of expertise in art," she answered. "This is the painting of an English nobleman. You can tell by the style, the pose, and the iconography. Shakespeare was a playwright. He would never have been painted in this manner."

Margaret laughed. "Maybe we should have brought her along from the beginning."

I scanned the area for Rose Brock and saw her preparing to give another tour. I waited until she noticed us and when she did I waved.

"Weren't you two here earlier this week with Marcus?" she asked when she came over.

"Yes," I said. "I'm Florian, and this is Margaret."

"Right," she said. "What are you doing back so soon? My tour's good, but it's not that good."

"I wanted to show my mother this painting," I said. "She's a preservationist at the National Gallery of Art, and I knew she'd find the story fascinating."

"Hello," said Rose, introducing herself. "It's nice to meet you."

"And a pleasure to meet you," said Mom. "Florian couldn't stop talking about the tour he had here. He told me I just had to come."

"I love that necklace," she said. "And those earrings. Where did you get them?"

"I've had them so long I don't remember," she said. "Back when we lived in Italy."

"I love Italy," she said. "I went to Verona to see the house where they say Romeo talked to Juliet on her balcony. I know she's a fictional character, but I couldn't resist. I try to go to Europe every year and visit the locations from Shakespeare's plays."

"You aren't from there, are you?" asked my mother. "Europe, I mean."

"Something far less glamorous," she responded. "Baltimore. Pikesville to be exact."

"I grew up not far from Verona, and when I was a teenager, my girlfriends and I made the same trip and stood beneath her balcony dreaming of our own Romeos."

The two of them laughed.

"Florian tells me that you used to work at the Library of Congress."

Rose gave my mom a look, like maybe she was pushing too hard, but Mom didn't back down.

"I ask because we're thinking of doing an exhibition together with the library and the National Gallery," she explained. "And I'm a little concerned about how they are to work with. The politics between institutions can be tricky."

"They're mostly good," said Rose. "Right now I'm actually working with them on a project for an upcoming exhibit about Shakespeare and the presidents. I'm calling it *The Bard of Pennsylvania Avenue*."

"That sounds really cool," said Margaret.

"It is," answered Rose. "We're going to display different copies of Shakespeare's works that were in the personal libraries of the presidents."

"So you've been working over there at the library?" I asked.

"I go over once a week," she said. "Luckily, the presidential libraries are all part of the Rare Book collection, and that's where I used to work, so I know it well. So they leave me alone for the most part."

A grandfather clock chimed, and Rose said, "That's my cue. It's time for the next tour. Are you going to be joining us?"

"I'd love to," said Mom. "But we have some errands to run."

"Here's my card," Rose said, handing her business card to

my mother. "Maybe in the future we can develop an exhibit between the Folger and the National Gallery."

"That would be delightful," said Mom.

Rose called her tour group together while we left the building.

"You were really good at that, Mrs. Bates," said Margaret once we were outside.

"Yes, Mom," I said reluctantly. "You were great."

"*Poverino bambino,*" she said, using the Italian for "poor baby." "You have to admit that your mother isn't useless."

We didn't have much time if we wanted to check on all four suspects in one day. Luckily, our next stop was right across the street.

"Who's next?" asked Mom as we walked toward the entrance of the Library of Congress.

"Alistair Toombs," I said. "He's in charge of the Rare Book and Special Collections Division of the library."

"He's also kind of awkward," said Margaret. "His whole life is the collection. He'd do anything to protect it. He's spent lots of money upgrading the climate controls and security system for the stacks."

"The question is, did he sell off some of his books to pay for those upgrades," I said.

"Got it," she said as we entered the building.

Most of the Great Hall was blocked off as workers set up tables for an event that evening.

"What's going on?" asked Margaret.

"The 'It's All About the Books' Gala," Mom said, pointing at a banner that was over the stage. "It must be a fund-raising event for the library." She looked around at the massive space. "It's certainly a beautiful location for one."

We navigated around the workers and up the stairs to the second floor. We were just about to go into the Rare Book Reading Room when Margaret reached over and grabbed me by the arm.

"Wait," she said. "We can't go in there."

"Why not?"

"Alistair Toombs talked to the FBI," she said. "He thinks Marcus stole the books, and we were with Marcus."

"You're right," I said, turning and leading us all in the opposite direction. "We've got to get out of here."

"No," said my mother, stopping. "You two have to get out of here. He doesn't know who I am."

"What are you going to do?"

"I don't know," she said as she walked toward the door. "I'll probably just be charming and see what happens from there."

She stopped and turned back to us. "How will I know which one he is?"

"Pale skin with a bad comb-over," said Margaret. "Oh, and it's probably faded by now, but on Monday his right arm was completely sunburned."

"Just his right arm?" she asked.

"Yes," said Margaret.

"Ciao," she said with a wink as she entered the reading room.

"I'm going to be honest," Margaret said to me as we stood there a moment. "I'm loving your mother."

"She has that effect on people," I said.

"Let's hope she has it on Alistair Toombs."

A large balcony wrapped around the second floor looking down over the Great Hall, and we stood there and watched all the people. There were the ever-present school groups and all the workers setting up for the gala. They were putting place settings on all the tables and the clinking of plates and silverware was almost musical.

"It really is a beautiful building," said Margaret as we looked over it all.

"Hard to believe there are spies lurking about," I said.

"Not really," she said. "With halls and tunnels that connect to the Capitol, it was bound to happen."

"Do you suppose that's how the secrets were stolen?" I asked.

"What do you mean?"

"Like you said, this building is connected to the Capitol. Workers here constantly go back and forth with carts of books to take to senators and congressmen. They enter all those rooms where secrets are hidden. Maybe that's how the secrets were stolen in the first place."

Margaret thought about this for a moment. "That makes a lot of sense," she said. "If you're a worker wheeling stuff in and out of a conference room day after day, I bet they stop noticing you."

"Yeah," I said. "That's what I was thinking."

We stood there for another fifteen minutes until my mother came out and saw us.

"Did you meet him?" asked Margaret.

"Alistair, yes."

"Well, what did you find out?" I asked.

"Like you said, he is very devoted to his collection. I told him that I work at the National Gallery and was curious about what measures he took to protect the books."

"I bet he loved that," said Margaret.

"Yes," replied Mom. "We talked all about temperature and humidity control. He seemed especially proud of his motion-control lighting system."

"Unfortunately, we already knew all that."

"Did you know that a computer tracks not only everyone who enters and leaves the stacks but also which lights are turned on when they're back there? He says it allows him to maximize efficiency in layout, all with an eye to protecting the books."

"We knew that, too," I said, disappointed by the lack of new information. "Come on, we better get going."

I started down the steps.

"Wait a second," said Mom. "Don't you want to know about the sunburn?"

I stopped and turned back to face her. "You know how?"

"Yes, I know," said Mom.

"He told you?"

"No. I figured it out," she said. "You're not the only one in the family with a logical mind."

"How?" I asked.

Mom flashed a smile. "I like this," she said. "I like figuring something out that you haven't yet."

"Are you going to tell us or not?"

"I'll tell you in the car," she said. "It'll make more sense."

26.

Preservation

MY MOTHER WAS IN NO HURRY TO TELL US ABOUT Alistair's sunburn. We'd left the Library of Congress and were headed up New Jersey Avenue toward the Petworth Library, where Lucia worked, and Mom was still milking the moment for all she could.

"You know, it's a really nice day today," she said. "Let's ride with the windows down."

First I rolled my eyes, then I rolled down the window.

"Feel that breeze," she said as we rode along. "Isn't it wonderful?"

"It's great, Mom," I said, exasperated. "Now, are you going to tell us how his arm got sunburned or not?"

"I just did," she answered. "Look at your arm, Florian."

I looked at my right arm, and it suddenly dawned on me. I'd rested it on the door now that the window was down, making it the only part of my body that was exposed to the sun.

"Your grandfather used to get that all the time," she said. "His truck didn't have air-conditioning, and he'd drive it for hours with the windows rolled down. I recognized it instantly."

I thought about this for a moment and couldn't think of how that might relate to the case. "So, Alistair drove around with his arm out the window. . . ."

"No, he didn't," said my mother. "He *rode* in someone's car with his arm out the window. It was his right arm. That means he was in the passenger seat."

"True," I said. "But I still don't think that gives us anything."

"I didn't figure it would," said Mom. "I imagine that's how most clues are."

"Still, it's impressive that you solved it," I said.

Just then Margaret blurted out from the back seat, "Brooke King!"

"We're going to see her last," I said. "After we stop by the Petworth Library and check on Lucia."

"No, no, no," she said excitedly. "Go to Dupont Circle, Mrs. Bates."

"It'll save time if we see Lucia first," I said.

"It doesn't matter," Margaret said. "We want to see Brooke first."

"Why?" asked my mother.

"Because the air conditioner is broken in her car!"

It took a second for me to understand her point. "She's right," I exclaimed. "Go to Dupont Circle!"

My mom turned the car, and we tried to explain why we were excited.

"When we went to see her, she had just come back from a trip to North Carolina, where she bought a bunch of antique books at an estate sale," said Margaret. "But when she was there, the air conditioner broke in her car, and she had to drive all the way back with her windows down."

"And this is important because . . ."

"Because Alistair was riding in the passenger seat," I said. "He showed us that picture he'd just taken of the lighthouse. Where was it?"

"Nag something," said Margaret.

"Nags Head," I said. "Where's that?"

Margaret did a quick search on her phone. "Nags Head is a town on the Outer Banks of North Carolina. Here's a picture of the lighthouse. It's the same one." She passed her phone to me to look at the lighthouse.

"Okay, we're getting somewhere," I said.

"Where?" asked my mother, feeding off our excitement.

I thought about it and said, "I have no idea. But it's something."

I plugged Palace Books into the navigation system on the car, and we worked up a strategy for Brooke King.

"Her specialty is book conservation and repair," I said. "So you two can certainly strike up a conversation about that. Do that charming thing again."

"Also, it's your birthday this week," added Margaret.

"It is?" she asked.

"We found a really great present there for your birthday," I said.

My mom picked this up so quickly, it made me wonder if solving puzzles was some sort of family trait. Margaret had been looking into her DNA hoping to find out more about herself. I wondered if my mom passed down the DNA that helped me come up with TOAST.

We opened the door to Palace Books, and a bell signaled our arrival. There were a few customers in the store, and Brooke King was behind the desk.

"Look who it is," she said when she saw me. "Are you back to pick up a birthday present?"

"Yes," I said. "And I even brought the birthday girl with me."

"Hello," said Mom. "I'm Florian's mother, Francesca Bates."

"Nice to meet you," said Brooke. "Let me get the book for you."

She went over to a cabinet behind her desk and pulled out the thin book. "I kept it back here to make sure no one else picked it up."

"What is it?" asked my mother, truly interested.

Brooke handed her the book, and my mother's eyes lit up.

"*La famosa invasione degli orsi in Sicilia!*" my mother squealed with delight. "I love this book. I haven't seen it in so many years."

"I told you," Brooke said to me.

"We are definitely buying this," Mom said to me as she happily flipped through the pages.

"I understand you're a conservationist," said Brooke.

"Yes," said my mother. "At the National Gallery of Art. And Florian tells me that you are a book conservationist."

"That's right," she said.

"Do you do that in addition to running the store?"

"Yes," she said. "I have a little studio set up in back. It lets me stay in touch with a lot of collectors and potential buyers, not to mention libraries and other institutions."

"That's fantastic," said Mom. "I don't suppose I could take a peek."

"Of course," she said. "Let me show you."

"What about your customers?" asked Mom.

"It's a small place," joked Brooke. "I can keep an eye on things from there."

She opened a door and revealed a small room with a workstation filled with all sorts of equipment, tools, and supplies. I didn't know what any of them were used for, but my mom recognized it all, and they started talking shop, only about half of which I understood.

I looked around the room for anything that might give me some additional insight into Brooke. I didn't see any pictures or personal items. The walls were mostly bare with the exception of a few posters for classic books like *The Grapes of Wrath* and *Pride and Prejudice*. One thing about the room, however, was that it seemed extremely organized. There were stacks of books in various piles around the room.

"I'm guessing all of these are stacked in a particular order," I said.

"Yes," said Brooke. "Everything on this side is work to be done, and everything over here is work that's completed and ready to go out. You can see that the completed piles are much shorter."

"Who do you work for?" asked Margaret.

"Let's see," said Brooke. "That stack is for the DC Public Library. That stack is for George Washington University. And that stack over there is made up of all the books I bought last week at an estate sale."

"Oh, that's right," said Margaret. "You were telling us about that. Was it out in Virginia?"

"No," she replied. "It was on the Outer Banks of North Carolina. Beautiful, but a long drive."

"Do you ever repair books for the Library of Congress?" I asked, going for broke.

"Once a week," she said. "That's why I'm closed on Wednesdays. I go in there to do that. This store isn't secure enough for those books."

"Well, it's all fascinating," said my mother.

"What type of work do you do at the National Gallery?" she asked Mom.

They started getting technical again, so Margaret and I moved out into the store to look around.

Ten minutes later they were done, and my mom bought

the Italian children's book. We said good-bye to Brooke and left the store.

We discussed the three suspects on our way to the Petworth Library, and Margaret explained the problem of our situation.

"There are things that make me think that each of them is guilty," she said. "And things that make me just as certain that each of them is innocent."

"I know," I said. "That's how I feel too."

"Well, we know it's not Lucia," said Mom.

"How do we know that?" I asked.

"Because Marcus's mother said so, and I believe her."

"We still have to check her out," I said. "And she's the only one who checks all the boxes."

"What do you mean?" she asked.

"One: She has access to the library. Two: She has a solid connection to Russia. And three: She could easily get into the basement at the Riverses' house."

We rode silently for a moment before Margaret added, "I hate to say it, but he's right."

There wasn't any parking near the library, so my mother dropped us off while she went to look for a space. At first we thought we'd struck out because when we went upstairs to check the children's department, another librarian was on duty. But then it turned out that Lucia was covering for somebody at the main circulation desk. We'd been in such a hurry that we'd walked right past her on the way up.

"I know you," she said as we approached the desk. "Did you go to Gorky's?"

"Yes, we did," I said. "Although we didn't end up making the piroshki. It was too difficult."

"What'd you do instead?" she asked.

"I think we're going to get everyone Alyonka candy," said Margaret.

Lucia swooned. "I absolutely love Alyonka."

"It's ridiculously delicious," said Margaret.

She had stacks of books in front of her and was sorting through them, putting them in different boxes.

"What's all this?" I asked. "I thought you worked in the children's section."

"We all have to pitch in and help at circulation," she said. "So right now I am sorting from the book drop."

"What's that?" I asked.

"These were all returned here. You can return a book to any branch of the DC Public Library. But once we get it, we have to send it back to the branch where it was checked out. There are trucks that go around all the time carrying books from one branch to another. I'm putting books in the right boxes for the next delivery."

"And how do you know which book goes to which branch?" asked Margaret.

"There's a code," she said conspiratorially. "Do you want to see it?"

She held up a book so we could see the back. There was a white tag on the top with a call number.

"The number at the top is the Dewey decimal number, which tells us where it goes on the shelf."

"Right."

"But you see those three letters on the bottom?"

"Sure," I said. "P-E-T."

"For Petworth," she said. "That means this book stays here at this branch. But look at this book."

I read the letters off the bottom. "T-E-N."

"This book goes to the Tenley-Friendship branch."

"That's pretty cool," I said.

"We're crafty in the library business; that's why we'd make such good spies."

It was an odd thing to say, and I was almost wondering if she was toying with us. Then my mother walked up. "I finally found a parking spot," she said.

"Is this your mom?" asked Lucia.

"Yes, it is," I said. "Mom, this is Lucia Miller. Ms. Miller, this is my mom."

Lucia's expression changed dramatically. "How'd you know my name was Lucia?"

I panicked. We'd been calling her Lucia so much I'd forgotten that we weren't supposed to know that.

"It's right there on your name tag," I said.

"Actually, my name tag says Lucretia," she responded. "That's my full name. But my friends and family call me Lucia."

"Oh," I said as I tried to cover. "I must've just misremembered it as Lucia. Lucky guess . . . I guess."

She still looked at me suspiciously, but there was nothing I could do about it. Thankfully, my mother came to my rescue.

"Did you guys find the books you were looking for?" she asked.

"Not yet," said Margaret.

"Well, you better hurry up," she said. "We've got to pick up your dad in twenty minutes."

We said quick good-byes to Lucia and hurried upstairs.

"I can't believe I did that," I said. "That was so stupid."

"Forget it," said Margaret. "It was nothing."

"It wasn't nothing," I told her.

"Well, there's nothing we can do about it, so that's that."

We killed time upstairs so that it didn't look suspicious, and when we came down, I was happy to see Lucia busy with a customer. We waved on the way out.

When we got home, we went down into the Underground. Mom even joined us for a while as we updated the caseboard and went through every possibility.

We wondered if Brooke and Alistair might be working together. We talked about Rose's trips to Europe and her still unexplained vaccine scar. We even considered the fact that more than anyone Lucia had a reason to want to hurt Marcus. And Margaret was still perplexed about why, with all the books to choose from, the spy had selected *Mrs. Hoover Speaks Mandarin and Other Fun Facts about the First Ladies*.

Finally, we practically collapsed on the couch in total exhaustion.

"What are we missing?" I asked Margaret.

"Maybe we're not missing anything?" she replied. "Maybe it just can't be solved."

I closed my eyes for a second, and then I heard my mom's voice behind me.

"Look who I found at the front door," she said.

We turned to see who she was with.

"Marcus!" Margaret said as she jumped up and ran to him.

She gave him a hug, and he embraced her tightly. I was hoping he'd come with a positive development, but when I saw his eyes, I realized that wasn't the case. He looked like he was fighting back tears.

"Have you solved it?" Margaret asked hopefully. "Because we're stumped."

"Not exactly," he said, moving over to sit in the chair across from the couch. "There's something that's about to happen, and I wanted to be the one to tell you."

"What's that?" Margaret asked.

He hesitated for a second and did his best to put on a brave face.

"I've decided to leave the FBI."

27.

Family Matters

MARGARET AND I JUST SAT MOTIONLESS ON THE couch for a moment before she finally asked, "What do you mean?"

"Exactly that," said Marcus. "I've decided to leave the FBI."

"When are you leaving?" I asked.

"Margaret's parents are working on some paperwork right now," he said. "I'd like to get it taken care of over the weekend so that I can clear out my office without a crowd watching."

"Why would my parents do this?" Margaret asked. "Why would you do this? You're Marcus Rivers! You just won the

Director's Award for Excellence! Why are you leaving the FBI?"

"It's extremely complicated," he said. "But just know that I'm doing it because it's the best decision for everyone."

"This isn't happening," she said.

"Yes it is," he said. "And you need to accept it just like I have."

"Can you explain any of it?" I asked.

"Everything has spun out of control," he said. "And those things are not going to magically get better. Margaret's parents and I sat down with Admiral Douglas, and we've worked out a solution that lets me leave the Bureau with my record intact and keeps me clear of any criminal charges."

"Well, of course you're clear," I said. "You didn't break any laws."

"True," he said. "But that doesn't mean that it might not look like I did. And if I let the investigation continue, my record might not look so good. Then I wouldn't be able to get a job anywhere."

"You already have a job," Margaret said. "Why are you giving up?"

"Kayla taught you the WAR technique, right?"

"Yes," I said.

"Well, I'm trying to defend myself. But they have no

weakness. I've been anticipating their moves, and I can't do anything to disrupt them. And they're coming at me from all sides, so I can't redirect their energy. My only defense is to give up."

"I don't want to hear this," said Margaret as she stood. "I'm going to go talk to my parents. They promised me they'd take care of you."

"They have," said Marcus.

She stormed off, and I went to go after her, but Marcus stopped me. "Let her go," he said. "She's upset."

"I'm upset too."

"At me?" he asked.

"Of course not," I said. "I'm just angry at the world."

"That makes two of us."

We heard the door slam as Margaret left the house, and then Marcus moved to sit next to me on the couch.

"You've got to bring her around," he said. "You know why I have to make this deal, don't you?"

I shook my head. "You didn't do anything wrong."

"Eventually they'd realize that I didn't steal the books, and I'd be exonerated," he said. "But Napoli and the organized crime team think I have some sort of connection to Nic the Knife. And if they keep poking around that, they'll figure out that the connection is Margaret.

"Then we should just go ahead and tell Margaret. Once the secret's out, it's over."

"The problem isn't Margaret finding out," he said. "It's Napoli. If he finds out, he will use her to get to Nevrescu, and he'll never stop. He won't care how it affects her life. He'll only care about closing cases."

"How do you know that?"

"Because that's what I would do," he said.

"You know that's not true," I replied. "If it was, you wouldn't be sacrificing your career to protect her."

"Well, there was a time when it might have been true," he said. "Nine years ago I did the stupidest thing in my life. I let the woman who I loved and wanted to spend my life with walk away from me because I put this job first. Well, I won't make that mistake again. I love you and Margaret like you're my family. I won't put my career ahead of that. Ever."

We sat there quietly for a moment.

"You really think it was the stupidest thing you ever did?" I asked. "Letting Lucia get away?"

He nodded.

"But what if she was guilty? I mean, it's possible. She may have even been the one who set you up again."

"No way," he said. "There's no way she did it."

"How do you know?" I asked. "The evidence points that way."

"I just know." He got up. "I've got to take care of some things. I meant what I said, Florian. You're my family. And I don't need to be working on cases with you and the FBI to make that true."

28.

A Knock at the Door

WHAT A DAY.

We'd been snatched out of school and taken to the FBI for questioning. My mother suddenly became a superspy and raced around town with us looking for clues. And now it had all come to a very bad ending.

Marcus was leaving the FBI, and there was nothing I could do to stop it.

The house was completely quiet as I sat in the Underground and stared at the caseboard trying to make sense of it. I was hoping for some sudden revelation that never came.

My parents had gone out for a dinner date they couldn't

cancel, and my plan was to reheat some leftover rigatoni and watch Italian soccer on television.

Then the doorbell rang.

I trudged up the stairs, and when I stood on my toes to look out the peephole, I half expected it to be Dan Napoli, Nic the Knife, or someone else ready to turn my world upside down. But it was Margaret. and she was looking surprisingly glamorous.

"Hey," I said as I opened the door. "What's up?"

"I just wanted to apologize for the way I acted earlier," she said. "I shouldn't have stormed out and slammed the door. That was very uncool."

I was still trying to make sense of what she was wearing.

"And for that you decided to do up your hair, put on makeup, and wear a fancy dress?"

"Oh, no," she said. "I'm dressed like this because I'm going to go to the Library of Congress, crash their fundraising gala, and break into their computer server so I can figure out who's setting up Marcus and solve the case. You want to come with?"

I thought about it for a moment and nodded. "Yeah. I do. Just give me a minute to change."

29.

Trapped

WE WERE CHASING A SPY. I WAS WEARING A
tuxedo. *This* was my James Bond moment. Except, rather
than racing a sports car along a cliffside road overlooking
the Mediterranean, we were crammed onto the subway
riding the Red Line toward Metro Center Station. And
instead of an evil supergenius with a secret island fortress
and a giant death ray, our enemy was either a librarian or a
bookseller who had key card access to the Rare Books stacks
of the Library of Congress. Still, when we switched trains
and I saw my reflection in a window, I couldn't help but
strike a 007 pose.

"I saw that," said Margaret, busting me.

I tried to cover. "Saw what?"

She started humming the Bond theme and said, "Just remember, I'm not Moneypenny waiting to be rescued. I've got skills just like you do."

"That's exactly what I'm counting on."

Our goal was the library's computer server, which kept track of anyone who entered the Rare Book and Special Collections stacks. If we could find out which of our suspects entered the area after we saw the Russian Imperial Collection on Monday but before two of the books wound up in the SCIF this morning, then we could discover who stole them and prove Marcus's innocence.

It was only a few blocks from the Metro station to the library, and as we got closer, my pulse accelerated. This worried me, because during this case I hadn't exactly been James Bond cool during pressure situations, a fact that had been upsetting me.

"I'm really sorry about everything," I said. "This is all my fault."

"What are you talking about?"

"My screwup with Andrei Morozov. If I hadn't run into him and said something in Russian, none of this would've happened. You could've taken his picture, and the FBI would've identified him through facial recognition software.

He never would have chased after you. Nic wouldn't have threatened him. Marcus wouldn't be in trouble. Everything would be better."

Margaret stopped. "You know that's ridiculous, don't you?"

"No, it's not," I replied, trying not to sound too emotional. "Every word I just said is true."

"I don't accept that version of the events," she replied. "Why did Dan Napoli start spying on us in the first place? I'm talking about at the awards reception the day before you ran into Andrei Morozov."

I thought about it for a moment. "I don't know."

"Then you weren't paying attention this morning in the SCIF," she said. "Moretti knew that we visited Nic to ask him about kidnapping when we were trying to find Yin. How could he have known that?"

"Nic's under FBI surveillance," I said. "I'm sure one of their agents probably saw us."

"Right," she said. "And it makes sense if that agent was Napoli. He's been here for six months, so he'd already transferred from New York. He saw two kids going in to talk to Nic the Knife, which I'm sure stuck out in his mind."

"And then when he saw those same two kids show up inside FBI Headquarters . . . ," I said, getting it.

"He was instantly suspicious."

"That makes sense."

She smiled. "And whose idea was it to go to Nic for help that day?"

Now I realized what she was doing. "I don't remember."

"Florian Bates, there isn't anything that you don't remember. It was my idea. We were at the Kennedy Center, and you pleaded with me not to go. So, using your way of thinking, I guess, this is all *my* fault."

"You were just trying to help Yin," I said.

"Just like you were trying to help solve this case the other day," she said. "You can't take one moment and turn it into something more than it is. What we do, *we* do. Both of us. It's plural. So stop taking blame for things that aren't your fault. Okay?"

"Okay," I said weakly.

"Okay?" she said, raising her voice for emphasis.

"Okay," I said.

"Good," she replied. "We may not have much of a plan, but we have something more important. You know what that is?"

I nodded. "We have each other."

"Now you're making sense."

This is when we reached the gala, which is where the

story began. A lot's happened since then, so I'll recap some of the highlights to refresh your memory.

We crashed the party pretending to be two middle schoolers who were so dumb they'd gotten locked out of the building by accident. (Ironic considering an hour later we managed to get locked *in* the building by accident.)

During the gala Margaret and I discovered *bulgogi* (which we loved) and were chased by Alistair Toombs (which we hated).

We hid in a room and locked the door to keep him from coming after us, but after he left, we couldn't open it. We also couldn't get any cell service to call for help. We were trapped.

Margaret started typing ten thousand different codes into the keypad while I looked for a book that might help and came across one called *Geek Mythology*. I was confused by the call number, and Margaret explained that unlike most libraries, which use the Dewey decimal system, the Library of Congress has its own classification system.

That's when my brain started putting together the puzzle pieces, and I asked Margaret for her phone so I could look through the pictures she'd taken during the case. There were two in particular I was looking for, and when I found them, I switched back and forth between them to make sure

I was right. And even though I was, I didn't know what it all meant.

I closed my eyes, and the pieces of the case flooded through my mind. FBI, CIA, NSA, Russian spies, Library of Congress, Albert Einstein, Alistair Toombs, and then . . . books. There were so many books throughout the case. Rare books. Science books. Children's books. Massive volumes of Shakespeare's works. A book that belonged to Thomas Jefferson. And now *Geek Mythology*. Maybe the hashtag was right. Maybe it was "all about the books." I remembered my mother once telling me, "No matter what you're searching for, you can always find the answer in the library. The secrets of the world are hidden in books," she'd said. "All you've got to do is look for them."

And then everything went dark, and I saw the answer right in front of me. I opened my eyes and looked at Margaret.

"We've got to get out of here!" I exclaimed.

"Yeah, I realized that a while ago. That's why I'm typing ten thousand different codes."

"No, I mean, we've got to get out of here because I may have just solved the case."

"Really? How?"

"It's hard to explain, but the first thing you have to understand is that *Geek Mythology* changes everything," I said. "Or rather, its call number does. This case is all about codes. That's what a Dewey decimal number really is, a code. And the Library of Congress system is just a different code. Two different numbers that are codes for the same thing. But if you turn that around, one number can mean two different things."

"I'm not following?" she said.

"Let me show you," I said. "Here's the picture you took of *Mrs. Hoover Speaks Mandarin and Other Fun Facts about the First Ladies.*"

I enlarged the picture and held up her phone so she could see.

"Okay."

"Read the Dewey decimal number," I said.

"Three fifty-two point twenty-three."

"Right."

I flipped through the pictures until I came to the one of the envelope in the evidence bag. I enlarged it as well.

"And here is the envelope for the letter Jarrett Underhill claims he never wrote to Alexander Petrov," I continued. "Read the zip code."

She gave me an uncertain look, but she read it.

"Three five two three."

It took her a second. "They're the same."

"It's one number that means two different things in two different codes," I said. "Petrov had this book and this envelope in his briefcase when Marcus tried to arrest him. There's no way that's a coincidence."

"What does it mean?" she asked.

"I'm not sure," I said. "But we've got to figure that out and show it to Admiral Douglas and Melinda Dawkins."

For a moment we were swept up in the excitement of the discovery, but our enthusiasm was quickly tempered by the facts of the situation. It didn't matter what we knew; we were still locked in the room. And if no one discovered us until work started on Monday, then it would be too late to help Marcus. He'd told us that he was turning in his resignation over the weekend.

"One time, I was visiting my cousins in Detroit, and we did one of those escape rooms," said Margaret. "You know, where you get locked in a room and you have to find clues and solve puzzles to unlock the door."

"How'd it go?"

"Actually, we didn't escape before time ran out," she answered.

"You're not filling me with confidence."

"But that was before you taught me TOAST," she said. "But also it makes me think we're looking at this all wrong."

"In what way?"

"We shouldn't think of it as a locked room. We should think of it as a mystery. We're no good with locked rooms. But we're great with mysteries. Let's use TOAST."

"That's good," I said. "Let's do that."

Earlier we'd been focused entirely on the locked door, but now we started searching the entire room.

In the corner there was a wooden desk and a chair with two stacks of plastic bins. Written on the red bins in big block letters was SENATE, while the blue ones said, HOUSE OF REPS. The desktop was pretty clean except for some basic office supplies.

"Scissors, tape, pens, and pencils, nothing particularly useful," Margaret said as she did a quick inventory.

"Let's check the drawers," I told her. "Maybe whoever uses this desk wrote down the combination for the keypad or hid a spare key in here."

I dug around the top drawer and found a package of index cards, a box of rubber bands, more pens, and a bottle of rubber glue. Meanwhile, Margaret sorted through papers in a file drawer.

"What's in there?" I asked.

"Three basic files: circulation reports, purchase orders, and book requests."

"Anything with the code?"

"No."

We looked some more but found nothing that helped us. I was sitting in the chair, and Margaret sat on the corner of the desk.

"Remember when Admiral Douglas took us to the SCIF that first time?" she said. "He told us that people think of rooms as separate places, but they're not. They're really connected to the outside world."

"Right, with things like windows, walls, and wiring," I said, remembering.

"How is this room connected to the outside world?" she asked.

"There's a door," I said. "But it's locked."

"There's electrical wiring," she said.

"Air-conditioning." I looked up at the ceiling, where there was a long narrow vent. "If only that was big enough to crawl through."

"Okay," she said. "How is it connected to the world in other ways?" she asked. "Why isn't there a phone on this desk?"

"That's a good question," I said. "Maybe it doesn't really belong to someone; it's just used by whoever's in this room at the time. You know, they get a book request, then come down here and find it. Put the books in a bin and take it back to either the Senate or the House of Representatives."

Margaret hopped up off the desk and started jumping up and down with excitement. "That's it. That's it. That's it."

"What's it?"

"That's what they do in here now," she said. "They come in with requests for books and put those in a bin to go back to the Capitol. But that's not what they always did in here. They used to take those bins and put them . . ."

"In the book tunnel!" I exclaimed as I shot up from my chair. "We've got to find where they plastered over the entrance."

After we'd learned about the book tunnels from Alistair Toombs, we had considered the possibility that it was how the burglar was getting into the stacks and stealing the books from the Russian Imperial Collection. I'd found a couple articles about the tunnels online and was fascinated.

They connected all parts of the Library of Congress with committee rooms and offices in the Capitol Building. In the pictures with the articles, the tunnel entrances were all about two feet by two feet and waist high on the wall. Margaret started at one end, and I started at the other, and we carefully rapped the wall every few inches, listening for anything that sounded different. It took about five minutes until we heard a hollow echo.

"Right here," she said.

"How do we break through it?" I asked.

We went back to the desk and looked for the heaviest and sharpest items we could find. We settled on an industrial-sized three-hole punch and a large pair of scissors. We smacked the wall with the three-hole punch until there was a cracking sound, then we started jabbing with the scissors. After about a minute we finally broke through a hole about the size of a quarter. We took turns peering through it using the flashlights on our phones to see.

"That's it," I said.

"Back up," she told me. She took off her shoes and posed like Kayla had taught us in self-defense class. "I'm going to kick through it."

"No," I said. "Don't."

"Why not?"

"Because you could hurt your foot. And you need it for soccer. I'll do it."

"What about your foot?" she said. "You've got tryouts coming up."

"It's okay," I said. "If I don't make the team, it won't be a big deal. But if you miss a bunch of games, that will be bad."

I got in position and gave it my best karate kick. It took

three attempts, but on the third try my foot went all the way through. My foot got caught in the plaster, and I almost fell, but Margaret caught me. We pulled back the plaster and drywall until we'd opened a space wide enough for us to crawl through.

"I just thought of something," Margaret said. "If all the entrances are covered, where do we crawl to?"

"I've already figured that out. In one of the articles, it said that there's still an opening in the Main Reading Room. There's an exhibit there about the history of the tunnels." I poked my head inside and looked up the incline toward a faint light.

"I can see it," I said. "About fifty yards away." I pulled back out and gave her a look. "Mostly uphill." (I left out the part about it being incredibly dark and scary looking.)

"Okay. You first. Start crawling."

"Why am I going first?" I said, trying not to sound scared. "You're the brave one."

"I'm also wearing a dress," she said. "I'm not crawling in front of you in a dress."

"I didn't even think about our clothes," I said. "What's crawling around in there going to do to my tuxedo?"

"Come on, 007, you can do it." Once again she started humming the James Bond theme, and I couldn't help but laugh.

I worked my way into the tunnel and started crawling, holding my phone up every once in a while to light the way. I heard Margaret get in behind me, and we were mostly quiet and focused as we crawled. It was cramped, and there was no room to turn around and go back. If we ran into a snag, we'd have to crawl backward.

When we were about halfway to the light, I began hearing music from the party.

"The gala's still going on," I told her. "I can hear the music."

"That's good," she said. "Maybe there's still some *bulgogi* left."

"Don't mention food. I'm starving."

Twenty minutes later we reached the tunnel entrance in the Main Reading Room, which was closed and entirely dark. We could hear the music coming through the walls from the Great Hall. We brushed off as much dirt and dust as we could and slipped through the door back into the party.

We didn't stop to look for food. We didn't worry about Alistair Toombs. We just headed straight for the main exit, catching some strange looks as we did. (Despite our best efforts, we were still pretty dusty, and I think I had some major cobwebbing in my hair.)

Once we were outside, I inhaled a couple lungfuls of fresh air and breathed a sigh of relief. Margaret did likewise.

"Nice work, Moneypenny," I said.

"You too, James."

We went down the stairs and sat on the edge of Neptune's fountain, enjoying the cool breeze off the water. I took out my phone.

"Calling your parents?" she asked.

"No." I pulled up the number I'd entered this morning when we left the SCIF and pressed call.

A woman answered, "Hello?"

"Is this Melinda Dawkins?"

"Who is this?"

"Florian Bates."

There was a pause on the other side. "Florian, how did you get my phone number?"

"Off the visitor's log," I said.

"Florian, it's inappropriate for you to—"

I cut her off. "We've cracked the code the Russian spies are using to communicate about dead drops. First thing tomorrow morning Margaret and I are going to the Hoover Building. If you and Admiral Douglas are there, we'll tell you everything we know."

"There are other members of the joint commission," she said. "I can't just—"

I cut her off again. "Just the two of you."

There was a long pause on the other side of the phone.

"Seven thirty," she said.

"And tell Admiral Douglas we'll need both evidence boxes," I said. "The one he showed us after the awards presentation and the one from Marcus's cold case."

"Why do you need them?"

"I'll explain it tomorrow."

"Florian," she said before I could hang up. "Don't tell anyone what you've figured out. This is dangerous information."

"Dangerous to whom?"

"To anyone who knows it."

"Yes, ma'am," I said. "See you tomorrow."

I ended the call and turned to Margaret. "She went for it."

"Okay, but you told her that we know the code," she said. "I thought you hadn't figured it all out yet."

"True," I said. "Let's hope we can solve it by seven thirty tomorrow morning."

30.

Codes

IT WAS SEVEN FIFTEEN ON SATURDAY MORNING, and some light rain was falling as my mother drove us to the Hoover Building.

"Are you sure you don't want me to go in with you?" she said. "I was pretty good yesterday."

"You were great yesterday," I said. "But it's just going to be the two of us, Admiral Douglas, and Melinda Dawkins from the CIA."

Mom pulled up to the curb by the entrance.

"Is it going to help Marcus?" she asked.

"I hope so," I said.

"Where do you want me to wait?" she asked.

"There's no telling how long this might take," I said. "I'll call when we're done."

We got out of the car and hurried across the sidewalk to keep from getting wet. An agent was waiting for us inside. He was young with a crew cut and a dark suit.

"Are you Florian Bates and Margaret Campbell?" he asked.

"Yes," we said.

"Follow me."

He walked past the reception desk.

"Don't we need to get visitor badges?"

"No badges."

We bypassed the normal bank of elevators and went around the corner to the one that Admiral Douglas had taken us on before.

"Subbasement four," the agent told the guard waiting inside.

No one spoke on the elevator. The silence was broken by the ding as we reached the floor and the doors whooshed open.

The agent walked us down the hall to the waiting room next to the SCIF, where there was a guard behind the desk.

"Cell phones," said the guard.

We handed them over, and I looked for the visitor's log.

"Where do we sign in?" I asked.

"You don't."

Admiral Douglas and Agent Dawkins were the only ones in the room. I was relieved to see the evidence boxes on the table. The mood was tense, and nobody said a word until the door behind us was firmly closed.

"Good morning, Florian, Margaret," boomed the admiral.

"Good morning, sir, Agent Dawkins."

"You know there aren't a lot of twelve-year-olds who can get us to show up somewhere this early on a Saturday morning," he said.

"No, sir, I don't expect there are," I said. "But I also don't think there are a lot of twelve-year-olds who can help you uncover a Russian spy ring that's been operating for at least nine years."

He laughed loudly and turned to Dawkins. "He makes a good point." The mood lightened some, and he leaned forward with his elbows on the table. "What've you got?"

"A deep-cover agent working out of the Library of Congress has been passing secrets to employees at the Russian embassy using a code that is ingenious in its simplicity. So much so that it has eluded detection for years."

"And you know who this person is?" asked Dawkins.

"No," I said. "We have it narrowed down. But we do know the code. And once you have the code, you can find the spy, the embassy employee receiving the information, and perhaps more importantly, other spies who use the same code."

The two of them shared a look.

"Okay," said Douglas. "Run us through it."

I stood up, opened the evidence box from the case nine years earlier, and pulled out the library book.

"*Mrs. Hoover Speaks Mandarin and Other Fun Facts about the First Ladies*," I said, reading the title. "This was found in the briefcase of Alexander Petrov when he met with Marcus to sell him two stolen books. It's kind of an odd read for a forty-five-year-old spy, don't you think?"

I passed the book to them.

"Yes, quite unusual," said the admiral.

"Agreed," said Dawkins.

"And this is a letter and envelope supposedly sent by an Alabama sculptor named Jarrett Underhill," said Margaret, passing them the evidence bags.

"Why do you say 'supposedly'?" asked Dawkins.

"Underhill claims that he didn't send the letter," said Margaret. "And the fact that the postmark reads 'Harrisonburg, Virginia,' and not 'Birmingham, Alabama,' backs that up."

"So we have a forged letter and a children's book," said Admiral Douglas. "What's the code?"

"They're the code," I said. "Look at the Dewey decimal number on the book."

Dawkins picked up the book and read it aloud. "Three fifty-two point twenty-three."

"And read the zip code on the envelope," said Margaret.

Douglas picked up the envelope and saw it. "Well, I'll be. It's three five two two three."

They held them up side by side to compare them.

"Could it be a bizarre coincidence?" asked Agent Dawkins.

"No," I said. "There's more."

I reached into my pocket and pulled out a sheet of paper that I'd printed off my computer.

"Margaret and I stayed up pretty late last night working out the specifics of how this code works," I said as I unfolded the paper and put it in front of them. "Here's a list of all the branches of the DC Public Library. We've circled nine of them."

These were the libraries that were circled:

Chevy Chase—5625 Connecticut Avenue NW

Cleveland Park—4340 Connecticut Avenue NW

Francis Gregory—3660 Alabama Avenue SE

Lamond-Riggs—5401 South Dakota Avenue SE

Parklands-Turner—1547 Alabama Avenue SE

Petworth—4200 Kansas Avenue NW

Shepherd Park—7420 Georgia Avenue NW

Tenley-Friendship—4450 Wisconsin Avenue NW

West End—2522 Virginia Avenue NW

"Why these nine?" asked Dawkins.

"Think TOAST," said Margaret.

Dawkins was confused, but the admiral smiled. "It's the technique they use for solving mysteries," he explained. "They call it the Theory of All Small Things, or TOAST."

It didn't take long for the admiral to see what we'd found.

"The streets," he said. "All of these libraries are located on avenues that are named after states."

"Exactly," said Margaret.

I reached back into the evidence box and pulled out one of the parking tickets and the ATM receipt. "The day before meeting Agent Rivers, Petrov got this parking ticket and withdrew two hundred dollars from an ATM."

"What was the money for?" asked Dawkins.

"The money's not important," I said. "What is important is the location. Both the ticket and the withdrawal were at different locations along Alabama Avenue. If you check that list, you'll see two of the libraries are located on Alabama.

"Petrov received the parking ticket across the street from the Francis Gregory branch, and he withdrew the money from a bank next door to the Parklands-Turner branch."

"I'm sorry," she said. "You've lost me."

"The zip code gives the Dewey decimal number," I explained. "But the state in the return address gives you the branch where that book can be found. The address is in Birmingham, Alabama. So he knew which street to use."

"But he didn't know which of the two branches," said Dawkins, getting it. "So he had to go to both."

"Right," I said. "And he found it at the Parklands-Turner branch."

"How do you know?" she asked.

"Two ways," I said. "The time printed on the ATM receipt is later than the time written on the ticket."

"And there are three letters underneath the Dewey

decimal number on the book," Margaret said. "P-A-R. It's the code DC Public Libraries use to make sure books get returned to the branch where they belong. It stands for Parklands."

"That's amazing," said Dawkins. "It's so out in the open, no one would even question it. But we don't know for sure that they used the code more than once."

"Actually, I think we do."

I opened the other evidence box and pulled out the book on the theory of relativity that started everything.

"This is the book in which Herman Prothro found the key to the post office box that contained the government secrets. He checked it out from the Tenley-Friendship branch of the library, which you'll see on the sheet in front of you is on Wisconsin Avenue."

Admiral Douglas picked up the book and looked at its spine. "The Dewey number is five thirty point eleven."

"And five three zero one one is the zip code for the town of Cascade, Wisconsin," said Margaret. "We looked it up last night."

"I think you have the ability to confirm that we're right, Agent Dawkins," I said. "I know that the mail is sorted by computers that take pictures of each letter in order to send them to their proper destination. I assume that either the

NSA or the CIA keeps track of all the letters that are sent to the Russian embassy. My bet is that if you go through the letters that were sent to the embassy in the days before Prothro checked out the book, you will find a letter addressed to Andrei Morozov from somebody in Cascade, Wisconsin."

"And the stamp will be upside down," said Margaret.

"Why?"

"Like on the envelope you have there," she said. "The stamp is upside down. That lets whomever is sorting the mail know that the letter has the code."

"You'll also find that the postmark is not from Wisconsin."

Douglas gave Dawkins a long hard look. There was no doubt he believed us.

"I can neither confirm nor deny that any agency tracks the mail sent to the Russian embassy," she said. "But I would like to excuse myself a minute to make a phone call."

She left us alone with Admiral Douglas, who shook his head as he turned to us. "You two never cease to amaze me."

"Thank you, sir," I said.

"You can't let Marcus quit," Margaret said to him.

"I can't stop him," he said. "I've tried to talk him out of it for two days. I've told him that all he has to do is ride it out, but he is determined to end this right now. He can be a stubborn man."

That's when I realized that Marcus hadn't told the admiral about Margaret and Nic the Knife. If the admiral knew that, then he'd understand why Marcus was being so insistent.

"How do the books work into this?" asked Douglas. "I understand passing the secrets back to the embassy, but why include the books? Maybe to help finance the operation."

"Actually, Margaret came up with the theory that I think works best," I said.

He turned to her. "What is it?"

"I don't think the books were supposed to be sold," she said. "I think the books were supposed to be returned to Russia."

The admiral gave her a curious look.

"When Alistair Toombs was showing us around the Library of Congress, he talked about the books being the DNA of the country," explained Margaret. "I think the spy feels like the books from the Russia Imperial Collection belong back in Russia. So I think he or she is placing them with the secrets with the expectation that they'll be returned home."

"In which case Alexander Petrov just wanted the money and figured nobody would ever know what he'd done."

"Exactly."

When Agent Dawkins returned to the room, she had a sly smile.

"What did you find out?" asked the admiral.

"Off the record?" she asked.

"In this room," he said, "everything is off the record."

"The day Prothro checked out the book on the theory of relativity, Andrei Morozov received a letter from a Josh Newhouse of Cascade, Wisconsin. The stamp on the letter was upside down, and the postmark was Harrisonburg, Virginia."

"That's great," said Margaret. "We can use the code to catch the spy. And when we catch the spy, we can prove that Marcus is innocent."

Both Douglas and Dawkins gave her grim looks.

"I'm afraid it doesn't work that way," she said.

"What doesn't?"

"We can't use this code to arrest anybody."

"Why not?"

"Because then they would know that we have the code and they'd stop using it. We have at least ten years of mail to sort through. We have countless letters in the future to look through. You two have given us something amazing to work with. You've helped the country tremendously."

"But what about Marcus?" Margaret asked.

"We have to put the good of the country ahead of one person's career," Agent Dawkins said. "When the British cracked Germany's Enigma code during World War Two, they had to let entire ships be torpedoed to keep the enemy from knowing it had been broken."

"It's the way it has to be," said Admiral Douglas.

"Then how do we help him?" Margaret asked. "You can't talk him out of it. We can't catch the spy."

"I don't know," he said. "You can probably help him best by supporting his decision."

"What if we catch the spy without the code?" I asked. "If we catch the spy and can prove that Marcus didn't steal those books, then all his problems would be solved, right?"

"If you do it without using this code," said Agent Dawkins, "then yes, I believe so."

I turned to Douglas. "Don't accept his resignation for twenty-four hours," I said. "For it to be official, you have to accept it, right?"

"Yes, but . . ."

"No buts," I said. "We just broke a code that you both said is vitally important to this country. I think the least we deserve is twenty-four hours."

He thought about it for a moment.

"Okay," he said. "I believe you deserve at least that much."

"Come on, Margaret," I said, getting up and heading toward the door. "I know where we have to go."

Margaret followed me, but before we left, I realized a problem with my plan. I stopped and turned back to them.

"Can one of you give us a ride? We sent my mom home, and we're in a hurry."

Admiral Douglas laughed. "I'll instruct an agent to take you wherever you'd like to go."

"And another thing," said Margaret. "We're going to need the FBI to pay for a wall to be repaired at the Library of Congress."

31.

Petworth

BECAUSE THE DAY HAD GOTTEN OFF TO SUCH AN early start, which caused both of us to skip breakfast, and because the Petworth Library wasn't going to open for another twenty minutes, Margaret and I decided to take full advantage of the admiral's instruction for the agent to drive us wherever we wanted to go. We made a brief pit stop at the Smoothie Shack and each got a large strawberry-banana smoothie. Much to our surprise, the agent insisted on paying for them.

"The admiral told me to take good care of you," he said.

"We appreciate it," I told him.

As we rode in the SUV and sucked down our smoothies,

Margaret and I worked out a plan that had two glaring weaknesses. First of all, we were doomed if Lucia refused to help us, which was very possible. Second, it all hinged on Marcus being right when he told me that there was no way she was guilty. I thought Margaret had discovered a third weakness at one point because she exclaimed, "Ooh, ooh, ooh, ooh!"

"What is it?" I asked.

"Brain freeze," she yelped as she started massaging a spot in the middle of her forehead.

The rain was clearing up, but because it was still sprinkling, the agent insisted we wait in the back seat until the library opened. When we saw someone from the staff unlock the door, we thanked him for the ride and got out.

We were halfway to the door when Margaret did another "Ooh, ooh, ooh!"

"More brain freeze?" I asked.

"No," she said. "I just thought of a problem. What if she's not working today?"

I stopped momentarily. "Then we'll just have to make it up as we go along. Just like we did last night."

"Okay," she replied. "But I hope we don't have to do any more crawling. My knees are pretty sore. Fingers crossed."

We both crossed our fingers, and Margaret did what I

could only assume was a good luck dance. I tried my best to mimic it. I failed miserably.

Because the door had just been unlocked, we were the first patrons of the day. There was no sign of Lucia at the main circulation desk, so we walked up the stairs to the second floor. We found her in the story time room arranging chairs.

"Our first stroke of luck," said Margaret.

"Let's hope it's not our last."

The advantage of being early was that there was no one else there to distract her. The disadvantage was that, with no little kids present, she was free to express her displeasure at seeing us.

"Well, look who it is," she said, her anger rising. "I don't know who you two are but—"

That's as far as she got.

"Marcus needs your help," Margaret said. "We're sorry if we've been less than honest with you, but he's like family to us, and you're the only one who can help him."

She had a confused look. "Marcus . . . *Rivers*?"

"Yes," said Margaret. "He's in serious trouble, and he needs—"

"Stop, right there." She studied us for a moment, trying to make sense of the situation. "Marcus sent you?"

"No," I said. "In fact, if he knew we were here, he'd be furious. But he can be a bit pigheaded that way. And whether he knows it or not, or you know it or not, you're his best hope."

She had moved past confusion to anger. "Well, then that's too bad for him."

She turned her back to us and went back to arranging the chairs.

"You know they went through his parents' house with a search warrant two nights ago," said Margaret.

She still kept her back to us, but I could tell she was listening.

"Mr. Rivers had to stay up half the night trying to put things back where they belong," Margaret continued. "Can you imagine how they felt, after all they've done, to have their son treated like a criminal?"

It was a brilliant move by Margaret, and not one we'd planned in the SUV. She knew that Lucia cared about Marcus's parents.

Lucia turned back toward us and sat down on one of the little story time chairs. She let out a long sigh. "Anntionette and William?" She shook her head. "What kind of trouble is he in?"

"All sorts," I said. "But basically he's being blamed for

stealing rare books from the Library of Congress, conspiring with organized criminals, and passing US government secrets to the Russian government."

She laughed at the magnitude of it all. "There's no way Marcus did any of that."

"We know that, and you know that," said Margaret. "But will you help us prove it?"

She crossed her arms over her chest as she considered this.

"I don't know if it matters," I said, "but yesterday he was trying to give me some advice, and he told me that what happened between you and him was the biggest mistake of his life. He told me to remember that people always matter more than careers and your heart always matters more than your brain."

There were some tears in her eyes as she stared at me. "Did he really say that? Or are you just trying to get me to help you?"

"Both," I said. "We *do* want you to help, *and* he really said that."

She scanned the library and saw that there were now a few combinations of parents and kids looking through shelves, but they all seemed to be taking care of themselves. Then she looked at us as she thought through everything.

"Okay," she said. "What do you need?"

Margaret and I shared a smile.

"There are two books that are essential to figuring this out," I said. "We know the last person to check out each. But we need to know everyone who checked them out before that."

It had dawned on me during our meeting with Admiral Douglas and Agent Dawkins that we never heard about the history of the book with the hidden key. The FBI was trying to create a time line of who'd checked it out before, but we weren't around when that information came back. And now we had *Mrs. Hoover Speaks Mandarin* to compare it to. If there was one common name for both books, that would be huge.

"I can show you the entire history of any book in the system," she said. "When it was checked out. How long it was checked out for. Where it was returned. But the one thing I can't tell you is who checked it out."

"Why not?" I asked, crestfallen.

"It's against the law for us to keep those records," she said. "The books you read are a matter of privacy and not something we keep track of."

It felt like we'd hit a dead end.

"But we can still tell a lot by what we can see," she said.

We walked over to her desk, and she logged onto her computer. As she waited for it to boot up, she asked, "You must care about him a great deal."

"Very much," I said.

"Believe it or not," she replied, "so do I."

"If we didn't already believe that, we wouldn't have come," said Margaret.

She searched for the information on *Mrs. Hoover Speaks Mandarin and Other Fun Facts about the First Ladies* and *Relativity*. There were multiple copies of both in the library system, but because we knew the dates that each was checked out last, she was able to find the borrowing history of the copies we were interested in.

"Okay, here's something," she said. "Each book was temporarily withdrawn from the system in the period before it was checked out."

"What does that mean?" I asked.

"If something's wrong with a book and it can't circulate, it's withdrawn from the system so that it doesn't come up when people search for it."

"Why would a book be withdrawn?" I asked.

"If it's lost or stolen; if a librarian wants to reserve it for a program; if it's damaged."

"Wait, what happens if it's damaged?" asked Margaret.

"It depends on the nature of the damage," she said. "If the damage is extensive, the book is removed from the collection permanently. But if it's fixable, we send it out for repairs and then return it to the system when it comes back."

"So you're saying these books might have been sent for repairs?"

She scanned their histories. "Well, neither of them was checked out for a long period, so they weren't lost, so yes, I'd say they were probably sent for repairs."

Margaret and I turned to each other and said it at the same time. "Brooke King!"

32.

The Stamp Act

AS WE RODE THE METRO TO DUPONT CIRCLE, we tried to formulate a plan. We felt positive that Brooke King was the spy, but it wasn't like the FBI would just take our word for it. Admiral Douglas had promised us twenty-four hours, so we were hoping to collect enough evidence to convince him we were right.

"What's our excuse going to be?" I asked. "How do we explain coming back for the third time in a week?"

"Why don't we tell her that the birthday gift was such a hit for your mom that now we're looking for something for Marcus?"

"That could work," I said. "Although do you think it's

a good idea to mention him? She's setting him up."

"Right, but she doesn't know that we're involved," she said. "I think it would be good to see her reaction to hearing his name. It might rattle her."

"She's been undercover in this country for most of her life," I said. "I'm not sure anything rattles her."

"What are we looking for at the store?" asked Margaret.

"A big pile of stolen CIA files would be nice," I said. "But other than that, we need to connect her to each aspect of the crime."

"And if Alistair Toombs rode with her to North Carolina, we need to figure out if they're in it together or if he's just a friend who doesn't know what's going on."

"That's a lot," I said. "Good thing we had those smoothies."

"No doubt."

The rain had stopped, but it was still overcast as we walked from the Metro to the bookstore. I kept running through our previous encounters with Brooke King in my head, trying to think of the pieces of TOAST to connect her to the crime.

"I just thought of something," I said. "The book on the theory of relativity was old, but the pocket on the back page had a stamp that said 'DC Public Library.' It looked brand-new. I remember thinking it was strange at the time."

"It's because she'd just repaired it," said Margaret. "She probably put on a new pocket and stamped it."

"You know all that equipment she had on the table in her studio? I bet she's got a rubber stamp in there. If we get it and give it to the FBI, they should be able to compare the two and see if it's the same one."

"I like that," she said. "That would definitely work. They could run an analysis and—" Then Margaret did something that only she could do. She interrupted herself. "Stop!" she said as though a bolt of energy had just run through her. "I just figured out how she got into the Riverses' basement."

"How?"

"When Marcus first told us about her, he said that one time his parents' basement flooded and a whole bunch of books, including the family Bible, had been damaged."

"And Brooke came and repaired them," I said. "While she was helping, I bet she got a key to the basement."

Suddenly the little pieces were coming together. Right before we entered the store, Margaret gave a coach's pep talk on the sidewalk. "We're going to find that key and find that rubber stamp!"

Unfortunately, we didn't find Brooke.

The only person in the store was a young woman in an

American University sweatshirt sitting behind the counter doing her homework.

"Hi," I said, trying to get her attention. "Is Brooke King here?"

"She's in the mountains," she said as she continued reading her textbook.

"Doing what?"

She finally looked up. "I'm sorry. Are you some close personal friend or something?"

"Oh, no," I said, scrambling. "I was just curious if she was going to another estate sale. Last weekend she did, and she got some great books. If that's what she's doing, I want to make sure to come back early next week."

She studied me for a moment. "You're a weird kid, you know that?"

"Yeah," I said. "I get that a lot."

"No need to rush back; she's just relaxing in her cabin."

She went back to her book, while Margaret and I pretended to browse the shelves.

"What do we do?" whispered Margaret. "We can't wait until Monday. Admiral Douglas only gave us twenty-four hours."

"One of us needs to get into the back room to look for the rubber stamp."

"You want me to try to distract her?"

"She's already pretty distracted," I said. "But I still think she'd notice me going back there."

"I've got it," she said, her voice rising slightly before she caught it. "Tell her you have to go to the bathroom. It's in the back room."

"Why me? Why not you?"

"Because you've already built a rapport."

I nodded and walked back over to her. "I'm sorry to interrupt you again, but I just drank an extra-large strawberry-banana smoothie and I really have to go to the bathroom."

"Our bathroom is for employees only."

I gave her my best desperate look. "It was really big."

She looked up at me and rolled her eyes. "Straight back and to the right."

"Thanks," I said.

Brooke had cleaned up her workstation, and I didn't see any rubber stamps out on the table. There were all types of glue and tape, as well as some little tools and machines that did who knows what. I was trying to make sense of it all when something occurred to me.

The room itself was about twice the size of my bedroom. There was the bathroom on one side. Her workstation was in the middle. One wall was bare with a couple book posters.

And there was a bookcase right next to the rear door. I was confident that I could see everything, which left me with a serious question.

Where was the safe?

When Marcus ran the financial records for all the suspects, he mentioned that when she'd opened the bookstore, Brooke had bought all sorts of equipment and furniture like bookcases. One of the most expensive items was a large safe.

But where was it?

I went back out in the bookstore and looked to make sure there was no area I had overlooked. There wasn't.

"Thanks," I said to the woman behind the desk. "Have a nice weekend."

She mumbled something and kept reading her textbook.

"Come on, Margaret," I said. "Let's go."

Margaret was reading a brochure about the store and looked surprised at my sudden wish to leave. But when she saw the urgency on my face, she followed suit.

"Did you find it?" she asked once we were outside. "The rubber stamp?"

"No," I said.

"The key to the basement?"

"No."

"Then what did you see?"

"It's what I didn't see that's got me thinking," I said. "I *didn't* see anyplace for a safe."

She looked confused. "But didn't she buy a big safe when she opened the store?"

"Yes," I said. "So where is it?"

"Maybe it's at her cabin in the mountains," she said, half-serious, half-joking.

"Right, except why keep your books in a safe so far from the store?" I said. "It doesn't make sense."

"Unless she's keeping something else there."

We looked at each other and said it at the same time. "A pile of stolen CIA files."

"Now we're getting somewhere," I said. "We've got to figure out where her cabin is."

"Well, this might help," she said, holding up the brochure. "It's about the store. Let me read you the little part about Brooke's bio." She read aloud from it. "'Brooke King is a native Virginian who has loved books since her childhood in Richmond. She carried this love on to college, where she earned dual degrees in English and art conservation at . . . James Madison University.'"

"Harrisonburg," I said. "That's why the letters are sent from there. That's where her cabin in the mountains is located."

"We've got to figure out how to get out to Harrisonburg," she said. "Do you think your mom would be game? She really got into it yesterday."

"She probably would be, but that wouldn't be enough," I said. "We have to figure out how to get the FBI to go to Harrisonburg with us."

"Which will be kind of hard considering we don't have any proof except our theory and a brochure."

We stood there on the sidewalk and tried to come up with something, anything. In some ways we were so close, but in reality we were way too far away. At least 120 miles.

"We could try to convince Agent Dawkins," she said.

"I don't think she'd go for it," I said. "She wouldn't want to risk us being wrong and blowing up the case she's building."

"What about Marcus?" she said. "He'd believe us."

"Yes, but he doesn't want us working on the case. And even if he did, I don't think he could get the Bureau to come along. They think he's guilty."

She let out a big sigh of frustration. "Well, you keep shooting down my ideas. Do you know someone who can get the FBI to go out to Harrisonburg?"

I grinned.

"In fact, I do." I found the business card in my wallet and dialed. Nic the Knife answered on the second ring.

"Hello," he said.

"This is Florian Bates. Margaret and I need your help. We need a ride out into the mountains."

He didn't hesitate. He simply asked where we were, and I gave him our location. He told me he'd be right there, and I said one last thing before I hung up.

"Make sure the FBI is following you!"

33.

Ferrari

WE HEARD NIC THE KNIFE BEFORE WE SAW HIM.

We were standing on the sidewalk in front of Palace Books when the roar of a sports car engine announced his impending arrival. We turned to look as he came around the corner in a matte black Ferrari.

He stopped right in front of us, his engine rumbling, and the passenger window slid down. Reading our expressions, he said, "What? You thought I'd come in a minivan?"

I peeked through the window and replied, "I thought you'd come in a car that had a back seat."

"This has a back seat," he said as he gestured toward it. "Just not a big one. Besides, you said you wanted me to make sure the FBI was following. This one stands out. It makes it easier for them to keep an eye on me."

"I got front!" said Margaret.

I squeezed into the back while Margaret luxuriated in the passenger seat.

"This is a Ferrari, right?" she asked him.

"Yes," he said. "I'm part Romanian and part Italian. Since the Romanians don't make a sports car I like, I decided to get this."

"Florian and I are part Italian too," she said.

I caught a glimpse of his reaction in the rearview mirror and could tell that just hearing this affected him. "Well, that's good."

"What's your favorite Serie A team?"

"Juventus, of course."

Margaret smiled. "Us too!"

"Great minds think alike," he said. "Now that I am here, what are we doing?"

"We're luring the FBI out to Harrisonburg, Virginia, to catch a deep-cover Russian spy and clear the reputation of our friend Special Agent Marcus Rivers."

I'd only told him we needed a ride when I called, and now I was worried he'd refuse. But instead he smiled and said, "Sounds like a fun Saturday afternoon."

He put the car in gear, and we took off down the road. "You know Juve beat Roma three to one today."

"Nice," said Margaret.

Despite feeling like a sardine in a can, I enjoyed riding in the Ferrari. It hugged the road during turns and felt cooler than any vehicle I'd ever been in. I also enjoyed watching Nic and Margaret talk. She thanked him for the improvements to the field, and he talked about how great she'd played that day.

"That's two times I've seen you play," he said, referencing the city championship, which he'd seen as well. "And both were spectacular."

"Thanks," she said bashfully. "I really love playing. And playing on the new field is wonderful. Why'd you do it? The donation for the field, I mean."

He was quiet as he thought about his answer, and for a moment I thought he might just break down and tell her the truth.

"In my life, I'm surrounded by a lot of bad things, you know that?"

"Yes," she said.

"I'm not a good person," he said. "But if I can do something that is good—something that helps other people—then at least there is a little bit of good in my life. Like when you see a flower grow in the crack on the sidewalk."

Margaret studied him. "Maybe you are a good person," she said. "After all, you helped with the case when our friend got kidnapped. Maybe if you just did the good things and stopped doing the bad things, maybe you'd have a much better life. Instead of a flower in the sidewalk, it could be like a whole garden."

He smiled.

"What?" she said.

"You have a good heart," he said. "And I would never hurt you or Florian, but you need to know this: I am not a good person."

"That doesn't mean you couldn't become one."

We were driving west on Interstate 66, and it was so cramped in the back seat, I had to wiggle and twist just to try to look out the back window.

"Are you sure they're following you?" I asked.

"Silver SUV four cars back in this lane," he said. "Plus the black sedan about a half mile behind him. They swap places every five miles or so because they think it keeps me from spotting them."

"Do you normally have two?" asked Margaret.

"No," he said. "Florian wanted me to make sure, so I made some calls because I knew they were listening. I made it sound like I was going out to the mountains to meet Carmine Santangelo, a mob boss they would very much like to find out about. They're probably alerting others as we speak."

It was such a strange situation. We were working for the FBI, yet we were getting help from a crime boss and tricking the FBI into following us. As crazy as it was, we needed to make sure we did whatever it took to help Marcus.

"Where are we going when we get to Harrisonburg?" he asked.

"That's the hard part," I said. "We're not exactly sure where she lives."

"Right," said Margaret. "All we know is that she has a cabin in the mountains near Harrisonburg."

"That's not much to go on," he said. "Why do you want the FBI there?"

"Because she has a big safe, and we think it's full of government secrets that she passes along to the Russians."

"And this affects your friend Marcus how?"

"They think he's corrupt," I said.

He gave me a look in the rearview mirror. "I have met him. He's not corrupt. That should be obvious to anybody."

"We know that," said Margaret. "But we have to prove it."

He thought about all of this for about a mile.

"What kind of safe?"

"What?" I asked.

"You said you think she has a big safe. Do you know what kind it is? How big it is?"

Margaret looked at her phone, where she'd taken pictures of all the evidence that Marcus showed us in the Underground. When she found the notes for Brooke's finances, she enlarged it and read it off to him. "It's called a Worldwide Super Fortress Safe."

He seemed surprised. "That's a very good model," he said. "Extremely big."

"You know safes that well?" Margaret asked, surprised.

"Well, in my line of work I have to know about them."

"Oh," she said. "Because you break into them?"

At first he looked surprised, but then he laughed deeply. "No," he said. "Because I run a construction company and build buildings like banks that have them."

Margaret looked horrified. "I'm so sorry."

"Don't be," he replied. "It's very funny."

He thought about it for a moment more. "You know, not just anyone can install a safe like that. You have to have special concrete, large equipment. It's not a job for a handyman or small builder. When did she buy the safe?"

Margaret looked at the picture. "Three years ago in March."

He went to turn on his hands-free phone, but first told us to be quiet for a moment. "We don't need anyone but the FBI to know you're in the car with me," he said.

"Got it," we both answered.

He called one of his construction foremen and described the situation. He said a woman in Harrisonburg installed a Worldwide Super Fortress Safe three years ago around March or April. He wanted the foreman to make some discreet calls to see if he could find out which company did the job and what the name and address of the customer were.

About thirty minutes later the foreman called back with the address, which Margaret typed into the navigation system.

"Did you get the name of the customer?" asked Nic.

"Yes," he replied. "Brooke King."

"Thank you, Radu," he said as he disconnected the call. "Is that the right name?" he asked us.

"Yes," said Margaret.

"Okay," he replied. "Now we're getting somewhere."

I got out my phone and started to type up a text.

"What are you doing?" he asked.

"Trying to make sure we have some friendly faces there for when this all goes down."

"Good idea," he said. "But you should probably leave my name out."

The text I wrote to Melinda Dawkins was simple and straightforward.

We came up with another way to find the spy. It's Brooke King. FBI agents from organized crime will be there. Would like to see you, too! Then I put her address. Right before I pressed send, I added two names to receive the text—Marcus and Kayla.

"Have you two eaten?" he asked.

"We each had a smoothie for breakfast," said Margaret.

"You must eat healthy and take care of your body," he said. "I know a place up here."

He pulled off at an exit and took us to a hole-in-the-wall barbecue joint.

"This is healthy?" asked Margaret.

"Well, it's good," he said with a laugh. He handed me two twenties and said, "Eat in there. Don't take too long."

"Aren't you coming in?" I asked.

"No, I need to make some more calls," he said. "Ones you two cannot hear."

We went inside, and I had the best pulled-pork sandwich of my life. Margaret got a chicken plate that looked equally delicious. While we were eating, I watched Nic making at least five or six different phone calls. He stood outside his car and kept his eye on the road leading back to the interstate.

Before we left, Margaret ordered him a pork sandwich like the one I had and a lemonade.

"Here," she said, holding it out for him as he finished a call. "You have to eat. You said so yourself. It's a pulled-pork sandwich and a lemonade."

"I love lemonade," he said, smiling. "Thank you, Margaret."

"You're welcome."

"But I eat out here," he said. "No food is allowed in the car."

He ate standing up, his eyes still watching the road.

"What are you looking for?" I asked.

"Our friends from the FBI," he said. "They are about a half mile down the road parked at a gas station. I made some more calls, and now they'll think this is a big meeting. They'll bring more than two cars."

We reached Harrisonburg about thirty minutes later. Just outside of town we turned onto a country road that we followed as it snaked up a mountain. Homes were spaced out with acres between them and eventually it led us to Brooke's.

It was a two-story wooden cabin at the end of a long driveway. It had a wraparound porch with a view of the mountains. There were two cars in the driveway.

"You think both of those are hers?" asked Margaret.

"Either that or maybe one belongs to Alistair Toombs."

Nic kept driving for a quarter mile until he passed a bend in the road. There he did a U-turn and parked it on the side so that we were looking back toward the cabin.

"What are we doing?" asked Margaret.

"Waiting," he said.

"Waiting for what?"

"For the FBI to get into better position," he said. "And hopefully for this woman to leave the cabin."

"Why?"

"It will be safer that way."

"What will be safer?" I asked.

"Just be patient, Florian. Just be patient."

We just sat there for about forty-five minutes, which in that back seat felt like hours. Nic tried to start little conversations to distract us. He asked us about school and what movies we liked. Finally, the conversation got around to our parents. I told him about my mom and dad working in museums. Then he turned to Margaret and asked, "What about you? What are your parents like?"

"What do you mean?" she asked. "They're just like parents."

"I was raised by criminals, Margaret. Not all parents are alike."

"Okay, what do you want to know?"

"Anything."

Margaret told him all about her dad coaching her soccer teams when she was little and about visiting her mother's relatives up in Michigan. She told the story of when she broke her arm and her dad literally carried her to the doctor's. She talked about how her mother volunteered to represent poor people in court cases and how much she looked up to both of them.

"They sound great," he said.

"I try not to tell them so they don't get bigheaded about it," she said. "But I want to grow up to be just like them."

I can't imagine what it was like for him to hear about the people who were raising his daughter, but he seemed genuinely pleased by all of it.

"You see, Margaret. They are what good people are like. There's a big difference."

A few minutes later there was activity at the cabin. Brooke came out onto the porch with Alistair. They got in one of the cars and drove off down the road toward town.

"Perfect," said Nic.

"Okay, I don't understand what we're doing here," I said. "Shouldn't we follow them?"

"You two have a problem," he replied. "You need the FBI

to enter that house so that they can see the evidence that this woman is a spy."

"Right," said Margaret.

"But the FBI cannot enter that house unless you can show them that a crime has been committed. And you can't do that."

"Okay," I said. "So what do we do?"

"Not we," he said. "*I* will give them a different crime. And then they can follow me in."

He got out of the car and turned back to us. "Florian, you can move up into my seat to stretch out your legs, but stay in the car. Do not get out and come toward the cabin. Do not get out until you see a friendly face."

I got out to move up to the driver's seat, and he went around back and opened the trunk. When he returned, he was carrying a tire iron.

"Get in the car," he said as he handed me the keys. "Just so you can run the air conditioner and listen to the radio."

I started to ask him something but didn't. "Thank you."

He didn't respond, and once again he virtually transformed before my eyes as he began to walk and carry himself much more menacingly.

"What's he going to do?" Margaret asked as I got in the car next to her.

"I don't know."

He walked down the road toward the house and picked up his pace as he did. He sprinted the last twenty yards, and when he reached the door, he started hammering it with the tire iron. Glass shattered. Wood splintered. An alarm went off. Finally, he kicked it in and entered.

"I don't understand," said Margaret. "What is he doing?"

And that's when the FBI and police started to swarm the building.

"He's giving them a reason to go inside," I said, realizing. "They've seen him commit a crime by breaking into the house. They think he's meeting with a crime boss, so they're not just going to wait around. They're going to go in there. And when they do . . ."

"They can find evidence that points to Brooke."

We sat and watched in amazement as the agents and police surrounded the cabin. We were mesmerized, and when there was a rap on the window, we almost jumped out of our skin. It was Dan Napoli.

The door was locked, and he signaled me to lower the window.

"Nic said not to get out until we saw friendly faces," Margaret said. "He's not friendly."

"I'm just going to crack it," I said.

I opened the window just enough so that we could talk.

"Get out of the car," commanded Napoli.

"No," I said. "We haven't done anything wrong. We're just sitting here."

"And my parents are both attorneys, so I'd be careful if I were you," added Margaret.

He took a deep frustrated breath.

"What's going on here?"

"Nicolae Nevrescu is delivering you a deep-cover spy who has been passing government secrets for at least ten years. Her name is Brooke King, and she's working with Alistair Toombs. She has CIA files stored in a safe in that cabin, and since Nic just broke the door down, you can go find them."

34.

Aftermath

WE STAYED IN THE CAR AND WATCHED AS THE drama unfolded. After Nic broke into the house, the FBI and police swarmed around and followed him in. Alerted by the alarm, Brooke King returned with Alistair Toombs to find total chaos. Sensing that her cover had been blown, she started to speed away, but she was blocked by agents who then escorted the two of them into the house. Soon after that Melinda Dawkins in a black SUV and Marcus in his maroon hybrid arrived.

I'd texted Marcus to let him know where we were waiting, and while Dawkins headed for the house, he came over to the car.

"Nice ride," he said as we got out of the Ferrari.

"Tell me you haven't handed in your resignation yet," I said.

"Oh, I handed it in," he said. "But for some reason Admiral Douglas has yet to accept it." He gave us each a look. "I don't suppose either of you know anything about that."

We shrugged and played stupid.

"Not at all," I said.

"How would we know," added Margaret.

He looked back at the bedlam unfolding in the cabin and shook his head. "That's going to take a while to straighten out," he said. "Why don't we hop in the car and chat?"

I moved back toward the Ferrari.

"My car," he said.

I looked at the sports car longingly. "I was really getting to like it."

"I bet you were."

As we walked over to the hybrid, Margaret went up to Marcus, and he put his arm around her and gave her shoulder a squeeze.

"I want you guys to start at the beginning and tell me everything," he said.

We got into the SUV and started talking. Margaret and I filled him in on every detail, even our escapade at the Library of Congress.

"You knocked a hole in the wall?" he said.

"It was a have-to situation," explained Margaret.

The real shock, though, came when we told him about Lucia.

"She gave us the final piece," I said. "Without Lucia we'd just know the code but not who was responsible."

He mulled this over for a moment. "She always came through in a pinch, so I guess I'm not surprised."

As we were filling him in on the final details with Nic the Knife, Dawkins walked out with Brooke in handcuffs. She led her to her black SUV and loaded her in back and put an agent in charge of watching her. Then she came over to us and rapped on the driver's window.

Marcus rolled it down, and she looked inside.

"Boy, you two sure know how to throw a party," she said to us. "We need the three of you to come inside and help sort something out."

As we walked toward the cabin with her, she filled Marcus in on some of the highlights.

"Somehow, Nic managed to open her safe," she said. "It was filled with stolen files that look like they go back at least twenty years."

"What about Toombs?" he asked.

"He claims not to have known anything about it, but

we're not just going to take his word on that. He's going to be spending time with some of our best people."

We were nearing the porch, and another agent came out leading Alistair Toombs away in cuffs. He had a look of total confusion on his face, made only worse when he saw us.

"You two?" he said, befuddled.

"I don't think the president's going to like this," I said.

He was loaded into another vehicle while we got up on the porch and walked through what was left of the doorway.

"What about Nic?" asked Margaret.

"That's what we're going in for," she said. "He wants all three of you."

Marcus gave us a look, and we both shrugged.

Dawkins led us to a living room where there were two couches. Nic was on one with his hands cuffed behind his back. Dan Napoli and his boss Mike Moretti were on the other.

"Here you go," said Dawkins. "I think we've got everybody in the room. Let's start talking."

"I don't know what there is to talk about," said Napoli. "We've got Nevrescu for home invasion and transporting minors across state lines against their will."

"Actually," I said, "not only were we willing; we asked him for the ride."

Napoli ignored me and turned to Marcus. "And that doesn't even scratch the surface when we get to Agent Rivers here. Once again, Marcus solves a case, and the mob's involved. How corrupt are you?"

"Enough!" said Nic. "Here are my demands."

"Demands? You're in no position to make any sort of demands!" said Napoli.

Moretti finally piped up. "Dan, let's just hear what the man has to say."

"Thank you," said Nic. "Number one, stop the ridiculous harassment of Agent Rivers and these two children. Two children, by the way, who just delivered you a Russian spy that has been operating under your noses since before they were even born."

He shot a look to Dawkins, and she nodded.

"Number two," he said. "Take off these handcuffs so that I may drive young Miss Margaret home." He turned to me and said, "I trust you can get a ride with Agent Rivers?"

"Yes," I said.

"That's it," he said. "Those are my demands."

"And what do we get in return?" asked Moretti.

"Everything," he said. "I will tell you all that I know, and you will put me in witness protection."

Moretti and Napoli were stunned.

"You would give us specifics and testify in open court against other criminals?" asked Moretti.

"Yes, yes, I know what is required," he said. "Perhaps it is time to see if I can be a good person."

It didn't take long for Moretti to agree to Nic's demands. When Napoli tried to protest, he overruled him. Nic stood up, and they unlocked his cuffs. Then he walked over toward Margaret.

"Miss Campbell, may I drive you back to Washington?"

"Yes," she said. "But why?"

"We need to talk," he explained. "And that should give us just enough time. I want to tell you about your parents. Your birth parents."

Her eyes opened wide. "You know something about my birth parents?"

He smiled. "I know everything about them."

"Who's my father?" she asked.

"I'll tell you that soon," he replied. "But first let me tell you about your mother. She was tall and beautiful, just like you."

Epilogue
A Visit to Fatou's

THE NEXT WEEK WAS ALMOST UNBEARABLE. Margaret barely spoke to me at all. When I saw her at school or in class she'd nod or say hello, but that was it. Just hello. She didn't sit with me at lunch. She didn't come by my house. It was like we weren't friends anymore.

On Thursday I met up with Marcus, and he caught me up on everything that was going on at the Bureau. Nicolae Nevrescu had come through as promised and was helping the organized crime unit build cases against some notorious gangsters.

"He's already been turned over to witness protection," he said. "You won't ever see him again. They're going to give him a new life and identity somewhere far from here. But how's this for amazing: he's not going alone."

"What do you mean?" I said. And then I figured it out. "Margaret's birth mother?"

"That's right," Marcus said with a smile. "It turns out they kept a sort of long-distance relationship over the years."

"As much as you guys followed him around, you didn't know that?" I joked. "I tell you, the FBI isn't what it once was."

He laughed. "And speaking of long-ago relationships, I went over to the Petworth Library to thank Lucia in person."

"How was that?"

"Brief," he said. "I didn't want to take too much of her time. I asked her to show me some pictures of her girls. And in addition to thanking her, I apologized for things that happened nine years ago."

"That's good," I said. "Very good."

"How are things with Margaret?" he asked.

"Terrible. She won't speak to me at all. Have you talked to her?"

"I think you're forgetting something. I kept the same secret you did. She wants nothing to do with either of us right now."

"That's going to change, isn't it?" I asked. "She will talk to me again someday, won't she?"

"Yes," he answered, although it wasn't entirely convincing.

On Friday I broke down and went over to her house. It was just after dusk, and I could see the light on in her room, so I knew she was home. I knocked on the door, and her mother answered it.

"Hello, Florian," she said warmly.

"Hello, Mrs. Campbell," I said. "Do you think that Margaret would be willing to talk to me? Just for a second?"

She reached out and placed her hand on my shoulder and said, "Not today, sweetie. I'm sorry."

"I understand," I said, even though I didn't.

I walked back to my house, went into my room, and just started crying. I'd never felt so low before. My mom heard me and came in to check on me.

"What am I going to do?" I asked her between the sobs.

"It's going to be all right," she assured me.

"She's the best friend I'll ever have, and she won't speak to me," I said, my words halting as I caught my breath. "How will that ever be all right?"

"She's in a lot of pain," Mom told me. "If you really are a good friend, you have to give her time to work through it."

That Saturday I went down into the Underground for the first time since we'd closed the case. I started taking down all the pictures from the caseboard. I wondered if we'd ever work another case together.

Then I heard my mother.

"Florian, you have a guest."

I turned to see Margaret on the stairs. We both just stood there for a moment and looked at each other.

"I'll be in the family room," Mom said as she closed the door.

Margaret took a couple of tentative steps into the Underground, but I stayed where I was. I was determined not to crowd her.

"You lied to me," she said.

I went to explain myself, but a voice inside my head told me to just admit it. "Yes."

"You lied to me about the thing I most wanted to know."

"Yes."

"Friends aren't supposed to do that," she said.

"No."

"I know you had reasons. I know that you even had good reasons. But you still lied to me."

"I'm so sorry."

"Good," she said. "You should be."

"You remember when you told me that when I needed to

apologize and make something up to you, I should buy you that Russian candy we got at Gorky's?"

"Yes," she said.

"I've got a case of it up in my room."

This caused her to laugh a little, and I felt it was a breakthrough. Small. But a breakthrough.

"So it turns out that I'm an African-American-Italian-Romanian daughter of a notorious crime boss," she said.

"You're still the same Margaret you always were."

"Evidence seems to indicate otherwise."

"Why would I listen to evidence when I know the truth in my heart?"

For the first time in a week I saw Margaret smile.

"Are you busy?" she asked.

"Not at all."

"Okay, why don't you come along with my mom and me?"

"Sure," I said. "Where are we going?"

"You'll see."

We went back to her house, and her parents both seemed happy to see the two of us together.

"Hello, Florian," said Mr. Campbell. "How are you today?"

"Much better than I was yesterday," I said.

"Florian's coming with us," Margaret told her mother. "Although he doesn't know where we're going."

"He's a good detective," said Mrs. Campbell. "He'll probably figure it out."

We drove over into Northeast Washington, not far from where Marcus's parents lived. And despite Mrs. Campbell's faith in my detective skills, I had no idea where we were headed.

And then I saw it. Fatou's Salon.

"The big chop," I said.

"I told you he'd figure it out," said Margaret's mom as she parked the car. "Have you ever been in a beauty parlor before?"

"Not that I remember," I said.

She laughed. "Oh, you'd remember if you had."

Judging by the pictures in the window and the women who were inside, Fatou's was exclusively for African-American women. Needless to say, I stuck out when we walked through the door. All conversation came to a grinding halt.

"Well, hello," said a woman in her fifties. "Who do we have here?"

"Hi, Miss Fatou," said Margaret. "This is Florian. He's my best friend."

She still considered me her best friend.

"Hello, Florian," she said. "Welcome to my salon."

"Thank you," I replied.

She read my facial expression and said, "It's the heat from the flat irons."

"What is?" I asked.

"That smell you're trying to place. We use the flat irons to help straighten hair, and it has a distinctive odor."

"Okay," I said, not knowing where to take the conversation from there.

"Well, I won't have to worry about flat irons today," said Margaret. "We're here for the big chop."

"Well, that's good news," said Fatou. "Let's get started."

Mrs. Campbell and I sat down as Margaret went over to a sink and had her hair shampooed. I looked around the salon at all the women who were there. So often Margaret was with me in a world where everyone was white except for her. It was eye-opening to have it the other way around. And despite the chill of the past week, it felt like she was letting me into her life more than she ever had.

"I didn't want to lie to her," I said to her mom. "I was just trying to protect her."

"And I appreciate that so much," she said to me. "And whether she ever says it to you or not, so does she."

Margaret moved from the shampoo sink to the chair and was sitting directly across from me but facing the other way so that she looked into the mirror. Her mother got up and walked over to her, but I stayed in my seat.

"Are you sure you want to go through with this?" asked Mrs. Campbell. "It's not like you have to do it today."

"I'm sure," she said. "I feel like my identity's gotten a little twisted and tangled lately." Then she looked up into the mirror and right at me. "Kind of like the Gordian knot. And you know, there's only one way to undo that."

She smiled, and I grinned right back at her.

"All right, Miss Fatou," she said as she closed her eyes. "Start chopping!"

Acknowledgments

It is a thrill and an honor to write books for kids, and there are so many people who make that possible. While some of their contributions may be invisible to the reader, they are all invaluable to me.

First of all, I want to thank the amazing TOAST team at Aladdin led by my editor, Fiona Simpson, and publisher, Mara Anastas. They are joined by a group of Simon & Schuster all-stars, including Jodie Hockensmith, Rebecca Vitkus, Katherine Devendorf, Laura Lyn DiSiena, Steve Scott, Sara Berko, Tricia Lin, and Stephanie Evans. You do all the hard work, and all you get in return are semiannual cupcakes from Magnolia Bakery. Thanks for welcoming me on the fourth floor.

Grazie mille to the one and only Rosemary Stimola and everybody at the Stimola Literary Studio.

ACKNOWLEDGMENTS

I'd like to give a huge shout-out to my hair and style experts, Fatoumata Diallo, Letitia Moye-Moore, and Anntionette Brown. I am so lucky to have you as friends. Also a major *spasibo* to Carey and Laura Cavanaugh for their Russian language skills and Terence Cavanaugh for his many creative suggestions.

My Golf Channel family is beyond supportive, and I'd especially like to acknowledge Keith Allo, Jay Madara, Chris Murvin, and Courtney Vargas.

This book is all about librarians, whom I worship in their many varieties. For their help researching this book, I'd especially like to thank the dedicated staff at the Library of Congress, including Michael J. North of the Rare Book and Special Collections Division and Sasha Dowdy with the Young Readers Center.

Finally, I'd like to thank my family, without whom none of this would be possible.

**FIVE KIDS FROM FIVE DIFFERENT COUNTRIES
ARE TRAINING TO BECOME REAL-LIFE SPIES.**
WATCH OUT, SUPERVILLAINS. STEP ASIDE,
JAMES BOND. HERE COME THE CITY SPIES.

SARA LOOKED AT THE WATER STAIN ON THE WALL and imagined it was an island. She wasn't sure if that was because it actually looked like one or just because she so desperately wished she were in some tropical paradise far from Brooklyn and this tiny room on the eighth floor of Kings County Family Court.

She sat across the table from her public defender, a massive man in a rumpled suit named Randall Stubbs. His bulky frame hunched over as he scanned her file. "This doesn't look good," he muttered, because stating the obvious was apparently something they taught in law school. "You're lucky they've made such a generous offer."

"They have?" Sara asked, surprised. "What is it?"

He looked up from the file and said, "You plead guilty to all charges and get thirty months in juvenile detention."

Two and a half years in juvie didn't sound generous to Sara, but it probably wasn't much worse than her last few foster homes. She was tough for a twelve-year-old. She could handle it.

"And, of course," he added, "you won't be allowed near a computer."

This, however, was unacceptable.

"For how long?"

"For the duration of your sentence. Maybe longer as a condition of your release. That'll be up to the judge."

"But all I did was . . ."

"What?" he interrupted. "Hack into the computer network for the entire juvenile justice system of New York City? Is that what you were going to say? Because that's not what I'd call an 'all I did' situation."

"I know, but I was only trying to . . ."

"It doesn't matter what you were *trying* to do," he said. "All that matters is what you did. You're lucky you're twelve. If you were thirteen they probably would've bumped you up to a higher court to make an example out of you."

The weight of this hit her hard and for the first time she

regretted her actions. Not because they were against the law. Legal or not, she had no doubt she'd been in the right. But she'd never considered that she could be banished from the one corner of the world that made sense to her. The only time Sara felt at home was when she was sitting at a computer keyboard.

"I'll never hack again," she said. "I promise."

"Oh, you promise?" he responded sarcastically. "Maybe you can cross your heart and hope to die once we get in court. I'm sure that'll fix everything."

Sara struggled when it came to controlling her anger, a diagnosis confirmed by multiple counselors and at least two school psychologists. Still, she tried to keep cool as she looked at the man who was supposed to be helping her. She couldn't risk angering him, because he was her only hope for a positive outcome. So she took a deep breath and counted to ten, a tip from one of those counselors whose name she'd long since forgotten.

"If I can't use a computer," she said, barely masking her desperation, "then I can't do the one thing I'm good at. The thing that makes me special."

"Yeah, well, you should've thought of that before you . . ."

She probably would've lost her temper right then and there if the door hadn't suddenly flown open and into the room stepped a man who was in every way the opposite of her attorney.

He was tall and thin with a thatch of unruly black hair. His suit was impeccable. His tie matched his pocket square. And, he spoke with a British accent.

"Sorry to interrupt," he said politely. "But I believe you're in my seat."

"You've got the wrong room," grumbled Stubbs. "Now if you don't mind, I'm having a conference with my client."

"Except, according to this Substitution of Counsel form, she's my client," the other man replied as he showed Stubbs a piece of paper. This brought an instant smile to Sara's face.

Stubbs eyed the man. "That doesn't make any sense. She can't afford a fancy lawyer like you. She doesn't have any money."

"Of course she doesn't have any money. She's twelve. Twelve-year-olds don't have money. They have bicycles and rucksacks. This one, however, also happens to have an attorney. This paper says I've been retained to represent Ms. Sara Maria Martinez." He turned to her and smiled. "Is that you?"

"Yes, sir."

"Brilliant. That means I'm in the right place."

"Who retained you?" asked the public defender.

"An interested party," said the man. "Beyond that, it's not your concern. So if you'll please leave, Sara and I have much to talk about. We're due before a judge shortly."

Stubbs mumbled to himself as he shoveled his papers into his briefcase. "I'm going to check this out."

"There's a lovely lady named Valerie who can help you," said the British man. "She's with the clerk of the court on the seventh floor."

"I know where she is," Stubbs snapped as he squeezed past the man into the hallway. He started to say something else, but instead just made a frustrated noise and stormed off.

Once Stubbs was gone, the new attorney closed the door and sat across from Sara. "I've never seen that before," he marveled. "He literally left the room in a huff."

She had no idea who might have hired an attorney for her, but she was certainly happy with the change. "I've never seen it either."

"Now tell me," he said as he popped open the latches of his briefcase. "Is it true? Did you hack into the computers of the city's juvenile justice system?"

She hesitated to answer.

"You needn't worry. Attorney-client privilege forbids me from telling anyone what you say in here. I just need to know if it's true."

She gave a slight nod. "Yes. It's true."

"Brilliant," he said with a wink. He pulled a small computer from his briefcase and handed it to her. "I need you to do it again."

"Do what again?" she asked.

"Hack into the juvenile justice database," he said. "I need you to make me your attorney of record before Mr. Stubbs gets to the seventh floor and checks for himself."

"You mean you're not my attorney?" she asked.

"Never set foot in a law school," he said conspiratorially. "So, chop-chop. I've got an associate who's going to delay him in the hallway, but she'll only be able to do that for so long."

Sara's head was spinning. She didn't know what to think. "Listen, I don't know who you are, but the court's supposed to assign me a lawyer. A *real* one."

"And the chap with the mustard stain on his tie is the one it assigned," he replied, shaking his head. "I don't know about you, but I'm not particularly impressed. Over the last nine years, that same court has assigned you to six foster families and nine schools. It's been one botch job after another with them. What do you say we try something new?"

She looked at him and then the computer. She was tempted, but she was also confused. "I don't think . . ."

"What did he say would happen?" he interrupted. "I bet he's already worked out a deal with the prosecutor."

"Two and a half years in juvie and I'm banned from using a computer."

He shook his head. "I can do better than that even without a law degree."

For reasons she didn't fully understand, Sara believed him. Maybe it was wishful thinking. Maybe it was desperation. Either way, she trusted her gut and started typing.

"Excellent," he said. "You probably won't regret this."

"*Probably?*" She raised an eyebrow. "Shouldn't you be trying to build up my confidence?"

"Only fools and liars speak with certainty about things beyond their control," he replied. "But I'm optimistic, so I'd rate your chances around . . . eighty-seven percent."

Sara smiled and continued typing. "What kind of computer is this?"

"Bespoke," he answered.

"I thought I knew all the computer companies, but I've never heard of that one."

"It's not a company," he said. "'Bespoke' means something has been tailor-made to the specific needs of an individual."

"Someone made this for you?"

He nodded.

"Well, whoever 'bespoke' it really knew what they were doing."

"Wait until you see the massive one," he said. "You're going to love it. That is, if we're not both behind bars by the end of the day."

Sara knew computers well but she'd never seen one like this. It was fast and powerful and she quickly shredded through the firewall that was supposed to protect the juvenile justice portal.

"They didn't even fix the backdoor I used the other day," she said in disbelief.

"Large institutions move slowly," he said. "Hopefully large attorneys do too."

It took her less than two minutes to reach the database for attorney assignments. She happily deleted the entry for Randall Stubbs and asked, "What's your name?"

"Excellent question," he said as he pulled three passports out of his briefcase. "Which sounds best?"

He read from the first one. "Croydon St. Vincent Marlborough the Third." He gave a sour face. "Seems a bit excessive, don't you think?"

She nodded. "Yes."

"We'll pass on that." He read from the next. "Nigel

Honeybuns." This one made him snicker. "Honeybuns? I quite like that." He tucked it into a pocket in his briefcase. "I think I'll save that one for another time."

"We're kind of in a hurry," she reminded him.

"Right, right, here we go," he said, reading from the last one. "Gerald Anderson. That sounds like a proper barrister. Dull. Boring. Imminently forgettable. Which is exactly what we want. That's my name, Gerald Anderson."

He handed her the passport so she could check the spelling as she typed it into the database.

"I just click 'update,'" she said as she finished, "and we're all set."

He flashed a nervous smile and paused to listen. "No alarms." He opened the door and leaned out into the hallway. "No one rushing in to arrest us. Very nice work, Sara."

"Except now I have an attorney who's never gone to law school."

"I've watched a lot of courtroom dramas on the telly," he said. "I can handle an appearance before a judge."

"Don't you mean, *probably*," she replied.

He smiled at this. "Right . . . *probably*. First, though, I'll need details about the hack."

"I'm sure they're all in there," she said, pointing at the file.

"This only tells me what you did," he replied. "I want to know the reason."

"The lawyer, you know, the one who actually went to law school, said it didn't matter why I did it."

"It may not matter to him. It might not even matter to the judge. But it matters very much to me."

She thought about her answer for a moment, trying to come up with the most straightforward way to tell it. She didn't want to get upset. She hated showing emotions in front of anyone. "My most recent foster parents . . ."

"Leonard and Deborah Clark?"

"Yeah, them," she said with a sneer. "They like to take in more kids than they have room for because the state pays them by the kid. More kids mean more money, whether they spend it on us or not. No one really checks that. We were crammed into bedrooms that were too small. Rather than give everyone a meal, they put food in the middle of the table, so it looked like there was more than there was. They called it 'family style,' which is a joke because they treated us like anything but a family.

"A new kid named Gabriel came about a month ago. He was scared. Sad. Lonely. Everything you'd expect from a five-year-old. He liked me because we were the only Hispanic kids in the house."

"You spoke Spanish to him?"

"Sometimes," she said. "Until they made us stop. Mr. Clark told me, 'You're in America now, so speaking English is something you're going to have to get used to.'"

The lawyer shook his head. "And what did you say to that?"

"I pointed out that Puerto Rico was already part of America, that I'd spent almost my entire life in Brooklyn, and that if *he* really wanted to speak English well, he shouldn't end sentences with prepositions."

The man laughed. "Cheeky."

"I'm not exactly sure what 'cheeky' means, but his cheeks turned red, so I guess so," she replied.

"Did you get in trouble?" he asked.

She nodded, the humor of the moment gone. "I could handle his punishment, though. It was Gabriel who couldn't."

"Why was Gabriel punished?"

She paused and saw him studying her expression. He wanted to watch her eyes as she spoke.

"One night he wet his bed," she answered, "and to punish him they locked him in the hall closet. I could hear him crying. They didn't care. They would've let him cry all night. So, I got up and let him out."

"And then what happened?" he asked.

"Then they locked me in the closet with him. Told me I had to learn my place. So, I picked the lock from the inside and let us both out." She was on the verge of tears so she stopped for a moment.

"And then?" he prodded.

"They locked us outside on the roof. They left us there all night. It was cold. It was terrifying. The next morning, I went to school, got a pass to the computer lab, and started working. First I hacked the juvenile justice database to see how many kids had been sent to the Clarks. Then I hacked their bank accounts to show how much money they were taking in and where they were actually spending it."

"You're not being charged with hacking the bank," he said, flipping through some pages.

She grinned. "Yeah, they dropped their complaints. I'm pretty sure they don't want the world to find out that a twelve-year-old girl beat their security system."

"Nice," he said. "I might be able to use that later. What'd you do with this information once you'd gotten it?"

"I sent everything to my social worker," she said. "And you know how stupid I am? When I saw the police coming up to the house, I thought they were going to arrest the two of them. For about forty-five seconds I was happy."

"But they arrested you instead?"

She nodded.

"The Clarks even had the other kids line up on the porch so they would see me being led out of the house in handcuffs." She closed her eyes tight, determined not to let a single tear fall. "They said, 'This is what happens to criminals.'"

He'd actually heard the story the night before, through a listening device. But he liked hearing stories twice. He wanted to see if they changed. That was always a good indicator of how truthful they were. Besides, seeing her face as she recalled it told him everything he needed to know.

"That's a good reason," he said. "I can work with that. I can make this a lot better."

"Don't you mean, *probably*?" she asked.

He smiled warmly. "No, I'm certain I can. But I'll need you to do something difficult. Something the reports in this file say you're completely incapable of."

"What's that?" she asked.

"I need you to trust me," he said. "No matter what I say or do, I need you to trust me."

"How can I trust you?" she asked. "I don't even know your name."

"Sure you do. It's Nigel Honeybuns. It's Gerald Anderson. Sometimes it's even Croydon St. Vincent Marlborough the

Third. It all depends on the situation," he said with a shrug. "But my friends and colleagues, and I do hope that's a group you'll soon consider yourself to be a part of, they all call me Mother."

For the first time since she'd been arrested, Sara laughed.

"Mother? That's an unusual name for a man."

"True," he said, smiling at her. "But I'm an unusual man, wouldn't you say?"